I0787983

# MISTAKEN IDENTITY

## CORSAC FOX
### BOOK 2

## BLAZE WARD

KNOTTED ROAD PRESS

**Mistaken Identity**
**Corsac Fox, Book 2**
Blaze Ward
Copyright © 2023 Blaze Ward
All rights reserved
Published by Knotted Road Press
www.KnottedRoadPress.com

ISBNs:
Paperback: 978-1-64470-393-9
Hardback: 978-1-64470-394-6

Cover art:
Jay O'Connell https://www.jayoconnell.com/
Illustration 108050035 © Raffaele1 | Dreamstime.com
Illustration 22850687 © Seamartini | Dreamstime.com

Cover and interior design copyright © 2023 Knotted Road Press

**Reviews**
It's true. Reviews help. Even a short one, such as, "Loved it!" So please consider reviewing this book (and all of the ones you've read) on your favorite retailer site.

**Never miss a release!**
If you'd like to be notified of new releases, sign up for my newsletter.

http://www.blazeward.com/newsletter/

**Buy More!**
Did you know that you can buy directly from the Knotted Road Press website?

https://www.knottedroadpress.com/shop/

# ALSO BY BLAZE WARD

**The Jessica Keller Chronicles**

*Auberon*

*Queen of the Pirates*

*Last of the Immortals*

*Goddess of War*

*Flight of the Blackbird*

*The Red Admiral*

*St. Legier*

*Winterhome*

*Petron*

**CS-405**

*Queen Anne's Revenge*

*Packmule*

*Persephone*

**First Centurion Kosnett**

*Encounter at Vilahana*

*Consensus at Aditi*

*Hegemony at Dalou*

*Princes at Ewin*

*Empire at Gloran*

*Domain at Yaumgan*

**Additional Alexandria Station Stories**

*The Story Road*

*Siren*

*Two Bottles of Wine With A War God*

**The Science Officer Series Season One**

*The Science Officer*

*The Mind Field*

*The Gilded Cage*

*The Pleasure Dome*

*The Doomsday Vault*

*The Last Flagship*

*The Hammerfield Gambit*

*The Hammerfield Payoff*

*The Bryce Connection*

**The Science Officer Series Season Two**

*Alien Seas*

*Buried Among the Stars*

*Captain Navarre*

**Last Stand**

*Lost Dreams*

*Ghost Towns*

*Games People Play*

*Prophet and Loss*

*Dandelion*

*Emergency*

*Warchild*

*Moot*

*Doomsday Girl*

*Princess*

*The Coven*

*Preacher Man*

## Captain Daring

*Revoked*

*Returned*

*Reborn*

## The Lazarus Alliance

*Escape*

*Return*

*Rebellion*

*Revolution*

*Liberation*

*Retribution*

*Alliance*

## Shadow of the Dominion

*Longshot Hypothesis*

*Hard Bargain*

*Outermost*

*Dominion-427*

*Phoenix*

*Princess Rualoh*

# CONTENTS

## WREN


Chapter 1 . . . 3
Chapter 2 . . . 7
Chapter 3 . . . 13
Chapter 4 . . . 17
Chapter 5 . . . 21
Chapter 6 . . . 25
Chapter 7 . . . 29
Chapter 8 . . . 31
Chapter 9 . . . 35
Chapter 10 . . . 39
Chapter 11 . . . 43
Chapter 12 . . . 47
Chapter 13 . . . 51


## Z'GOSZA STATION FOUR


Chapter 14 . . . 61
Chapter 15 . . . 67
Chapter 16 . . . 73
Chapter 17 . . . 79
Chapter 18 . . . 87
Chapter 19 . . . 91
Chapter 20 . . . 95
Chapter 21 . . . 101
Chapter 22 . . . 109
Chapter 23 . . . 113
Chapter 24 . . . 119
Chapter 25 . . . 123
Chapter 26 . . . 127
Chapter 27 . . . 133
Chapter 28 . . . 139

# CORSAC FOX


| | |
|---|---|
| Chapter 29 | 145 |
| Chapter 30 | 151 |
| Chapter 31 | 157 |
| Chapter 32 | 161 |
| Chapter 33 | 165 |
| Chapter 34 | 167 |
| Chapter 35 | 173 |
| Chapter 36 | 179 |
| Chapter 37 | 187 |


# COMPASS ROSE


| | |
|---|---|
| Chapter 38 | 193 |
| Chapter 39 | 197 |
| Chapter 40 | 201 |
| Chapter 41 | 205 |
| Chapter 42 | 207 |
| Chapter 43 | 209 |
| Chapter 44 | 213 |
| Chapter 45 | 215 |
| Chapter 46 | 219 |
| Chapter 47 | 223 |
| Chapter 48 | 227 |
| Chapter 49 | 229 |
| Chapter 50 | 231 |
| Chapter 51 | 235 |
| Chapter 52 | 239 |
| Chapter 53 | 243 |
| Chapter 54 | 247 |
| Chapter 55 | 251 |
| Chapter 56 | 255 |
| Chapter 57 | 257 |
| Chapter 58 | 261 |
| Chapter 59 | 265 |
| Chapter 60 | 269 |
| Chapter 61 | 277 |

Chapter 62                                              281
Chapter 63                                              285
Chapter 64                                              289
Chapter 65                                              293
Chapter 66                                              297

## KHILE HEAVY

Chapter 67                                              309
Chapter 68                                              313
Chapter 69                                              319
Chapter 70                                              323
Chapter 71                                              329
Chapter 72                                              337
Chapter 73                                              345

Read More                                               351
About the Author                                        353
About Knotted Road Press                                355

WREN

# ONE

"All hands to action stations," the call came over the speaker.

Captain Ulysses Fortier—Uly—was already on duty, listening to his own voice echo around his bridge as everyone hyped up to that next level.

Combat imminent.

*Corsac Fox*, the former Ononguli pirate starship that he and his new crew had stolen out of an Auga police impound orbit when they broke out of jail, had been quietly trailing the other ship under his command, the *Cargo Vessel 00429490477*, now known as *Wren*.

Back home, in the *Institutional Republic of Batyr*, he'd been a mere naval Ensign, an O-2 three years out from his commission, originally serving as a peon officer on the Forward Cruiser *Vanguard Lesauvage* until that ship had needed to go into extended drydock for repairs after a battle with ships from the *Combined Crowns of Danumash*, also known as the Seven Kingdoms.

His father had gotten him transferred to the Forward Cruiser *Marshall Castillon* instead.

That was when things had gone wrong.

Maybe.

Hard to judge, even with hindsight. Captain Dimka Savatier, his new commanding officer on *Marshall Castillon*, hadn't liked Uly. That much had been obvious from the start.

Dan Sheridan, his new Second-in-Command these days, had figured that Savatier saw him as a spy for the Industrial Protectors Party.

In any case, Savatier had dumped him, Dan, engineer Kolya Roux, plus security troopers Emil Beranger and Gennady Travers onto a newly surrendered *Danumash* cargo vessel as a prize crew to sail it home, then left them there.

Maybe that was when things had truly taken a turn for the worse.

But he'd also rescued the Mazhin slaves on the vessel *King Hewitt II*. Made friends with them, even. Convinced them to join him in repairing the badly damaged freighter so that they could all escape whatever retribution *Danumash* might have been sending.

It had helped that all of the *Danumash* officers and about half of the midshipmen on *King Hewitt II* had been killed instantly with a through-and-through shot from a wavebolt. Uly had inherited a group of teenage boys and a small crew of enlisted men and civilians. Plus the medical staff for his freed slaves.

Uly pulled himself out of the rabbit-hole of memory, and looked at his screen.

He didn't need to spend time on the trials and tribulations where *King Hewitt II* had been in turn captured by this very vessel, when it had been known as the *Iron Wasp*, under the command of a Conductor rather than a Captain. Adrian Sobol.

Subsequent capture by the Auga Empire. Jail, then jailbreak before the Auga could get around to *processing* that last group of prisoners. The one that included Uly and his by-then greatly expanded crew: Human, Mazhin, Emro, Thogin, and even a group of now-former Ononguli pirates, mostly engineering specialists who had thrown in their lot with Uly rather than spend time in an Auga prison.

"Cartographer," Uly called, causing Sterling Huff to look up and nod. "Status?"

"Enemy vessels have taken the bait, Captain," Huff replied crisply.

His voice didn't even break when he spoke. But then, Huff was fifteen and finally starting to grow into himself, physically as well as emotionally.

There were times when Uly would have liked to find some mystic necromancer, just to bring *King Hewitt II*'s former commanding officer back from the dead, in order to slap the man for the way that fool had treated his crew.

Probably for the best that he couldn't. Uly already had a long enough list of enemies that he was planning to get even with, one of these days.

"How many?" Uly queried sharply.

*Corsac Fox* was heavily over-armed for an Interceptor-class vessel. Almost a dreadnought frigate for firepower. At the same time, he barely had enough crew to sail it and fight at the same time. Were the ship not so automated, he'd have never attempted something this crazy.

"Two signals at present, sir," Huff replied. "Roscoe was just bringing *Wren* into the edge of the system when they slipped in and blipped him out of warp. *Z'Gosza* itself is close enough to see us with a long light-speed lag, but they don't have anyone in a position to intervene."

"That's why we're here, Huff," Uly grinned.

He turned to the Mazhin officer next to Huff.

*Corsac Fox*'s bridge had four main stations in an arc facing inwards towards the Conductor, letting Uly see each of them when they looked up. More stations outside that arc that faced the bulkhead.

Haydar Ramezani was running sensors today, having been functionally blackmailed into the job, at least until they could hire or recruit enough people to let him go back to being a scientist.

"Have they seen us yet?" Uly asked.

Haydar was Mazhin. Erect biped who could pass for a skinny human in bad lighting. At least until you saw his head.

The Mazhin didn't have hair. Instead, they had sensory tentacles covering most of the same space. Those were stirring like sleepy snakes, but several pointed at Uly now.

"They have not," Haydar replied with a grin. "Two Probes or Ultra-Bombers from the size. They appear to be entirely focused on the vessel they are in the process of ambushing. Amateur mistake."

Uly had never gotten the entire story from Haydar. And the other

Mazhin had only been willing to hint at pieces. Uly assumed Haydar was blackmailing them, in turn, for their silence.

He did know that the middle-aged Mazhin gentleman had been far more of a pirate in his youth, some thirty or forty years ago. He had an interesting skill set that most of the rest of the crew lacked.

At least today.

Uly nodded.

"Wavebolt Gunner Kovalchuk," Uly turned to the Ononguli crew member next. "As they are small, keep the 6dm tubes loaded for shield detonation. Instead launch a pair of the 1dm bolts when we drop. Also set them to detonate on shields, rather than punching through. Understood?"

Kovalchuk gulped and nodded.

"Aye, Conductor."

The man was qualified to stand bridge watches, but most of the time that had meant either engineering or maybe life support. Today, he was manning the big guns.

*Corsac Fox* mounted a forward turret with a pair of 6dm tubes. The wavebolt torpedoes were deadly packets of coherent plasma with a control circuit built in. Normally, a ship this size might be expected to have a single 4dm in a turret forward with possibly a second aft, plus the four 1dm defensive weapons mounted on the corners.

*Corsac Fox* had a lot of firepower for its size. Uly simply didn't have the crew to man everything with experts. Or even trained crew. He would take what he could get.

Needs must when the devil drives.

"Bring the electroshields full and reinforce on the forward array," Uly ordered, waiting for Kolya Roux to nod.

One of Uly's three enlisted senior engineers, and the only one with significant experience in combat operations, Kolya was forward handling shields and monitoring things while the other two were aft, whispering to their systems.

Uly took a deep breath to center himself.

"Huff, take us in."

# TWO

Uly had the Conductor's screen set to a fairly broad view of the zone in front of *Corsac Fox*. The warp bubble dropped almost as quickly as it spun up, but they'd been following *Wren* at a safe distance, sniffing the trail that the ship's Variable Pulse Spatial Generator left as it sailed through space at Fast FTL speeds.

That trail was how pirates caught civilian ships. And how the police caught the pirates. Uly wasn't sure which he was today.

Two such generators could not operate in close proximity, so both ships would be tossed out of the bubble, back into regular space. If the attacker left their own generator on standby, you had to get far enough away from them if you wanted to escape.

Huff had let the two pirate ships trap *Corsac Fox* by sailing right up to them, just as they had done to *Wren*, then letting their generators kick him out. But he was going to keep his own generators on as well.

Those folks didn't get to escape him.

Contact.

*Wren*, sitting dead in space, surrounded by a pair of ships so tiny that they looked like guppies threatening a whale.

Two pirates, sailing close on their Navigation Displacer thrusters. Definitely Seeker-class. Small ones, at that. As Haydar had said, possibly

Probes. Maybe Ultra-Bombers. Could even be nothing more than armed freighters.

*Wren* had no guns to challenge them. And hardly any shields. It was a massive cargo carrier that he'd stolen, fully loaded with emergency supplies sufficient to keep Uly and his crew fed and operational for a long time.

He wasn't here to steal more food.

"Captain, we've caught them entirely by surprise," Haydar announced laconically.

"Kovalchuk, one torpedo only on each enemy," Uly ordered. "Maybe we can convince them to surrender instead of being annihilated today."

Kovalchuk moved smoothly once they were committed. As a rule, the Ononguli man tended to think too much ahead of time but locked in hard on the task when things got serious.

Which was why he was manning the guns today.

Uly heard the two beeps indicating shots sent downrange.

"Haydar, are they not looking up at all?" Uly asked.

"So it would appear, Captain," Haydar replied with a rude chuckle, looking up with eyes as well as about half of his tentacles. "Oh, my, they've even dropped their electroshields in order to send over boarding parties."

"Warn them," Uly said sharply. "Challenge them. Something. Those bolts are about to slam into raw metal hard."

"Pirate vessels, this is your only warning," Haydar announced in a crisp, news-announcer sort of voice. "Surrender immediately or be destroyed."

The two 1dm wavebolts weren't moving at light speed, but an appreciable fraction. Those two ships had about eight seconds before they exploded.

There, both had panicked and raised shields. One of them was even managing to fire back with their Neutron Omnipulsar. Wildly inaccurate at present, but something.

Shieldless, 1dm bolts would have crushed those ships like aluminum drinking cans.

"We surrender!" someone called on an audio channel.

Haydar had routed it to the bridge speakers, so Uly heard it fully, instead of as a tinny echo from that station.

"Kovalchuk, kill both bolts," Uly ordered. "Then keep the Sixes centered in case someone decides to play possum."

The Ononguli man pressed a pair of buttons, then looked up in confusion.

"Possum?" he asked.

"Never mind," Uly shook his head. "Stay prepared."

Kovalchuk nodded.

On Uly's screen, both wavebolt icons faded.

"Pirate vessels, this is *Corsac Fox*," Uly said. "You will immediately put your entire crews in suits and evacuate your ships to stand outside on the hulls. Unarmed. We will search your vessels. If there is anybody hiding aboard, or any of my boarding crew are injured, all your lives are immediately forfeit. Am I clear?"

Uly muted the line and drew a breath. He hated this part of life. The terrible pirate warlord damning lives on a whim.

He'd been an adult and an officer for three years before he'd taken command of *King Hewitt II*. And had just turned twenty-five last month. Yet, he was in command here. Responsible for nearly one hundred lives. Everyone looked to him to lead them.

He had to do a good job of it.

Once upon a time, he'd promised that he would get everyone home, wherever that turned out to be. But the Mazhin didn't belong to planets, the Thogin cousins were itinerant, and three of his Emro crew were traveling scholars. The fourth, the Emro woman Anari Supasei, had been Moss School, because the Auga thought she was too smart to be Sabre School, when Suka Kuri, the Moss School elder who was an Exemplar of the Arts—a literal *Living Legend*—said that Supasei might rise to that level herself, given time.

And his combined Human crew had all thrown in with him as pirates, mostly because one group didn't want to go back to *Danumash*, and whatever punishment they might face.

His *Batyr* folks had gotten a little pissed to have been abandoned out here by Captain Savatier.

Uly was on his own, far from home, and trying to make the most of it.

At least he'd found some friends to help.

"Uly, they've turned off engines, electroshield arrays, and targeting systems," Haydar spoke after a long moment. "I'll assume that they are done. At least for now."

"Do we know who they are?" Uly asked.

"The first person I spoke with sounded Ugotha from the accent," Haydar nodded. "Sensors suggest a broad mix, all medium-sized, however."

Uly nodded. Thogin were tiny by comparison to Humans or Mazhin, lean and running around a meter and a half tall on average.

At the other end of the spectrum, the Emro—of all schools or walks of life—ranged upwards from two meters, to as much as two and a half, with Hiko Seiichai, the Seeker of the Moss School, apparently near the high end at two hundred and forty-nine centimeters in his bare feet.

Hiko was not, however, a warrior by any stretch of the imagination. Or even a dancer. One hell of a painter, though.

Uly turned to the wing station where a ship's Knight would sit on a *Danumash* ship. Dan Sheridan held that title for now, along with First Officer and Second-in-Command. All of them were wearing too many hats.

Today she wore a suit of boarding armor with the helmet on a cord at her hip and a serious look on her face.

"You are remaining aboard the *Fox*," Dan announced as she rose from her station, brooking no argument.

Uly simply nodded.

He had argued with her enough on the topic before today. It was still a pain in his ass when she was right.

He still took her in with a long glance as she turned to exit.

A few centimeters taller than him at one hundred and eighty-eight. Heavier, too, at seventy-five kilograms, but Uly had always been tall and skinny. Sheridan Chastain was made of muscles.

Extremely dark skinned, even compared to Uly's Turkishness and curly brown hair, her skin was a rich, deep brown. Black hair curls kept buzzed tight on the sides and a little fuzzy on top.

Square face with a flat nose and thin lips. Eyes that came out to sharper edges than his, in a manner he'd once heard called *Afro-Siberian*.

Beautiful woman. Smart, too. Deadly dangerous. Highly competent.

But he was the commanding officer around here, so all he did was watch as she left, hoping that nothing went wrong.

He needed her as a Second-in-Command.

And as a friend.

# THREE

Dan double-timed down the staircase to the lowest deck. Her boarding team was already there, waiting patiently in their armor, including a suit they'd found buried in *Wren*'s supplies that was big enough for Anari Supasei to wear.

The woman towered over everyone, but was still the greenest rookie today.

Okay, bad choice of words. Emro were already green. With straight, black hair and dark eyes.

Supasei looked another half of Dan tall and two of her wide. Then you stuffed the woman in boarding armor that added to her bulk.

If she snuck up on someone, and she could, they might think that a building had been suddenly erected behind them.

Not necessarily wrong, either.

Dan counted noses. Beranger and Travers had been with her for years at this point, having helped her capture or steal *Danumash* vessels in the before time.

Before Uly. Before *Corsac Fox*.

*Before.*

Nils Shevchenko led a small team of armed, Ononguli engineers mostly there to handle unfamiliar equipment.

Dan was for combat.

She turned to the last two. Both Mazhin.

She could have ordered Nasrin and Piruz the Horse Thief to remain aboard the *Fox*, but two ships meant she had twice as many directions to pay attention to.

Dan focused on the male first. Piruz was many things, but even he was happy to say he was more lover than fighter, though she didn't think he'd ever wandered outside his own kind. At least recently.

Not her type, anyway. Too slick.

"You do know which end goes boom?" Dan asked, gesturing to the Exoripper carbine the man held on two hands.

"Aye, sir," he nodded, grinning fiercely.

His qualification scores were good enough. For now. He could probably manage to not hurt anybody he didn't intend to.

Dan had a Heavy Exoripper pistol tucked into her own armor, outside on her left thigh, and an Icemace collapsed down into carrying mode for now on her right.

She turned to Nasrin next.

Known to the former pirates and most of the crew now as *The Songbird*. Also pretty good in close combat, she and Dan having taught each other their respective unarmed forms over the last few months.

"Is there a reason you checked an Omnibow out of the armoury, Nasrin?" Dan asked, nodding to the weapon.

This one used a coiled spring to fire a grenade, springbolt style. It was currently unloaded, but the Mazhin woman had a bandoleer strung across the front of her armor with an even mix of Painspheres and Firespheres.

And she held the weapon with easy familiarity.

"If they give us any grief, I can hit two or three of them at once," Nasrin replied evenly. "I'll be loaded with Firespheres by the time we exit the airlock."

Dan bit back any comment. Painspheres were great, nonlethal weapons, but only inside an atmosphere where the shock waves could propagate evenly. Almost worthless in a vacuum, except for the guy you shot. At least a Firesphere took all that and added flames.

Of course, anybody looking at a bright red grenade on the tip of Nasrin's weapon would probably have quick second thoughts.

"Okay, people, helmets on," Dan announced.

Around her, everyone got fully enclosed and went to inside air. The suits were all quality stuff, stolen from the Auga who had originally staged them aboard *Wren* for whatever emergencies might necessitate a call up of the ship. Lots of useful things aboard.

"Channel three," Dan said, holding up three fingers as she did and checking that everyone's helmet status indicators were showing green on the outside.

It took a few moments, then everyone was finally ready.

Scratch crew. Scratch assault team. Making it up as they went. She was the pro around here.

"Travers, into the airlock first," Dan ordered, making sure everyone got in ahead of her. She could trust Travers and Beranger to know what to do.

Now was when things could get tricky.

# FOUR

Dan had shepherded her team out of the airlock, riding on short-range, compressed-nitrogen thrusters. *Corsac Fox* had moved close, once the two small ships had come to rest and the crews had abandoned.

"Haydar, what's their status?" she asked over the command line.

"Twenty-four sailors in suits," he replied evenly. "Eleven and thirteen. Closer ship appears to be an upgunned Probe. Farther one came off the assembly line as an Ultra-Bomber, about the time my grandsire was first discovering girls."

Dan chuckled. Mazhin tended to live about as long as Humans, so she could assume that the ship was probably close to one hundred years old by now. Haydar had been cagey about his age, but had always struck Dan as being about as old as her own father, back home on Aurtan.

"Any problems?" she asked.

"Lot of localized chatter on channel one, if you care," Haydar replied. "Nothing interesting at present. Will yell if they start planning something. I've got sensors on all local channels, just in case. No weapons I can see from here."

"Thank you, Haydar," Dan said. "Closing now."

She was in no hurry to cross the two hundred or so meters separating the *Fox* from the Probe. The Ultra-Bomber was another hundred or so beyond that, with *Wren* off to one side. Roscoe had as skeleton a crew as he could get to fly that ship. Just enough, barely, to bait this trap.

As a result, she had time to watch the two crews adjust to seeing her mob closing. And listened in on channel one as they recognized the immense size of an Emro coming at them, and rightly assumed a Sabre School warrior was involved.

And one who was probably still not in the top three most dangerous people approaching, though Dan didn't tell them that.

*Killer* was a state of mind. Anari Supasei was still getting there, but first she had to overcome several years of Moss School thinking as the Auga had tried to make her an engineer.

Round peg, square hole.

Kinda like a lot of people on the *Fox*.

"Everyone to channel one," Dan ordered on three as they started to come to rest.

None of the close group of pirates were armed, as near as she could tell. Hopefully, the far group hadn't gotten stupid, either.

"You have all surrendered," Dan reminded them in the most ugly, implacable tone she could manage. With a lot of practice back home. "You are now under arrest."

She had to pause there, because all twenty-odd of them were suddenly yelling, screeching, howling, or something.

A wall of noise so painful she had to dial her speakers down some until they got over themselves.

Dan snapped out her Icemace to its full, two-meter length and let her thrusters ride her a little closer. The pirates were all standing on their own hull with magnetic boots, so she was flying about four meters in front of them.

Icemace wouldn't be all that effective through a normal armored suit like hers, but most of these guys weren't in anything that heavy. Mostly basic suits, so atmosphere and a few plates on important joints. Clubs and Exorippers would be normal weapons they'd have taken aboard *Wren*, if this had been a simple capture.

Instead of Uly's trap.

"HEY!" Dan snapped back finally, pointing the Icemace, now two meters long, into the face of the closest one, who shied back. "Most of you should only be going to jail. Unless you think that living is too much right now, in which case, you go right ahead and let me know."

She drew the Heavy Exoripper in her left hand and pointed it at the mob. Fairly standard plasma bolt weapon, but hers was configured for boarding and zero-gravity, so it used a tiny portion of the bolt's power as a counter-thrust to neutralize recoil.

*Batyr*'s navy had a lot of practice taking *Danumash* ships, after all. That had been her job.

The pirates fell to silence. No doubt, others in her team had weapons pointed at the pirates, including Nasrin and her Firesphere.

"Any heroes?" Dan prompted.

Didn't feel like it. Still, she waited. Watched like a hungry kitty.

"Okay, all of you step off your hull," Dan announced, again waiting for the cries of disbelief to fade. "Piruz, hand them a rope so nobody gets lost."

Quickly, they all hung in space, grabbing that line like their lives depended on it. Might, if they gave her grief.

"Beranger, take Shevchenko and his group in to confirm everything aboard Number One," Dan ordered. "We're doing this by the book."

None of the other species had a book like that. Apparently, Humans were at least as bureaucratic as the Auga in many ways. And way more combative. Much more so than most of the others.

Including a group of pirates on the farthest fringes of Imperial Sector Fifteen.

Dan remained outside and watched, but her little birds on a line were cowed. For now.

She'd see how they behaved after both groups got properly put into cells on *Corsac Fox*.

# FIVE

Uly had stayed on the bridge while Dan had rounded up all the pirates. Both ships were smaller ones, and *Wren* was huge, so Shevchenko and his people were in the process of landing the vehicles aboard *Wren* in one of the big flight bays that ship had.

Prepared for any emergency. Including landing smaller craft from orbit. Not that he would land today, but Haydar and Huff had probably stolen the single greatest cargo ship that Uly could have wished for.

It had certainly made his life a lot easier.

"Uly, I'm finally picking up communications chatter from *Z'Gosza* Orbital Control," Haydar spoke up sharply, his tentacles writhing at a faster pace than normal. "The light-speed wavefront has finally gotten to the station and they are watching us capture these two pirates. About forty minutes lag."

"They still have nothing big in the way of local defenses?" Uly asked the man.

"Stations are armed," Haydar replied. "Mix of one, three, and twelve DM weapons. Nothing much past that. Mostly search and rescue, or escort cutters not even as well armed as our two new friends here."

"Send them a note that we're friendly and coming over to chat shortly," Uly said. "Something diplomatic, because I'd like them to not be shooting at us."

"Understood," Haydar nodded, tentacles curling back down to focus on his various screens.

Uly opened a line to his other ship.

"*Wren* here. Roscoe speaking."

"How's everything at your end, Drew?" Uly asked.

The man was Uly's Sailing Master. Originally a civilian trainee on *King Hewitt II*, working towards his *Danumash* certificate under Hylda Hobbs, who had owned that ship. She'd been killed in the same shot that took out the officers, with Roscoe and Huff having been safe on the Secondary Bridge.

The only reason they had survived.

"Landing both vessels now," Roscoe said. "We staying or leaving at that point? I have two courses plotted."

"As soon as you are ready, we're going to drop down to get close enough to the planet to communicate to them with only a short lag," Uly replied. "I don't know if they will be friendly enough to talk to us, or if they'll immediately open up with their big guns, so plot me something where I don't have to worry about a 12dm chasing."

"Understood, sir," Roscoe acknowledged. "I'll need about ten minutes at my end, then we should be ready."

"Excellent news," Uly said. "Huff will be in charge here. I'm headed down to see about Dan's prisoners."

Uly cut the line and turned to Sterling Huff. Fifteen and he'd already fought and won a battle against a ship like the just-captured Ultra-Bomber over there. Turning into a fine officer.

At one point, Uly would have been happy if Huff's next *Danumash* Captain had nice things to say about how Uly had trained the young man, but like the others, Huff was planning on staying put.

"You are in command, Huff," Uly said formally.

"I acknowledge transfer of command, Captain," Huff said in a sober voice.

Uly grinned and Huff grinned back. It was the things you did now that became automatic when the shit hit the fan.

"Back shortly," Uly said, rising to see what Dan had found for him.

He didn't need bodies that desperately. And wouldn't have trusted captured pirates for the most part.

What he needed was information. Intelligence that would let him know what his options were, so many light-centuries from home and getting farther with each week.

Had they finally gone far enough?

# SIX

Dan had her prisoners rounded up and taken care of. Easy enough. Each group of six had gone into the airlock and been ordered to strip back down to regular clothing before they were allowed in to where Travers and Supasei were waiting inside with her.

They were down to the last group now, watching the first three groups. Nasrin had swapped for Painspheres when she joined them.

Nobody would be getting stupid looking at that. Not with a Sabre School warrior in their faces. Or them in her chest, which was about the scale here.

Dan watched the airlock open for the last group as Uly emerged from the staircase up.

Dan hadn't depolarized her faceshield, so these pirates had no idea what species she was. Only Supasei stood out, and that for her size.

Uly was wearing the threadbare remains of his original *Batyr* officer's uniform, a little worn and patched along a seam on his leg. Soon, they needed something for everyone, but they'd been too busy sailing here and setting up this ambush to bother.

"What are you?" the closest pirate demanded almost hysterically, lurching just enough that his step froze untaken when Dan slipped her Icemace across his path and growled over the speakers.

This one was Ugotha. Looking at him, Dan was reminded of an ant, if you scaled it up to human size. Soft chitin over an endoskeleton. Two compound eyes. Four antennae, two up above the eyes and two down near the mouth.

The species was generally a muted orange she'd once heard called burnt umber. It clashed horribly with the maroon pants and copper shirt he'd chosen when he got out of bed this morning.

"Human," Uly replied.

They were getting good at starting conversations off that way, as they were nearly two full Imperial Auga Sectors from home by now. An astonishing distance.

"I am also the Conductor on this ship, and you are my prisoners," Uly continued.

"But this is *Iron Wasp*," the man replied, confused. "Where's Sobol?"

"In an Auga prison somewhere, doing time and hoping that the clan elders back home consider him important enough to trade for at some point," Uly said. "And the ship is no longer *Iron Wasp*. After I captured it, I renamed it *Corsac Fox*. Keep that in mind."

"Captured?" the Ugotha gasped.

The others joined in like some weird Greek chorus, but Dan didn't see anybody psyching themselves up for violence. Not like her people had already done several hours ago.

"Captured," Uly agreed. "Like I captured all of you. And now we are going to turn you over to the local authorities and let them deal with you like the pirates you are."

Dan liked that hint of terror that came into the eyes she could see, though the Ugotha had a fantastic poker face. His hands gave it away instead, clenching and unclenching in fear, rather than rage. She still had the Exoripper ready to open fire.

"You aren't a pirate?" the Ugotha asked in a quiet voice.

Dan had the impression that this one might have been the leader of the group. He'd been on the Probe, but the ones off the Ultra-Bomber had all given her the impression of followers.

And all of them were at least as threadbare as Uly was today. So not all that successful in their chosen field of endeavor.

"Privateer," Uly replied, possibly with a hint of a sneer. "Freebooter, if you will. I'm hoping that the locals will see their way to hiring me to help clean up this sector of space. Maybe deal with some of the pirates running around. I'm given to understand from others that many of you are slave traders. Several of my crew are former slaves, so they have strong opinions on the topic, if you feel like discussing ethics with them some time. Or giving me grief."

A bit heavy handed, but Dan liked it. Uly was the only real officer around here. The rest of them were either enlisted folks filling billets way above their normal pay grade—like her—or civilians doing military jobs because somebody had to. Haydar, for instance.

The pirates had all clenched up then froze like bunnies when Nasrin rotated her Omnibow to cover the middle of the group, already understanding that the three Humans would be killing everyone closer if the pirates started something right now.

Dan could only imagine that Nasrin's smile, still hidden behind the polarization, was as terrible as her own was. The moment passed and the pirates deflated.

"Right," Travers yelled over his outside speakers, causing everyone to jump. "You lot will form two lines and march to my orders. I will provide you directions. You will follow them. Am I clear?"

Right out of the book. Heads hung, but nodded. Bodies started into motion.

Most of these men—and a handful of women of various species, though no Emro—looked like they already knew what a jail cell smelled like.

Travers began marching them, headed aft to that spot where Dan and Uly had been imprisoned after *Iron Wasp* had captured *King Hewitt II*.

It was a strange circle, but Uly had a plan.

# SEVEN

Uly stood off to one side and watched each pirate walk by, measuring them as he did. It was doubtful that any would make good recruits, depending, but a little over half had turned out to be Ononguli, like most of his own crew, so his people might have old comrades over there that they'd be willing to speak up for.

He'd let Shevchenko say something if that turned out to be the case.

Once they were all by, he followed Dan. All the hallways except one were closed off and locked to anything this group might do until they got where they were going. Hopefully, he wouldn't be responsible for them for all that long.

The whole point of this operation was to make friends here in *Z'Gusza*, which notes from Ethir Ewen—the leader of his group of Thogin delinquents—referred to a *mercantilistic oligopoly*.

Ethir hadn't used the term. Uly had supplied it from his own studies of political systems, part of a well-rounded officer's education.

Quickly, Dan and her folks got the pirates shepherded into the prisoner facility. They had bathrooms and bunks. There would be food at some point if he had to keep them long enough.

What he would do with them was still up in the air.

Beranger locked the hatch.

"That's that, sir," the man announced. "Mister Ramezani is monitoring the room for sounds of riot or emergency. None of the personal gear they brought with them will get that hatch open from their side."

Uly nodded. He'd spent too much time on the other side of that hatch, thinking and planning. It had saved them all later but he doubted that the folks in there right now were that sharp. And still in shock. It had taken Uly a week to even settle.

"Well done, everyone," Uly nodded as helmets came off and smiles greeted him.

Slowly, they were becoming a single crew, but it would take time. And little successes like this along the way.

"What's next?" Dan asked, mostly for the benefit of the folks around them.

"Now, we move closer to the planet itself and see if they are interested in some captured pirates," Uly replied. "And maybe, just maybe, hiring themselves their own privateers."

That got a quiet cheer. His Ononguli crew were already pirates, trying to be reformed. The others were learning. The Humans would be teaching, starting with Dan, but also including Beranger and Travers.

He nodded to the group.

"You get changed and report to your duty stations," Uly ordered. "Dan, I'll see you topside shortly."

# EIGHT

Uly studied the screen again, as *Corsac Fox* dropped out of a bubble. Not on top of the largest station. Not even that close to it.

Those folks would still be watching the wavefront from out where he had captured and loaded two small ships. And their crews.

That was why he'd taken his time moving, so they saw all that before he was suddenly standing on their front porch with a warship.

Folks might react negatively.

Here, it at least helped that nothing they had mobile was a threat to *Corsac Fox*. That didn't stop him from having everything primed for combat. It just meant that he stayed over here.

"What's the lag, Haydar?" Uly asked.

"Five seconds, give or take," the man replied with a nod that included almost all of his tentacles.

Still weird to see.

"Good enough," Uly said. He opened a channel. "*Z'Gosza* Orbital Control, this is Uly Fortier, commanding the vessel *Corsac Fox*. Please reply on this channel."

He muted things and left it at that. There was no way to predict the reaction. They might go ahead and fire 12dm wavebolts at him from there, though those could be easily evaded or destroyed at this range.

And they might be friends with the folks he'd captured. Nobody was ever willing to admit the truth, according to Dan. Not when hiring or dealing with pirates.

He glanced over and she nodded back at him. Sober and serious. She'd done the hardest part in capturing those pirates.

His job was the diplomatic side.

"*Corsac Fox*, this is *Z'Gosza Station*," a deepish voice replied. "What are your intentions?"

Uly went ahead and brought live the camera to send his image, presuming that the next question would be explaining his species. At the same time, that short-circuited other things.

Hopefully in a good way.

"*Z'Gosza Station*, we have captured a pair of pirate vessels intending to attack one of my freighters," Uly replied. "I have no use for captured pirates, nor their ships. I would like to turn them over to local law enforcement authorities. After that, my wish is to open a dialogue with your government about trade."

There, leave it at that. Trade would be a squishy term, and he had no idea how they might interpret it. *Corsac Fox* might get hired to escort other freighters. Or even to haul some cargo, though they didn't have nearly the volume to make it all that profitable.

Better if they hired him as their own privateer to attack whatever pirates he could find. Or any enemies they had.

If he had a safe base from which to eventually recruit, while selling off captured cargoes from his own piracy, without selling slaves, he could make a living at this.

At least until he figured out what he was supposed to do with a crew representing half a dozen different species in a stolen warship.

"What species are you?" the man on the other end asked, voice a little shaky.

The image came live on Uly's screen, showing a Khet male. Similar looking to the one that had been in command of the Ultra-Bomber that had nearly killed him when he'd first stolen *Wren*.

Amphibious species. Or an erect fishman with webbing between fingers and toes. Aqua skin with scaly ridges in places and orange highlights. Eyes more towards the sides of the head like prey, instead of forward like a predator. Crest from the center of his forehead to the back of his skull.

"Human," Uly replied. "Originally from the far side of Imperial Sector Seventeen."

He left it at that.

"We saw you capture those two ships, *Corsac Fox*," the Khet replied after a lag. "You intend to turn them over to law enforcement?"

Hell of a way to have a conversation, but he wasn't about to sail any closer to a battery of 12dm tubes.

"As soon as someone can fly out a small ship capable of collecting the disarmed pirates," Uly said. "And two pilots who can retrieve those ships as evidence. Until then, I will remain at this distance from your station."

He didn't mention that Roscoe's folks were busily copying the data-cores off of both ships using specialized tools Haydar had invented and built. Or that engineers were disabling the weapons systems on both vessels. They didn't need to know what sorts of resources Uly had if they weren't going to be friendly.

He was also outside of the range that they could threaten him. To say nothing of his 6dm tubes being able to even hit the station from here.

The pause was longer this time. The image froze as well. Folks over there having an argument about things, most likely.

He didn't mind. If this didn't work, he could try the same stunt elsewhere. He'd selected *Z'Gosza* because Ethir and the cousins had been through here at least once and knew more about the culture than the records he had inherited with the ship.

Other systems would be happy to see piracy cut down. Or destroyed. Nobody liked pirates, once you got beyond the gloriously *faux* image that was mostly from videos. Not when you found out how it really worked.

Ships like *Corsac Fox* were expensive to own and operate. Either a planetary government paid for everything, or you had to have a positive income. Uly had never been a merchant, having grown up the son of a high Party official instead.

He did understand that a warship was ten times as expensive as a comparably-sized freighter would be to operate.

And if he didn't have someone else paying the bills, piracy was probably his best bet.

A new voice came over the speakers now, after a wait of nearly four minutes.

Not quite long enough that he was expecting trouble, but perhaps enough that he'd reconsider this system and its culture.

"*Corsac Fox*, this is Administrator Rabiu Khadijan," the newcomer said. "We will deploy a vessel shortly to rendezvous with you at your current location. I will accompany that vessel to meet you in person."

Uly didn't hear anything like *please* in there, but that was acceptable. If the man was coming out here, he at least had courage. And, according to Ethir's notes, an Administrator was about the middle of the upper levels of the local government bureaucracy, below the Governor, Trade Factors, and Directors.

A man of some importance, but probably not high enough ranked to escape being a sacrificial victim if it came to that.

Still, Uly could work with that.

"Looking forward to it, Administrator," Uly said. "We will communicate again when you launch."

He nodded to Dan. She'd had time to take a quick shower after shedding her armor, and put on her maroon uniform that looked much like his.

It would hopefully help them look like an organized navy.

Or something.

# NINE

Haydar noted that the four Humans with him today all wore the maroon uniform of the *Batyr* navy. The same one that had rescued him from his most recent stint of incarceration.

He, too, had gone ahead and dug out one of the nicer outfits that he'd liberated from ship's stores. Dark blue pants that tucked into calf-high boots, black with a low, walking heel. Pullover tunic in a muted green with a black leather belt holding various pouches for things completed the outfit, since the pants lacked pockets entirely.

He was not armed. Haydar didn't do guns anymore, except when Uly asked him to fire the wavebolts. Hopefully, they would be able to recruit enough folks at some point such that he could go back to his lab. Roshan was getting an unfair lead on him for inventing things, since that gentleman never left his lab, save to eat or sleep.

Roshan wasn't helping fly the ship.

At least the rest of his people hadn't insisted that Haydar continue to *Speak* for them. Uly was handling that quite admirably, and he had Piruz if he needed a used camel salesman for whatever reason.

Thus, Haydar was standing off to one side as some sort of data officer, rather than as a warrior.

The shuttle from the station was docked against the airlock port forward on the lowest deck, after Haydar had assured himself and everyone else that the small vessel was unarmed and only contained the pilot and two passengers.

Uly had called the situation a potential Trojan Horse at one point, and made Haydar look it up.

Interesting way to surprise someone, at least as a pirate. Not particularly ethical, but Haydar supposed that it would be a quick way to capture a ship without boarding it under fire.

The lock thumped one last time and the inner hatch began to beep as it opened.

Haydar stood a little taller and looked around: Nasrin, standing off to one side, though she'd slipped the Omnibow around her back for now. Ethir Ewen, but not his three Thogin cousins. Both young Emro women: Yanouk Miyoshi and Anari Supasei.

The former was Moss School, but had been trained as a dancer, and Haydar could see the various Human forms of dance in how they fought, so it wasn't much of a stretch.

Anari had been forced by the Auga to pretend to be Moss School, and an engineer, but really the woman was Sabre School. And would be utterly deadly at it, one of these days.

After she got properly trained by Dan Chastain. Look what the First Officer had done to turn Armsman Solomon Wyndham into a deadly sailor. That young Human would only get better as he grew into the size his hands and feet promised.

Wyndham and the rest of the crew of the former *King Hewitt II* were aloft at the moment or on the other ship, operating both bridges and keeping watch against anyone getting frisky. Uly trusted them.

Hell, Haydar trusted them. It helped that all the assholes had gotten themselves killed along the way, including Midshipman Quartermaster's Mate Thorley Eldridge, may the Creator of All piss excessively on his grave.

Haydar caught Nasrin's flinch at his own anger and sent her a quick scent that all was well. She nodded and returned her attention to the hatch.

Khet. Less common in the sectors where Haydar had originated. And most of his new clan.

More common in Imperial Sector Fifteen and points beyond. Like Uly and Dan, Haydar was a considerable distance from the place where he'd been born.

Fortunately, it wasn't a planet he would miss. And as far as he knew, most of the crew of that vessel were in various prisons these days. Or dead.

Piracy was a hard life.

The first Khet through was a flunky. That was obvious from the way he was dressed. Formal, but bland in brown. The next one to emerge was obviously an important bureaucrat.

Or perhaps self-important. His fashion sense seemed a bit over the top for a mere Administrator, as Haydar understood the local political structure from Ethir.

Gauzy robes in gold, trimmed with white. Several layers deep, each progressively darker. At least it didn't clash with his orange highlights.

Much.

"Administrator Khadijan," Uly said. "Welcome aboard."

Uly stepped forward. The other three maroon-draped Humans stayed back.

As intended. Khet would know about Mazhin, Thogin, Emro, and especially Ononguli.

Humans would be the surprise. That much was obvious from Khadijan's eyes.

Sideset eyes on a skull that looked more wedge shaped than round. Able to see at least two hundred and seventy degrees at once. Those eyes were up and studying the walls and ceiling. The welds and shape.

This was an Ononguli ship, if you knew what to look for. Uly had made a few, mostly cosmetic, changes, but they didn't have the crew to do much, so the lights were set to Ononguli standards. As were the hatches.

The Administrator bowed his head politely and diplomatically.

Probably going to be on his best behavior, once he realized that there were Mazhin in the room, if he knew Haydar's kind.

The man smelled like fish, but there wasn't much flop sweat present.

Not yet.

"Conductor Fortier," Khadijan said. "I have been tasked by my Director to determine how we should proceed."

Haydar approved. Keep it simple. Sacrifice a mid-level piece if they had to, but also it gave the locals the ability to measure a brand-new species.

Always a business opportunity, and Uly had called them businessbeings first, and bureaucrats a distant second, after reading Ethir's notes on *Z'Gosza*.

"I note that you didn't bring pilots with you," Uly offered blandly. "Were you and your assistant intending to fly the captured ships home yourselves?"

"You were serious about turning them over to *Z'Gosza*?" the Khet asked, surprised. "Just like that?"

"Perhaps we will come to an agreement to sell them to you for one Imperial Guilder each, Administrator," Uly countered, sounding like Piruz was whispering in his ear or something. "And certain, mutually beneficial, additional considerations."

The Khet Administrator looked like someone had just bonked him on the nose with a noodle. Haydar had to fight to keep from grinning. Nasrin's scent said the same.

"I see," the Khet managed.

"However, let us move to a conference room where we might chat under relaxed circumstances," Uly said. "This is my First Officer, Sheridan Chastain. And my Data Officer, Haydar Ramezani."

Haydar nodded and let his face take on a relaxed pleasantness.

"Greetings," the Khet offered.

Whatever the Administrator had been expecting, he hadn't gotten it. Haydar watched the man attempt to recalibrate his entire day from scratch, having met polite alien pirates who wanted to talk like businessfolk.

This was going to be so much fun.

# TEN

Uly watched Dan sort out security. Technically Wyndham's job, but he was busy on the bridge, pretending to be the Security Officer while watching too many boards at once and hoping he didn't make any irreparable mistakes.

Uly remembered those days.

"Beranger and Supasei, on duty here," Dan ordered.

That left him Yanouk, who had size, and Travers, who looked like a human/troll crossbreed, with long arms and a wiry build. And a face that could curdle milk.

Dan led them to a nearby conference room. Based on Adrian Sobol's notes, it had been the place where he could drag captured officers off of ships he took and deal with them in private. The man had understood the difference between honey and vinegar, and often got such prisoners to talk and double-deal, if they were away from their crew, who wouldn't then know that they hadn't been tortured into revealing things.

Today, it made a nice space to bring his guest. Big, square table, adjustable to height, but set by default to Ononguli scale, which was close enough to Human. Chairs for Ononguli as well, which Haydar liked to bitch about because they were built all wrong for Mazhin butts.

Ethir had built his own booster to get him to proper height once he climbed up.

Suka Kuri hadn't been there to greet the Administrator. Instead, she had taken upon herself the role of Tea Master today, having fixed a pot she claimed would be the sort of thing a Khet would enjoy.

As an Exemplar of the Arts of the Moss School, Uly had simply nodded at her pronouncement and stepped back. The scent filled the room with a warm earthiness that caused his own stomach to wake with a quick rumble of anticipation.

He settled the Administrator, then took a spot a quarter of the way around, with Dan across from the Administrator and Haydar, Ethir, and Suka Kuri filling in once she served the tea.

The other Khet had a spot on the wall behind the Administrator, looking like a child as he stood next to Yanouk.

"I have many questions," the Administrator began, having sipped his tea and gotten yet another surprise.

"We took this ship away from the Auga Empire," Uly said simply. "It was formerly a pirate vessel. Some of the crew escaped from the Auga with me, while most of the original crew are in prisons now. The non-Ononguli folks have been with me much longer, having been marooned or captured along the way until I freed them."

He left it at that. This person didn't need to know the full truth. Not any time soon.

And having a senior staff representing five different species—so far —would lend credence to his tales. Apparently, it was almost unheard of, by any of his experts.

Administrator Khadijan absorbed all that and sat silent for a moment.

"You captured a pair of known pirate vessels when you arrived," the Khet said.

"I laid a trap for them," Uly smiled. "I don't particularly like pirates, Administrator, though circumstances have forced me into something of a parallel role. At least at present. It was my hope that by capturing those ships, or destroying them had they forced me to, I would be able to convince your government to deal with me on better terms."

Another pause. Longer. Uly's smile remained warm.

"What terms?" the Khet finally asked.

"We'd like to use *Z'Gosza* as a friendly port," Uly offered. "Sell materials that we have acquired to you at a reasonable rate, including ships that we take in the course of our own activities."

Uly liked the way the Khet's eyes got even bigger than they normally were. He even sputtered once, briefly, before he got himself under control.

"You want us to finance you as you commit piracy?" he finally asked, possibly aghast from the tone. Possibly carnivorous with potential profit. It was hard to separate the two.

"Close," Uly countered. "I want to hunt other pirates down and put them out of business. In the process, I'll probably end up owning a lot of materials previously stolen elsewhere, ships that need to not immediately return to piracy after we leave, and pirates. I have no idea what *Z'Gosza* does with such folks, though I am told that you don't generally believe in the death penalty for most crimes. And I suspect that most pirate crew members can probably be rehabilitated, if you cared enough to try. I might have to deliver them elsewhere, if you aren't interested in that part, but wherever I'd send them would be better than the Auga Empire, as I'm given to understand it."

"What about smuggling?" Khadijan asked carefully.

Uly shrugged, understanding that *Z'Gosza* was a major shipping port that dealt with a broad swath of planetary systems.

"Smugglers, as I understand it, are working around customs enforcement to deliver goods in high demand," he said. "Rarely are they going out and hurting people, except as criminal networks might use force to protect their own turf against others and law enforcement. Those folks are lower on my list. Small ships with a few bottles that nobody had paid appropriate taxes on are not my concern."

He left it at that, leaning back.

Ethir leaned forward.

"I've been to *Z'Gosza* before," the Thogin announced. "You people are rank amateurs at the art of smuggling. Hell, you might be better off to hire us as consultants on all the ways you could tighten things up around here, if you really wanted to. However, considering who's in charge, that's highly unlikely, isn't it?"

Khadijan studied Ethir with eyes gone huge. The Thogin smiled mischievously.

Ethir nodded and looked at Uly.

"Oligarchs," Ethir said clearly. "Them folks that have written the laws around here such that they don't pay shipping taxes on anything, let alone their fabulous income. Taxes are for little people."

Hell of a double entendre, but Uly let it slide. And Khadijan didn't take the bait.

Uly leaned forward again.

"Also, Administrator?" he asked. "I'd like to negotiate permission from whomever, as part of our larger deal, to occasionally recruit crew members around here. As you can see, we're already extremely diverse, though I do not at present have any Khet or Ugotha in my crew."

"I can't make those sorts of deals," Khadijan stammered.

Whatever he'd expected, he hadn't gotten it, but Uly wasn't surprised.

Near as he could tell, *Corsac Fox* was an entirely new thing in the galaxy.

"I'm aware of that, Administrator," Uly nodded. "If you have two Imperial Guilders, let's start by selling you a pair of retired pirate ships while you return to the station and talk to your superiors about the pilots for them. And the former crews."

# ELEVEN

Dan watched as the airlock slammed shut, with the Administrator and his flunky aboard and ready to go do whatever folks like that did.

She turned to Uly.

"Think they'll go for it?" she asked.

"I have no clue," he shrugged deflating a little. "It's a good deal. And a nice opening if they want to grasp it. *Z'Gosza* is a place where money talks, as they used to say."

He paused and looked at all the folks around him listening.

"I think we're going to be here a while, so let's go ahead and feed the pirates now," he ordered. "Dan, you take charge of that. Haydar, could you and Ethir join me on the bridge while we wait at the speed of bureaucracy for something to happen?"

Dan laughed and gestured her folks to join her.

As with everything else, there weren't enough bodies to go around to handle all the things that needed to be done. Adding in two dozen extra mouths to feed wasn't going to drain their supplies all that quickly, but it meant that folks would have to actually cook.

They stopped at the armory, checking things back in, then headed aft.

Vahid Siah—aka *The Spatula*, the name given to him to identify him separately from his twin brother Azad—was in his kitchen. Dan had had him cross train most of the security people to cooking, since the Ononguli were all engineers first. They'd eat almost anything you put in front of them and generally didn't understand that other people wanted to actually enjoy their food.

"Orders from the top," Dan said as she entered. "Uly wants the guests fed now while we wait for the locals to decide how they want to reply."

Around her, Yanouk and Anari started putting on aprons as big as sails. Beranger and Travers were remaining on duty, so they'd kept pistols against some bizarre prison break.

Maybe like the one that had seen this crew escape Auga custody.

"Which kind of dinner were we feeding them?" Vahid asked.

Dan turned to the Mazhin with a scowl.

"Dinner like you'd feed the rest of the crew," she said distinctly.

He and his tentacles both nodded at that.

Dan remembered being fed when they'd been prisoners on this ship. Just enough food to keep everyone alive, but not enough that they could plan anything dangerous.

Sobol had been planning to sell all his prisoners to agricultural colonies or mining stations at some point.

Slaves.

Dan had prisoners now. In that same room.

She'd treat them like she should have been treated before.

Vahid understood.

Then he grinned and walked to a big pot simmering on the stove. Lifting the lid, he fanned the smell in her direction.

"I am NOT, however, letting them have my chicken soup," Vahid announced.

He'd learned the recipe from *Danumash* slavers who had captured them originally. Dan had a precise count of how much chicken broth they had left in stores.

At some point, she was going to need to buy or steal chickens from a Human colony, so she could start a breeding program and never be without chicken soup. That or locate an alien critter with the same taste and texture when cooked. Maybe a snake?

"Nor should you," Dan agreed. "That's for us. They can have simple carbohydrates and trace minerals. Bread and stew is good enough."

"Coming up," Vahid nodded, turning to the two giant women and starting to issue orders.

They had an immense store of food that they had captured when they'd stolen *Wren*. In cans that were cube-shaped, which meant that they held a quarter more material for the same volume than the cylindrical ones she was used to.

*Wren* had been packed to the gills with emergency materials. Ready to fly to the scene of any tragedy or accident and feed a lot of workers for a long time.

Years, at the rate of consumption that this crew was at, even with additional pirates.

Dan nodded to Vahid and made sure that everyone else was prepared. Nasrin had gone off duty. The Emro ladies were on duty to cook. Travers and Beranger were armed because the pirates might get stupid and Dan knew her men would open fire without hesitation.

Yanouk and Anari were getting there, but they were still rookie troopers, not even fresh out of training camp, while Beranger and Travers had been at this for years.

She had everything under control.

At least these things.

She headed forward and up to see how Uly was doing.

# TWELVE

Uly had watched the shuttle return to the station from his bridge. Encrypted communications had flown heavy and thick, but neither he nor Haydar had the key to crack them and listen in.

Suffice it to say that things seemed serious. At the same time, Uly assumed that Administrator Khadijan wouldn't want to say certain things over a radio, where there might be listeners around who could understand.

*Corsac Fox* was an entirely new thing in the galaxy. Uly found himself disappointed at that idea, but he supposed that the *Combined Crowns of Danumash* were more like the Auga Empire that way, with a ruling elite selected by blood ties and marriage.

*Batyr*—specifically the Industrial Protectors Party—intended that the best form of government was a republic of meritocracy. Common schools and curricula. Tests to identify strengths and weaknesses. Excessive levels of taxation to prevent the accumulation of fortunes that could be handed down to children.

Everything to create an ongoing social leveling and socialization specifically to prevent power falling into the hands of fools and fascists. It had been good enough to let the smaller *Batyr* keep the much larger *Danumash* at bay for a century.

As a result, he was here trying to make the galaxy a better place, rather than merely trying to get rich, which seemed to be what most pirates were after, to hear his crew talk.

That, or hurt as many people as they felt needed it.

Which was why places like *Z'Gosza* needed him. Uly simply needed them to understand that there might be a better way to do things. One that didn't necessarily involve inviting the Auga Empire in to handle security for them.

With all *those* associated costs.

He nodded to himself and turned to Sterling Huff.

"Status of the station, Mr. Huff?" Uly asked.

"At present, they are maintaining a certain level of alert, sir," Huff replied. "Down a step or two from where they'd been before, if I read the signals correctly, but still prepared to unleash unholy hell on us if we were to get any closer."

"Agreed, Mr. Huff," Uly said. "Maintain us at this distance, with *Wren* ready to flee at the first sign of trouble and us ready to fire on anything, then run."

"Are we expecting anything like a Striker or Devastator, sir?" Huff asked, using the Auga terms for what he and Uly might have once called cruisers and battleships.

"We are not," Uly shook his head. "*Z'Gosza* doesn't maintain a formal navy, and none of the local vessels are hardy enough to engage us, unless they got crazy and tried to swarm. Even then, I suspect that the twin sixes would wreak a terrible havoc. That was why we started here."

"That," Ethir spoke up, his voice almost a birdlike chirp, "and they're so corrupt around here already that they won't necessarily mind dealing with ex-pirates like us."

"There is that," Uly agreed. He paused to consider. "Huff, you go off duty for now. Get a snack and maybe take an hour of downtime, in case this ends up running longer than we anticipated. Roscoe can fortify himself with enough coffee over on *Wren*, but he won't have to do anything except fly."

"Understood, sir." Huff rose and made his way aft. Vahid ought to have food ready for everyone, since they were all more or less on duty until this got sorted out.

Uly simply didn't know which way these folks would jump.

# THIRTEEN

Administrator Rabiu Khadijan appreciated that Director Bukra, his boss, had given him the opportunity to go out and meet with the aliens. Even if they were completely insane.

Go out and hunt pirates? Where was the profit in that?

Except that if this *Corsac Fox* was successful, *Z'Gosza* merchants might not have to pay such high rates to insure hulls and cargoes. What would that look like on a quarterly report? Or annual profit sharing?

The shuttle that had borne him to meet the aliens had landed and docked. He exited the vessel quickly, his Deputy falling in silently as he walked. Kyauta Alhaji was more competent than gifted. He would make an excellent Administrator, one of these days, but Rabiu didn't see the man ascending higher than that.

Not like Rabiu intended to do. If he could play this situation to his benefit.

How could he work this to his advantage?

They passed through a mister-gate and Rabiu let the extra dampness soak into his pores like warm sun on a glorious morning. Refreshed, he ascended from the docking level to where the Director would be waiting.

Director Bukra's Deputy sat at a desk when Rabiu entered the office space, gesturing them to seats near the door as that one rose and made her way to the hatch and entered.

A moment later, the woman emerged again.

"The Director will see you, Administrator," she said coolly.

Kyauta Alhaji remained seated, reviewing and expanding upon the notes he had already taken as part of the meeting with the aliens. Rabiu entered to see his boss seated at a desk almost large enough to land shuttles on. It was perfectly clean, too.

"Sit," Director Bukra ordered, pointing to the nearer chair.

Rabiu did, adjusting his robes just so. Perhaps a bit showy, but he'd intended to make an impression on the aliens.

He wasn't sure if he had. The situation hadn't gone anything like he'd planned.

Bukra studied his face for a long moment, turning his head right and left to let each eye focus in turn.

"They sold you the two pirate vessels for one Imperial Guilder each?" Bukra began, skipping all the preliminaries in a single blink.

Not that Rabiu was surprised. Director Bukra tended to cut to the heart of any matter quickly. Rabiu had learned to follow the man's leaps of intuition.

"Affirmative, sir," Rabiu acknowledged. "I went ahead and paid with cash that I happened to have on hand. Presumably, you will reimburse me from divisional funds, so that it doesn't look like I'm starting my own pirate clan as a side business?"

*Z'Gosza* was deeply into the shipping business. The lords of finance would not look favorably on him moonlighting. Especially like that. At the same time, getting those two ships out of circulation would put a gold star next to his name on his quarterly and annual reviews. Especially at the cost.

"I'll expect an expense report as soon as you return to your office," Bukra nodded. "And your signature on a formal transfer of property, though I'll need to consult with legal to understand how they want that handled."

Rabiu nodded. He'd been instructed to play this mission a bit fast and loose, simply because the Director had also had no idea how it would unfold.

Nobody did. Still didn't, but at least Rabiu had taken the measure of the *Corsac Fox* enough to understand that the Human had a great deal of the sorts of personal charm and charisma that would make him a successful Director in his own right, had he been part of *Z'Gosza* society.

"Talk to me about their plans," Bukra continued. "I've read the preliminaries you sent, and frankly, they are insane."

"I would tend to agree with you, Director," Rabiu nodded. "At the same time, this *Corsac Fox* seems to believe that he can succeed in his self-appointed mission. And the officers with him also seem committed."

"Hunting pirates for money?" Bukra asked.

"The term he used was *Privateer*, sir," Rabiu explained. "Formal documentation from the Governor and his Government, issued in his name, to attack enemy shipping, in this case being the pirates that he considers the enemy of all civilization. His words, by the way, not mine."

"Has nobody told him what a fool's errand that is?" Bukra replied, somewhat amazed and possibly a bit annoyed.

"His advisors include more Humans like himself, as well as Mazhin, Moss School Emro, and Thogin, Director," Rabiu said. "Normally, I would agree. At the same time, does it cost us anything, if we do send pirate hunters out?"

"Do they know how many local conglomerates they might make as enemies?" Bukra rasped.

"No," Rabiu acknowledged. "However, none of their pirates are formal employees. Instead, I'm given to understand that funds tend to be transferred as either insurance against future attacks by enemy vessels, or ransom for lost ships and cargoes."

Bukra eyed him sourly, but the Khet hadn't just spent an hour chatting with this *Corsac Fox* to understand the being.

"May I speak freely, sir?" Rabiu asked.

He knew it was a calculated risk on his part. At the same time, this might be the sort of radical, cultural transition that let a boss like Lawal Bukra leap over Senior Director and move straight to the rank of Factor.

From dangerous to world-shaping. If done correctly.

That Rabiu would be able to ride his coattails to glory meant that he could make Director and possibly get filthy, stinking rich in the process.

Always something useful. Money really was power to *Z'Gosza* society.

"Go ahead," Bukra grunted.

"If we were to feed coordinates and intelligence to this *Corsac Fox*, he might be good enough to crush some of the pirates we have to deal with, Director," Rabiu began, pausing there until he got a simple nod. "The ones we don't like. And there are many conglomerates with unofficial piracy divisions. What would happen if some of them, perhaps your own enemies or at least rivals, were the ones that were hit? While perhaps others were ignored? This *Corsac Fox* is one man with one medium-sized warship. He cannot clean up the entire Sector by himself."

"But he might make war on my enemies for me?" Bukra laughed harshly. "Or create an opening where some of that protection money flowed into my coffers instead of some pirate?"

Rabiu nodded in a most compact manner. If nothing else, Lawal Bukra had spoken the words. He could own them later if someone was listening on an electronic device right now.

"Worse," Rabiu offered as the afterthought nearly engulfed him in flames. "He might succeed, if we put the right public relations people on the task."

Rabiu slammed his lips shut at the thought, but the words had been spoken. And heard, from the way Bukra's headcrest suddenly stood upright.

Bukra blinked but didn't call down the wrath of the creators on Rabiu's head. Rabiu took that as an opening and proceeded, damning the torpedoes, as the ancient saying went.

"Piracy is supposedly glamorous," Rabiu offered carefully. "Partly, that's a tool the oligarchs use to give the proletariat an emotional outlet for the fact that their lives could be so much easier if the tax structure was applied to everyone, regardless of income or social status. Could we instead somehow combine the exoticness of this new, alien warlord with a mission as a law enforcement officer, hunting pirates? Create some new cultural touchstone?"

Rabiu stopped right there, understanding how close to heresy he was treading, with a suggestion that all creatures might have been created equal. Or that the law might apply equally to all citizens.

The *Corsac Fox* had spoken as something of a radical republican. Certainly, his command staff did not fit any model Rabiu was familiar with.

Bukra's eyes had grown speculative.

They were talking revolution here, at least in the eyes of certain classes that might take affront. And had the power to do something about their pique.

Bukra suddenly had a thought. He pulled a data reader from a drawer and starting flipping through some document, no doubt looking for a particular detail.

Rabiu waited, glad that he hadn't already been handed his head. Metaphorically or literally.

These could be dangerous waters for a mere Administrator.

At the same time, this might be the thing that made Rabiu's career. And Bukra's.

If they had the gall to grasp it. There was a phrase this *Corsac Fox* had used at one point.

Audacity.

*Z'Gosza* society tended to the careful deliberation of bureaucratic warfare.

Except when something came along and upended all formal calculations.

How rich could he get? And how far could he fall?

"Ah," Director Bukra barked. "There. Tell me about this command staff you met with. Mazhin, Emro, and Thogin?"

"And I was given to understand that perhaps as much as half of the crew were Ononguli, but sailors that had been captured when this *Corsac Fox* stole the ship away."

"It really is the *Iron Wasp*?" Bukra asked.

They knew of such a ship. That had been part of their worry when it suddenly showed up here. Worse, when it attacked someone, except that it had been attacking pirates. Other pirates.

And it wasn't *Iron Wasp*.

A bizarre case of mistaken identity, to be sure.

"It appears to be that vessel, Director," Rabiu nodded. "The hull was certainly Ononguli design. They had no mister-gates, and the corridors were generally that odd scale that the Ononguli build because of their horns."

He paused there, recalling all the details.

"The Emro woman was introduced as a Moss School Exemplar of the Arts, Director," he continued. "And certainly impressed me so with her age and sophistication. Plus, there were two more Emro women in the security detail."

"And the Mazhin?" Bukra asked.

"Two of them at the table, both male, plus a female with the security team," Rabiu said.

"Security?" Bukra asked. "Females?"

"Indeed, Director," Rabiu grinned. "The other Human in command, introduced as the First Officer, was a woman. This *Corsac Fox* seems to not mind being surrounded by competent, deadly females."

"Bizarre," Bukra muttered, but Rabiu understood.

*Z'Gosza* society tended to be heavily unbalanced to the male, leaving the female out of government and most business jobs, save when they were scions or heirs of some industrial power or wealth. Or carved themselves out a role.

Perhaps the women on that ship were in the process of doing the same. He made a mental note to confirm later.

"The Mazhin males were both sharp," Rabiu continued. "The elder was smart in the sense of technical brilliance, and was introduced as the ship's Data Officer, while the other one seemed extremely facile. A born merchant trader, that one."

"Data Officer?" Bukra asked. "What an odd job for a pirate."

"Elder statesman advisor, Director," Rabiu offered. "*Of Counsel*, as it were. The others all struck me as young, save for Suka Kuri, the Emro. This is a young team."

"Then they haven't yet learned that they cannot change the galaxy," Bukra laughed.

"Indeed, Director, but I have a question," Rabiu said, waiting for the man to nod. "What if they can?"

"Can what?"

"What if we used them as much as they intend to use us?" Rabiu continued. "What if we did put a public relations team on the task? What if they could succeed?"

Bukra sputtered some more, then fell silent.

There was a long pause, where Rabiu began wondering if he'd finally overstepped and was about to get his fins singed. Possibly demoted such that Kyauta Alhaji became his boss and he the deputy.

Risks and rewards in a bureaucracy were hardly ever obvious.

Bukra's scowl was ugly and dangerous, but then it cleared some.

"Write me up a project plan about how you would do such a thing, Khadijan," Director Bukra ordered in a terrible voice.

"Sir?"

"How would you make this *Corsac Fox* a hero?"

# Z'GOSZA STATION FOUR

# FOURTEEN

Uly had been in his office, six steps away from the bridge in case of an emergency, but not breathing down Huff's neck for the moment.

It had been...just over two hours since the Khet Administrator had left.

His comm beeped.

"Sir, we have traffic from the station," Huff said. "You'll want to read and reply."

Uly was already in motion. He emerged from his office a step faster than Haydar and Piruz entered via the main hatch, so they must have been close by and gotten the same call. Possibly playing a Mazhin game similar to Human chess over tea.

Everyone threw themselves into stations and buckled themselves in, but the ship had not changed alert status.

Huff looked a little worn and frazzled, but that was time being in command of the entire vessel by himself. At fifteen.

Uly didn't think he'd have even done as well as the young man. But then, Uly hadn't had a senior officer trying to make him the best naval officer possible at the time, either.

"Thank you, Mister Huff," he said honestly.

"On your screen, sir," Huff replied, relaxing a shade.

Uly unlocked it and read. Then read it a second time.

"Seriously?" he asked the room.

Haydar was reading the message as well, from the way his tentacles were writhing madly.

"Haydar, I realize that you don't know the Khet as a species all that well, nor do you know *Z'Gosza*," Uly said. "Your thoughts?"

"Ask Ethir," Haydar said. "He's the one with any way to determine if this is an honest offer or a trap."

Uly nodded and found the button on his arm rest.

"Ethir, this is Uly," he said, listening to the system play his voice back a second later. "I need you on the bridge soonest."

He left it at that. Then read the message again.

Ethir Ewen wasn't an engineer, so he didn't bunk with those folks aft. He and his cousins were generally excellent at manual labor that required eight hands but not a lot of strength, so they did basic maintenance and occasionally helped cook.

Nobody sat around on a warship in service, but not everyone should be elbow deep in a drive system, either.

Ethir appeared quickly, still wiping his hands on a rag that he stuffed into a pocket as he did.

"What've you got?" he asked brightly.

"Message from the station," Uly said. "Invitation. Here, you read it."

Ethir slipped around next to him and muttered. Then whistled.

He looked up at Uly and nodded.

"Wondering if it is a trap?" Ethir asked.

"Undoubtedly," Uly nodded back.

"Think they're on the level here," Ethir said. "See this line? They want you and one of your folks to fly the two captured pirates down, rather than them sending pilots out. Keeps folks around here from getting inspired to maybe make a run for it with armed warships."

"Why would they do that?" Haydar asked from his station.

"*Z'Gosza* can be a shitty place, if you aren't rich," Ethir turned to him. "Three sets of laws on the books, depending on how you read them. Me and the boys got thrown in jail for twenty-four days for vagrancy, merely because we didn't have that next month's rent already in our pockets when stopped by a cop. Would've, but they don't understand that sort of thing. We were no better than thieves in their eyes."

"Which was, of course, impossibly far from the truth," Uly noted dryly.

Ethir grinned.

"Maybe," he shrugged. "You can't con an honest man, and we also didn't have the cash for a quick bribe. After our time, we took the offer of a cheap transit somewhere else, because at that point we were on their scanners and they'd have started looking for reasons to pick us up. Eventually, we'd have probably all ended up in a labor battalion or something."

"Circle back," Uly ordered. "We fly two ships over to them. How do we get back?"

"Oh, that's part of the negotiation," Ethir replied. "They want to see how well you fly, to see if you're seriously capable of taking on pirates."

"Is it a trap to capture Uly?" Haydar asked.

"Don't think so," Ethir said, then shrugged. "One way to look at it is that they slot you in somewhere as a mid-level peon. Not rich enough to fawn over. Not irrelevant enough to ignore. Somewhere in the middle, where they normally put the artisans and small-scale merchants who don't compete with the industrial conglomerates that own and run the economy, if that makes sense. Skilled folks without fortunes, looking to make them."

"And this person they are inviting me to meet?" Uly pressed. "According to your notes, a Director is extremely high ranking. Two down from the Governor, depending on how you slice it."

"Those are big steps, boss," Ethir cautioned. "Factors are major players, but they come in a thousand caste flavors. Directors are the ones that really make the economy and government work. If you can separate the two."

"Separate?" Uly asked.

"Sure, this Director Lawal Bukra of the Khet is a bureaucrat," Ethir nodded. "He also is going to have direct ties to at least one major corporate organization. Probably several, all loosely allied. They'll need favors done. He needs money. Both sides have an ongoing arrangement."

"And us offering to hunt pirates might disturb that?" Uly asked. "You told me that it would be a good opening around here."

"Oh, it is," Ethir laughed. "They'll send us after their enemies first. We'll open holes in other economies where they can slip friendly merchants and ships in, thereby making them more money. Or we'll crush some of the pissant junior varsity players running around, like those boys we nailed down when we got here. They don't belong to anyone local, or they wouldn't be preying on shipping this close to home. Someone already likes us lots for that, even before they have a name."

Uly considered it. It made no sense, but he'd been prepared for that. If you looked at the oligarchs around here in the same light as you saw *Danumash* nobles, there were a great many parallels visible. Inherited wealth and power. Multiple legal systems, most of which really didn't bother the wealthy all that much, while crushing any dissent.

But everyone hated pirates. Not enough to actually do anything about them besides buying them off, according to Ethir, but they weren't popular with the oligarchs.

Merely the cost of doing business.

Until the *Corsac Fox* came along.

"Then answer me this, Ethir," Uly said. "We're extremely short-staffed around here. And stretched even thinner by operating both ships at the same time. Now, I need to fly down to the station aboard one of the pirates. How many people do I take with me, leaving everyone else to carry that much larger of a load while I'm gone? And how much of a threat are they to me personally while I'm there?"

"I think you're going to be under a solid safe conduct passage," Ethir said, pointing to the message on the screen. "That's how I read this part. Even if nothing else, this offer of a reset means that we're stuck with the pirates, and you return to your ship and depart, assuming no deal can be struck after selling the ships. But the rest of this language really feels to me like they want to cut a deal. Like, bending over back-wards here, compared to what I'd normally expect."

"How soon will they expect a response?" Uly asked.

"At minimum, not for an hour," Haydar spoke up sharply. "We need to review their offer and consider our counteroffer. Or some bullshit like that. I wouldn't wait more than six hours, because that seems to be the end of their regular business day, from the time-keeping signal that station is broadcasting."

"So I have time to think?" Uly asked.

"Absolutely, boss," Ethir nodded enthusiastically. "How can I help?"

Uly considered it.

"You stay here with Haydar and Sterling, keeping watch," Uly decided.

"Where are you going?" Haydar asked.

"To consult with an expert," Uly replied.

# FIFTEEN

Uly had checked with the system and located Suka Kuri aft in one of the small gymnasiums that Adrian Sobol had maintained for training his boarding troops, back when this vessel had been a pirate. Dan still held similar classes here, teaching and learning various forms of close combat fighting, with and without weapons.

Uly didn't attend that often, instead focusing on pure endurance training and fighting with his Shadowwhip sword. Being an officer took a lot of his time. Being the only trained officer aboard meant that he was overseeing five or six times as much work as that asshole Savatier had, back on *Marshall Castillon*.

Today, Suka Kuri was teaching a class in painting. Or rather, supervising while Hiko Seiichai painted a masterwork that Uly would have proudly hung in his office or quarters. Two of the Thogin cousins, Waltin Gysby and Ralphye Byne, were also painting with more enthusiasm than skill. The third, Hobse Baldo, was no doubt off having a nap somewhere while this group sat on stools and concentrated on easels.

There were even a couple of Ononguli engineers in the class. At least trying to paint. Dedicated to at least committing some level of art. Uly wasn't good enough to judge, other than Hiko was that amazing.

It was a shame that Hiko had left feet when it came to dance or close combat, which was probably why he was Moss School, when his immense size and bulk would have made him truly intimidating in Sabre School.

Suka Kuri looked up when Uly entered, then smiled.

She gave the impression of being tiny and hunched with age, but the woman was still two hundred and eight centimeters tall and one hundred and forty kilograms. It was only when she was standing next to one of the other Emro that she looked small.

"Conductor?" she asked quietly.

"I was hoping I might borrow you for a few minutes, madame," Uly nodded. "Your wisdom and worldliness."

She got a mischievous glint in her eyes and a grin that suggested how much of her vast experience might not have been entirely wholesome, but that was exactly why he wanted to talk to her specifically.

Everyone else here, not counting Haydar, were young. Approaching middle-aged at most.

Only Suka Kuri was old and wise, however much she might deny the second part.

"Hiko, you continue painting, but get up every once in a while and answer questions," she instructed.

Hiko was also shy. Would happily squirrel in on the easel in front of him until someone poked him in the ribs and reminded him that the dinner bell had already gone off and that he should eat.

Suka Kuri approached and Uly backed into the corridor, smiling up at the woman as he moved to a nearby office. None of the furniture fit an Emro, so she sat on the desk instead, leaving him at her knee like a supplicant.

Not entirely wrong, either.

"How can I help you, Uly?" she asked simply.

"I have an invitation from the station to meet with a Director and discuss piracy," Uly said, taking a few moments to go over the gist of the message with her. "Ethir thinks I'm safe to go down and meet. That the worst would be they put me on a shuttle and send me back."

"I think he is correct in that assessment, Uly," Suka Kuri nodded. "And?"

"And I need a second pilot," he said. "Plus an indeterminate number of crew members accompanying me. We're stretched thin. This will make it worse, at least until we get back. Doubly so with twenty-four captured pirates."

"I spoke with Nils Shevchenko," Suka Kuri said. "He thinks that there might be as many as seven that could be recruited out of that mob. Five men and the two women who he knows by reputation. He was intending to talk to you at dinner."

Uly nodded. His Ononguli crew were still a lot in awe and a little nervous approaching him directly. Partly, that was them remembering being the slavers who had captured Uly and his people. That had killed Thorley Eldridge, though none of them had been there. They were still feeling their way into a relationship with Uly and his more-established crews.

They would get there. It was just taking time.

"Have Haydar and Piruz interview them," he decided. "And you assist, if I may impose upon you."

Suka Kuri threw her head back and laughed. Uly grinned.

An Exemplar of the Arts was a title awarded by acclaim. Broad acclaim. Once given, it freed the possessor from all strictures. They were as free as Emro society allowed, to go anywhere or do anything that would further their art.

That Hiko and Yanouk had been her personal students when they had originally been captured by *Iron Wasp* just let Uly know how much potential Suka Kuri saw in the two.

She had told him, more than once, that he could give her orders. And he had reminded her, more than once, that she might not choose to listen. And hadn't, more than once.

They shared a smile.

Then her eyes got so deadly serious that he could see where this woman might have become Sabre School, a lifetime ago. Sabre were artists in their own way, just as Moss were warriors in theirs.

Suka Kuri's chin came up and her eyes focused on some distant point.

"You will have Dan fly the other ship," she said soberly. "Nasrin will join you, as will Yanouk. And Katya Zehlennko."

"Why her?" Uly asked, wondering most about including an

Ononguli woman engineer that he could only pick out of a lineup because there were exactly three Ononguli women in the current crew.

"When Administrator Khadijan joined you to talk business, I was watching him," Suka Kuri said in a strong, deliberate voice. "That was why I chose to act as Tea Master. It put me beneath his notice. I doubt that he understood how open his face was when he spoke, however twisted and convoluted his words might have been."

"Okay?" Uly prompted when she fell silent.

"Ethir has spoken of the gender imbalance in their culture," she continued. "How most all of the people you will meet with will be male."

"He did."

"You had women handling your security," Suka Kuri laughed. "These poor men wouldn't ever do something like that."

"Dan's the best," he said simply.

She was. He couldn't have done any of this but for her supporting him. Her being there when he needed someone to talk to. To rely on.

Someone who was his friend, and not just a crew subordinate.

"She is," Suka Kuri agreed. "So are Yanouk and Nasrin. Add in Katya and there will be one male officer, surrounded entirely by female warriors. Competent, deadly ones, because Katya is the best of the three Ononguli at that. Now, these Khet must account themselves for a new world where an alien species nobody has ever heard of has a team of alien women, representing four different species themselves, advising and protecting him. I'm just sorry Ethir didn't bring one of his female cousins with him."

"None of them were crazy enough to travel with those four goofballs," Uly pointed out.

"True. Very true," she grinned. "Still, perhaps we should make it a point to find you such. To form for you an advisory council that are only women, representing as many species as we can find. Excluding the Auga, at least for now."

"Any particular reason for that?" Uly asked.

"They are the opposite of Humans, in many ways," she nodded. "Humans will strike out into the unknown to see what is out there. Look at you. The Auga tend to move with exceptional planning and great bureaucratic detail. You will not find many Auga criminals to begin with. Female Auga criminals will be like that one mythological creature you mentioned. The one with a single horn in the forehead."

"Unicorns," Uly nodded.

"Yes, unicorns," she agreed. "You might find one out there somewhere, as this is a vast galaxy, but we should not waste much time chasing those sightings. Instead, we will listen and if she exists perhaps she will come to us."

Uly leaned back in the chair to study the woman. An Exemplar of the Arts was granted that title for their lifetime of wisdom. He could hear it in her words, however insane the idea was on the surface.

Any crazier than sailing into a strange port and offering to hunt pirates for money?

No.

He nodded.

"This is why you bring such joy into my life," she said, causing him to start with surprise.

"Me?"

"You will listen to the crazy ideas of an old woman, Uly," Suka Kuri laughed.

"Ah, but that's a survivorship bias," he said, standing now, though it still left his eyes below hers. He took her hands in his. "You have seen and learned many things. It is in my interest to listen, because you save me from mistakes. And teach me new ways to think."

They shared another grin.

"Now what?" she asked.

"Now, I go find out just how interesting the Khet of *Z'Gosza* want to be."

# SIXTEEN

Dan had brought Katya with her, sending Yanouk and Nasrin with Uly on the Probe.

The Ultra-Bomber was disarmed, with parts missing and left on *Wren* against some future need, so she was piloting the craft towards a heavily armed station with nothing more than her Heavy Exoripper and her Icemace.

And Uly.

"*Fox Three*, this is *Fox Two*," his voice came over the comm. "Approaching the landing bay now. On terminal approach."

"Understood, *Fox Two*," Dan replied.

The station was huge. Almost a small moon, orbiting in a high geosynchronous orbit over the main city on the planet below. According to Haydar, a significant chunk of their government was below, but all the important people were up here.

And he'd told her that the place could easily hold two hundred thousand people, without crowding.

A city in space.

*Batyr* had military stations that size, but those were bases intended to build and repair major fleet elements, so they were long and massive.

And mostly hollow. *Danumash* preferred many smaller stations, strung out like pearls in the night sky.

*Z'Gosza* had it all in one place.

She could see where that might make them a little nervous when a pirate arrived. Or when two small raiders were sailing close.

They were invisible, but Dan could feel the monstrous 12dm wave-bolts tracking her. And, no doubt, they were vectoring her and Uly into an armored spot on the station, well away from the important people if this was all some elaborate trap.

That was how she would have done it.

The Probe slipped into a bay large enough to hold a dozen small ships just like it, aligning with a set of landing lights on the far left. Uly was also a good pilot, but Dan understood that junior officers like him frequently were assigned to command vessels that size fresh out of school.

Uly's father had probably pulled strings to get his son assigned to a Forward Cruiser. Or someone wanting to court favor with the man. Same as he'd been transferred to *Marshall Castillon* when *Vanguard Lesauvage* went in for major repairs that might last a year.

Hell, that ship might even be back on active duty by now, all things considered.

And she knew Uly wouldn't want to go back. Not now, possibly not ever. He had too many people—too many species—counting on him to do the right thing.

Including her.

"*Fox Two*, we have successfully landed," Uly said over the comm.

"Beginning final approach now," Dan replied.

Like Uly, she was a pretty good pilot. Capturing enemy vessels often required boarding them in a shuttle, unless some berk like Savatier sent them across in suits. And officers didn't fly those shuttles. Enlisted punks like her did.

Dan made sure to come in exactly along the same lines, flying the same formation. By the book, because there would be folks over there keeping score.

*Gotta make Uly look good.*

The Ultra-Bomber was a weird craft. One turret with a Neutron

Omnipulsar. Wavebolts in launch tubes under the wings, but only two of them, so more of a threat than a danger.

This one was simply a badly configured freighter now. Or a transport for a small crew and a set of passengers.

No longer a warship.

She landed on the tracking lights and shut everything down, nodding to Katya.

Like the rest of her species, she had bright red skin and long goat horns, twisted and pointed up and slightly back. Black eyeballs with red irises that glowed slightly in the dark.

Human-sized bipeds. Katya was shorter than Dan and Uly. Not as curvy as Olimpiada or Taisiya, being built more square from shoulders to hips, without a lot of waist in the middle.

Closer to normal height for a female Human, plus the horns. A little nervous but hiding it well.

"Relax," Dan reminded her with a smile. "You'll do fine."

"As long as I don't have to shoot anyone," Katya replied nervously.

"There will be more training when we get back to the *Fox*," Dan nodded. "For now, you just stand around and look menacing."

"Compared to a Mazhin and an Emro?" Katya laughed. "Sure."

Dan shared the laugh. Yanouk was big. Nasrin had brought her Omnibow. Katya with an Exoripper carbine would not add much to that.

At the same time, Dan did like Suka Kuri's idea of a security team made up entirely of females.

Anari would get there soon. Omid Adl, the other Mazhin, was much more of a homebody, and a middle-aged one at that. She ran the laundry and cleaning services with an iron hand, and all the Mazhin were thankful.

Dan hadn't met a Khet female. Or even seen pictures of one, come to think of it.

They both rose now, adjusted weapons, then moved to the hatch as the big, outer bay door slid shut and the entire volume began to fill with air. To a human, the atmosphere would be heavy, cool, and wet, but that was Khet preferences, and down on the surface it would be even worse, reflecting their aquatic heritage. The station was a compromise, allowing all other species to trade with *Z'Gosza*.

Dan waited until the outside air pressure stabilized before opening her hatch. They'd discussed traveling in suits, but Uly had decided that he needed to act like he trusted the locals, regardless of the truth, so they were in uniforms.

At least the two of them. They really needed something new, and enough of the outfits for everyone. And not Imperial Auga red and gold, though they had a lot of those uniforms. She'd be happy to sell or trade those for something else, one-for-one.

Dan emerged with Katya a step behind her and off to one side. They joined Uly as he exited the Probe ahead of Nasrin and Yanouk, looking like the start of a joke.

*A Human, a Mazhin, and an Emro walk into a bar...*

Uly nodded calmly at her, but she could see the stress in his eyes. And his hands. However, she supposed that only someone who knew him as well as she did would, so it was good.

She nodded back, and his four, female, badass bodyguards started towards the main hatch, all armed. Even Uly was wearing his Shadowwhip sword, though he'd left off the Lamellar vest.

*We're pirates. And we're not afraid of you.*

As a look, it seemed to work.

Yanouk had brought a boarding ax. Like Dan's Icemace, it was a variable-length weapon, but it only shrank down to one meter, and could deploy all the way out to three, making it a halberd, according to some definitions. Bearded ax for an edge, with a massive hammer face opposite that.

She had it midway, so the weapon wasn't even as tall as she was when walking, but Dan knew Yanouk would have to duck under most doorways.

Only the Emro built ships to that scale. And the Sabre School tended to prefer small attack craft, rather than big Strikers.

Still, what would a Sabre School Devastator look like?

Dan made a note to ask Anari at some point. Or Haydar. He might know where to find historical records, if it had ever been done.

They exited the flight bay and Administrator Khadijan greeted them, with the same Deputy as before. There was a small security detail in one corner, but nobody was holding weapons at present, which was good.

Two other Khet stood off to one side. It took Dan a moment to realize that the closer one was holding a camera, and the other had some sort of boom microphone on a backpack-deployed, stabilized arm.

It almost looked enough like a weapon that she'd gone for her Exoripper.

Dan shifted to keep them visible in the corner of her eyes, just in case. Nasrin and Yanouk could step into hand-to-hand combat and move to any of several unarmed or armed forms fast enough. Katya would pull her carbine around front. Uly had his sword.

"Conductor Fortier," the Administrator greeted them. "I've taken the liberty of inviting a documentary crew to join us and record this first contact between our two civilizations."

*You've what?*

# SEVENTEEN

Uly felt Dan and the other women bristle behind him. He focused on remaining outwardly calm and perhaps a touch aloof.

Ethir had mentioned that *Z'Gosza* society tended to be extremely finely graded socially, so Uly simply decided that he was superior in rank to a mere Administrator, though not necessarily to the man's Director. That put him in a position of power here.

Especially if Khadijan was going to throw curveballs like this at him.

He turned to the camera, noting it, then ignoring everything but the Khet in front of him.

Administrator Khadijan, the being who had invited him to travel to the station in order to make a deal about hunting pirates.

Privateer. Freebooter. Something.

"Administrator," Uly acknowledged the man coolly. "I'm looking forward to our negotiations."

For an awful lot of other species, this might be their first exposure to Humans. Imperial Sector Seventeen was a long ways away from here, so he would be setting future expectations until more Humans arrived. Uly supposed that this would be some sort of immortality.

For good or ill.

Before the Khet could speak again, Uly decided to throw his own curveball back.

"My advisors," he said, gesturing to the women Suka Kuri had suggested. "Sheridan Chastain, my First Officer. Nasrin Monfared of the Mazhin. Yanouk Miyoshi of the Emro. Katya Zehlennko of the Ononguli."

He didn't mention that Yanouk was Moss School. Everyone would assume Sabre, considering that she was armed. One of these days, he'd bring two such giant, green women with him, doubling the impact when he did.

Khadijan was certainly off-centered again.

"This way, Conductor," Khadijan managed after a beat too-long to let his brain catch up.

Uly let the man lead. The Deputy moved to the end of the line. The film crew shut down their gear for now and fell in last, but Uly could already sense the Khet in charge wanting to take him aside and ask all manner of questions.

Probably the sort of thing that would set the fellow up for whatever was their most prestigious journalism award, to be there for a true First Contact, however much it wasn't, since he'd first been captured by Adrian Sobol, then the Auga Empire.

Still, good press. Wasn't that what he was after, offering to destroy piracy in this region?

The trip took a while. Up forty levels in a lift that was a bit crowded with Yanouk hunched over. At least she was smiling.

Eventually, after possibly crossing half the station on slidewalks, they were escorted into a meeting hall, but only after the camera crew got in there first and set themselves up to capture more footage.

This time, Uly let Nasrin lead, followed by Yanouk then Katya. Dan was a step ahead of him and the Khet filming seemed pleased with the footage.

There was an older Khet seated when they entered. He didn't rise, so Uly assumed this to be the Director. The being who could rank him, in the made-up system Uly was applying to his day. Ethir had said that Directors got things done, using Administrators as their hands.

This then, was the person in charge.

The four women took up spots behind Uly along the wall. The film crew moved to shoot over the Director's shoulder in such a way that Uly was centered on his team in the picture.

Pretty, if nothing else. Deadly, if necessary.

"Conductor Fortier, it is my pleasure to introduce you to Director Lawal Bukra," Khadijan began. "My superior, and the person who has purchased the two pirate vessels you captured when you first arrived in the *Z'Gosza* system, in the name of the department."

Uly nodded. Playing to the crowds who would see this footage. And history, he supposed.

He still didn't know who this Bukra represented, although there was apparently a department involved.

It was an opening.

"Thank you for the welcome, Director," Uly replied. "It is my hope that I might be able to turn over the captured crews to local law enforcement as well. I'm not entirely familiar with your customs, but it is also my hope that they face nothing more than incarceration, as opposed to some of the systems I've visited where those beings would be immediately executed for their crimes."

He liked the gasps. And the calculations in the Director's eyes, entirely invisible to the camera behind the being. This was a person who was here to deal. And now understood that Uly had indeed been to a variety of places and met many cultures.

Uly didn't need to mention that he'd been a prisoner for most of them and a pirate for the rest.

Not yet, anyway.

Uly let himself be drawn into small talk at that point. He mentioned a few systems. Talked for the cameras about rescuing the Mazhin, Emro, Thogin, and Ononguli who made up his crew, though again, he didn't go into too many details.

Icing, rather than cake.

After a time of verbal fencing, he felt Director Bukra mentally step up and grow more serious. Khadijan had remained largely helpful off to one side, without contributing materially.

Like Dan in her current *faux* role as a *mere bodyguard*, Khadijan wasn't here to talk. Which was a shame, as Dan had more experience at the piracy side of things than he did. As did Haydar, though he didn't like to talk about it.

Uly had to be on point today. Making decisions and contacts that would set the pattern for how things would proceed from here.

"Conductor, how did you come to be in possession of your other vessel?" Director Bukra asked in a leading voice, almost nodding to the camera. "The one I believe is called *Wren*?"

Uly smiled. He'd been waiting for this opening for hours at this point. Ethir and Haydar had both had useful ideas.

"I took it away from the Auga," he said simply. "We had captured the ship once known as *Iron Wasp* already, and I determined that taking possession of the cargo carrier *Wren* would put us in the best position to not have to turn to piracy to make our way."

"You took it?" Bukra asked, his voice stuttering down to nothing. "Away from the Auga?"

"That's right," Uly nodded, smiling. "Sailed into the port where it was being held, boarded it with a team, and sailed it away."

Khet, like Humans, blinked rapidly when the brain suffered a cognitive overload. Khet eyes were much larger, so it was far more obvious. Plus the way the gills flapped on the sides of the neck.

Uly watched his statement being processed.

The Auga Empire was the single largest and most powerfully dangerous political entity anybody knew of. Only the fact that they moved with slow deliberation and deep bureaucracy in all things had prevented them from conquering the next ring of Sectors out. That, and the number of smaller nations surrounding them that were fighting against that rising tide.

The Ononguli were fractious at the best of times, as he'd been told, but would all assemble into vast war fleets to fall on any Auga force attempting to enter the regions of space the Ononguli considered theirs.

The Khet of *Z'Gosza* were far enough away from the Auga that they hardly ever saw them. And then only as diplomats and traders, not as military formations.

And the Auga had a reputation as a ruthless, militaristic society.

Of course, nobody had ever met the Humans of the *Institutional Republic of Batyr*, either. Uly was willing to grant that his society was at least as dangerous and violent, if so much tinier that they didn't matter.

Except when he'd stolen a warship, then a cargo carrier, from the Auga.

Director Bukra shook himself once and came back on-line.

"And you intend to go hunting pirates?" he said, almost sounding normal again.

"That's right," Uly replied. "I would like to negotiate a treaty with your government that grants my vessels safe harbor here at *Z'Gosza*, plus the ability to dispose of materials that we will capture in the course of such activities."

"Such as?"

"Enemy warships we take," Uly turned serious as he spoke. "Third-party vessels we end up liberating from where said pirates had previously captured them. Cargoes and supplies that are surplus to my military or commercial needs. That sort of thing. I've prepared a draft for your legal advisors to review."

He glanced back and Dan stepped forward, handing him a data card that he put on the table. She looked like a pure war goddess with the fierce scowl on her dark face.

Deadly beauty, carved in the darkest bronze.

Uly could have had the card in his own pocket, but she'd been right that having her carry it around elevated Uly in the eyes of the locals.

He had *staff*. Better, they were armed and dangerous women. Beautiful ones, at that, though Uly had never considered that he might look on an alien woman that way. To say nothing of several different species.

Exotic, though, which just added to the mystique he was intending to bring to *Z'Gosza*.

Uly slid it across the table to where Director Bukra took it. Standard size. Standard everything. The Auga traded with a great many planetary systems and star nations, and their tech had permeated out a immense distance, even reaching places like *Danumash* and *Batyr*.

Uly had never really known how vast the rest of the galaxy was. How populated. But then, *Batyr* was on the far edge of Imperial Sector Seventeen from the more cosmopolitan regions, with most of *Danumash* between them and the Auga. And everyone else.

They'd be in his way if he ever did decide to return home. Or, at least, to go back to the world where he'd been born.

Bukra seemed to have fallen into a sort of shock.

*Expecting barbarians for whom indoor plumbing and Variable Pulse Spatial Generators were magic, were we?*

Uly kept his smile compact and polite, rather than triumphant. He would need Director Bukra, or someone like him, to pull this stunt off. And Ethir and Haydar had been most helpful in filling in some of the blanks in the plan he and Dan had come up with.

"Given the bulk of materials we've proposed, I'm certain that your staff will need some time to digest it all, Director," Uly noted dryly. "With that in mind, how would you like to proceed?"

He leaned back and did relax now.

Bukra looked like a person that someone had whomped upside the head with a stick. Administrator Khadijan probably earned his quarterly bonus by stepping into the fray.

"Conductor Fortier, as you are a stranger to this region, I have laid out a variety of activities to keep you entertained," Khadijan spoke up. "Tourist sorts of things, intended to give you a greater understanding of the Khet of *Z'Gosza*, with both cultural elements as well as simple recreational activities. Were you in any hurry to return to your ship while we undertook to digest your proposals?"

Uly turned to Khadijan and smiled.

"I was not," he said simply. "Though some of my crew might be disappointed that they aren't granted shore leave at present. Still, I would love to get a better understanding of your culture if we're likely to go into business together."

He noted that the camera in the corner hadn't turned off at any point. Hadn't flinched. Nothing. Recording all of this for posterity.

Uly figured he'd look good. And the two Khet at the table were handling things well.

And he'd said the magic word that would smooth over any number of complications later.

*Business.*

"Director," Khadijan said, turning things back to his superior. "With your leave, I will see about getting Conductor Fortier and his staff settled. Then they can look over the list of activities and we can plan our response accordingly?"

"Yes," Bukra said, his voice finally firm again. "That sounds like an excellent suggestion, Administrator Khadijan. Make certain our guests are well treated."

Khadijan rose, so Uly did as well. The Director had several hundred pages of a proposed treaty to go over before he could even begin to really start negotiating, but those were lessons Uly had learned from his parents.

Anselm Fortier was an Assistant Deputy Secretary of the Party on Gralbo itself, the capital of *Batyr*. Tamsin Simon might have been more of a *housefrau* than a bureaucrat, but Uly knew just how sharp and smart Mom was, assisting Father's maneuvering in subtle ways to get him only a few steps below the Secretariat itself.

Uly figured he would be using those lessons here.

If he wanted to survive.

# EIGHTEEN

Haydar looked over the game board with something bordering on despair. Piruz just grinned.

"Okay, I admit it," Haydar surrendered. "I'm not concentrating well enough to give you a good game. You win."

He leaned back and picked up his tea, noting that he'd gotten so distracted that he'd let it grow cold, too.

Rising, he took it with him and moved to the sink to dump it out. Piruz had left the board and joined him, so they poured more tea as they stood there.

"Anything in particular?" Piruz asked, as much with words as scent and tentacles.

But then, the Mazhin weren't as limited in their communications as most species.

"Worried about Uly," Haydar admitted.

Piruz nodded in agreement.

"He will be dropping a small bomb on them with that treaty," Piruz noted. "I wonder how long it will take them to understand that signing it makes Uly his own national actor. That is a treaty between nations, after all."

"I expect them to redline most of that language out on the first pass," Haydar chuckled. "Ethir and I put it in there to give their lawyers something to do, after all. No, I wonder if we're asking Uly and Dan to do too much here. It's too easy to forget that he's younger than you are, Piruz."

Piruz blinked once, then nodded.

"Yes, he is," he acknowledged. "How do we take some of the load off his shoulders?"

Haydar considered his options. And that last meeting with Uly's inner team, including Suka Kuri.

"It's time to go talk to those folks that Nils identified as potential recruits," Haydar decided. "See if we can trust them enough to add them to the crew. It's not much, but every little bit helps."

"Following you, old man," Piruz bowed mockingly.

Haydar made an obscene gesture with his tentacles and headed out. Sterling Huff and Drew Roscoe were handling the two ships well enough for now, but those were technical tasks.

Haydar needed to handle some of the subtler things.

He headed down and aft and gathered up Suka Kuri to assist.

Gennady Travers was guarding the hatch where the pirates were being held. He came to attention as Haydar approached.

"Should you be armed, sir?" Travers asked as Haydar considered the hatch.

"No," Haydar replied. "Shoot anyone making a break for it. If they gang up, shoot all of them."

A bit bloodthirsty, but Travers nodded crisply and turned into the sort of deadly serious creature who would carry out such an order. Piruz sobered. Suka Kuri had a growl on her face utterly at odds with how the woman normally held herself.

Haydar opened the hatch and stood where Travers could shoot past him if necessary.

Twenty-four beings didn't fill the vast space any more than Uly and his various crews had, when the situation had been reversed.

"Vova Naumov, present yourself," Haydar ordered the room.

An Ononguli male popped up from a bunk off to one side, looking around confused and maybe a little scared.

"Stand there," Haydar pointed. "Klavdiya Chaykovsky. Serafima Sobol. You will join Naumov."

The only two females present. Both Ononguli.

The remainder was an even mix of Ononguli, Ugotha, and Khet. Males. Most of them hardened criminals. Most of them not worth talking to, though Nils Shevchenko had several more that he spoke well enough of to consider. It was still a sliding scale.

"You three, come with me," Haydar ordered in a voice he hadn't used all that much since he'd stopped being a pirate. Possibly about the time these three youngsters were learning to tie their own shoelaces.

The remaining pirates had stirred, but nobody jumped up and demanded to know what was going on. Even the Ugotha who had been nominally in charge of this raiding party.

But then, that one hadn't impressed Haydar as a leader of any kind. Merely a bully willing to use his bulk and craziness to get the others to obey.

Exactly the opposite of what Uly needed, if they were all going to be successful at this.

The three came to rest. Haydar backed out of the doorway and gestured them to join him, then shut the hatch and locked it.

"Nils Shevchenko has been willing to speak up for the three of you," Haydar said to their confusion. "And a few others. My friends and I are going to interview you individually. If we like what we hear, you might be offered a job as part of this crew, once I can speak with the Conductor."

"And if not?" Naumov asked.

"You'll go into an isolated cell until I talk to everyone on my list," Haydar replied. "Then, when I'm done, you'll go back in there with the rest and be turned over to the local authorities. That's jail instead of death, at least in *Z'Gosza*. Am I clear?"

He hated coming across as the heavy. It had never been his favorite role in the old days, even when it had been necessary.

It was necessary here, though, so he would do it.

The three gave off the scent of nervous fear, but he wasn't surprised.

What would be telling was when they started answering questions, and if they understood that his kind could smell their lies.

# NINETEEN

Administrator Rabiu Khadijan wondered, yet again, if he'd dreamed too big. Set himself up for utter failure in such a way that even being demoted to Deputy might be too much to ask.

"What in the Dark Rift is an Admiralty Court, anyway?" Bukra grumbled under his breath, paging through the printed document.

It was nearly a finger thick, this printout. Reset margins and with spacing to provide the ability to mark it up with the requisite purple ink that most bureaucrats bled when pricked.

"Appendix Seventeen," Rabiu said, flipping his copy over to get to the reference. "*After capturing, the privateers can bring the seized prize before a designated Admiralty Court for condemnation and transfer of ownership to the privateer, with said prize then being added to the privateer's forces, or sold at auction, either public or private, with or without the associated cargo, to be determined by the privateer at the time they take possession.*"

"And we have to set one of those up?" Bukra snapped.

They'd been at this for several hours. Rabiu hoped that the hotel he'd hired for the *Corsac Fox* and his crew was adequate for now, as he suspected he would be in with the Director all evening. Unless he arranged a dinner to break things up.

Which sounded like a smarter and smarter idea every time it popped into his head.

"We will, Director," Rabiu said. "However, I think that we can adapt the existing Probate Court structure without much effort, since most of the time they tend to be dealing with estates that do not have proper heirs. This isn't that different."

Rabiu nearly flinched at the scowl Director Bukra sent his way, but fortified himself with the knowledge that the Khet across the table didn't have any better idea what he was doing there than Rabiu did. Idly, he wondered if this *Corsac Fox* had set them up.

Or rather, how well had he done so?

He decided to take another risk. After all, if the only limits here were his imagination, how far could Rabiu dream?

"Plus, Director, I'm sure that the Governor will need to look into taxes to be assessed on the sale of condemned vessels emerging from such a Court," he offered. "And judges will need to be hired, with their associated staffs."

"Go big or go home, Khadijan?" Bukra asked with a sudden smile, sounding more like a hunting shark now, which was good.

"There would appear to be, on the surface of things, a tremendous amount of money to be made, Director," Rabiu replied. "Especially if the *Corsac Fox* can start capturing pirates and own captured ships. Those will be new hulls that can haul more cargo. Or be turned into some sort of local gendarme, so maybe you will need to contact Factor Bitrus about forming some sort of private or maybe even a semi-public militia navy."

"Whatever for, Khadijan?" Bukra pressed, confused again.

"Assuming the *Corsac Fox* is successful, he's going to make enemies, sir," Rabiu replied. "More enemies. Those forces might be sufficient to consider an attack on *Z'Gosza*, if only to attempt to recover warships they have previously lost. Or to take possession of a small armed fleet. Better if we were already building such a fleet ourselves, isn't it? Perhaps other adventurers might see what the *Corsac Fox* has done and start attacking other pirates themselves. Could we make *Z'Gosza* a regional hub of used starship sales? Plus, servicing and repairing many new ships probably will also require an investment in orbital shipyards dedicated to small warships, instead of turning out cargo carriers. Or in addition, perhaps."

Rabiu grew nervous when Director Bukra put down the papers on his side of the table and stared at Rabiu for nearly a minute.

"How big, how utterly stupid, were you planning to get with this, Rabiu?" Bukra asked quietly.

Rabiu took a deep breath, aware that he was about to put his entire career onto the table in front of the one who could make it. Or break it.

"Could you become a Factor yourself, Director Bukra?" he asked.

The Khet gasped in response. Rabiu nodded.

"This *Corsac Fox* appears to be a new thing in the galaxy, sir," Rabiu said. "The Auga would never be able to understand him well enough to react quickly. Most of your competitors might not as well, but doesn't Factor Bitrus count on you and your organization to find him openings that he can exploit for wealth and power? More wealth? More power? The *Corsac Fox* comes to us and asks for a legal imprimatur that he captured these ships properly from enemies of civilization. He will then sell those ships that are surplus to his needs, but his profit margin will be exceptional if he didn't pay for them in the first place. Thus, hopefully we can pick up hulls and materials cheap, thus furthering our own subsequent profit. Again, cheap, because this *Fox* should have a certain friendliness with the organization that helped him get started."

Bukra had paled, but not interrupted. Rabiu wasn't sure if that was a good sign, or a bad one.

"How do we keep him from turning on us eventually?" the Director asked.

Rabiu smiled. This one, he was prepared for.

"Appendix One, sir," he replied. "A Letter of Marque and Reprisal, as he defines it, is a legal warrant that includes permission to cross an interstellar border to conduct a reprisal—defined elsewhere as taking some action against a previous attack or injury—and that the privateer so empowered was authorized by an issuing jurisdiction—namely ourselves—to conduct such reprisal operations *outside of our borders*. Specifically, he cannot attack shipping owned by any *Z'Gosza* enterprises, which covers our commercial fleets."

"However, nobody's pirates are on the books," Bukra nodded,

understanding coming into his eyes. "And therefore are not covered by this document. Are we starting a war with the other conglomerates, though?"

"No, sir," Rabiu said simply. "We've been quietly at war with each other for centuries. This might be us putting ourselves in a position to win such a war."

"Because you are also going to get the public enthralled with this pirate hunter," Bukra noted. "This *Corsac Fox*."

"If we win the public relations war, we win the public with it," Rabiu said. "Isn't it time for a little revolution?"

# TWENTY

Dan had explained to the hotelier that Uly would require one major suite, with several sleeping chambers off of a central hub, rather than stretching them all along a hotel corridor. It had taken a bit of work, right up until Yanouk had loomed over the man and growled.

Moss School didn't teach its students to growl, but Dan supposed that she'd been spending time learning to be an actress, in addition to her roles in security, maintenance, and everything else. The woman didn't understand power systems, and had no interest, just as Anari had made it plain that she was done being an engineer entirely, since Uly was going to let her become Sabre School.

Now they just needed a Sabre Elder to teach Anari. Or rather, Dan was also filling that role, but she'd worked with Yanouk for much longer, and that woman was ready to be armed on public station.

For the moment, they had gotten through to the fool Khet. Uly was in the Ambassadorial Suite, along the outer edge of the station itself with a fantastic view of deep space. And the planet below if you stuck your nose and one ear against the viewshield.

One major room with a kitchen on one side and a conference table on the other. Sofas and comfortable chairs in the middle. Six small sleeping chambers off the sides. Two restrooms.

Uly's room in back was large enough for small sporting events, but Dan understood from Ethir that foreign dignitaries frequently required a lot of space to contain their egos.

Uly normally slept in a chamber smaller than the one Dan had taken for herself, but they were all out front right now.

The colors in here tended to be bright. Off-white walls and ceiling. Emerald-green carpet that looked a lot like grass. Azure and navy fabric on the furniture.

She'd have preferred some wood veneer, but wondered if that might strike the locals as a bit barbaric. They were, after all, originally evolved from fish in the same way that Humans had come from arboreal tree shrews.

Yanouk and Katya were on duty enough to be watching the locked main door to the suite. Dan and Nasrin had settled Uly on the biggest couch to let him decompress.

"Do we presume that we're being watched and recorded?" Dan asked as folks sat.

He shrugged. That was one of the things she loved about the man. If he didn't know, Uly wasn't one to speak just to hear his voice. Or to have an opinion.

"According to Haydar, we should be safe in here," Nasrin offered.

Dan turned to the Mazhin woman. Young, but exceptionally smart. And sneaky, which was even better. Too many boffins had zero social skills, once you got them out of their immediate expertise.

"We've tried to convey Uly as an ambassador," Nasrin continued. "Business espionage seems to be the central hobby around here, but we're political, so they'll take a different tack. At least that was the consensus Haydar and Ethir seemed to come to."

Dan nodded. She'd heard the same things but hadn't placed them into the right context until now. It was good.

"How badly are they going to be confused?" she asked Uly.

His grin was like the sunrise.

"You and I put some good military stuff in there," he nodded. "Ethir and Haydar, after consulting others, added a bunch more. If they sign it, we're a foreign nation trading with *Z'Gosza,* which they might actually go for, as it keeps us out of their local politics. I don't expect acceptance, though."

"I agree," Dan said. "I mean, yes, I saw all those bits, but Haydar and Ethir seemed to think that most of it would be excised by Director Bukra's lawyers in the first round."

Uly shook his head.

"They're thinking like civilians, which they are," he replied. "You and I are military. We've framed the relationship as a military one, which puts us outside of their normal understanding. At least for now. They don't have a national navy. Only local defense forces against pirates like us, plus ground militias that can be called up in an emergency or alien invasion."

"Are we forming the basis of what might later become some sort of planetary navy?" Dan asked.

She'd wondered at the time, but Uly seemed more convinced.

"The ancient term is *condottieri*," he nodded. "Mercenary captains of military forces hired by various governments, in an era where wars were small and fought by professionals. It was only later, in the first Industrial Age, when populations grew large enough, and educated enough, to call out mass levees of troops with a formal draft. If they go for this treaty, they set themselves up to hire us and whoever else comes along. At the same time, unless they purposely set out to do so, they won't build up a naval force large enough to threaten other systems."

"Because you need battle lines and fleets of heavy warships," Dan nodded back, understanding. "But pirates don't think on that scale. Would they accept the sorts of formal discipline that a true navy requires?"

Again, he shrugged.

Nasrin spoke instead.

"If they wanted to be formal and disciplined, they wouldn't be pirates," she offered. "That would be too much like growing up and acting responsible. Also part of the reason that ships like *Iron Wasp* were about as big as such operations could maintain. More likely, you have random groupings of smaller ships, like our two friends we captured. A double handful of crew. A commander with some ability and some charm. Or at least size and threat. But operating a warship for a long period of time requires a significant logistics chain and planning that far out isn't something most of them want to do."

Dan wanted to ask her deeper questions but withheld. She knew that the Mazhin didn't generally live on planets these days, from comments all of them had made at various points.

Was the entire species largely living on board starships? Warships?

An entire nation of pirates? Haydar certainly had done colorful things in his youth, though you had to pry those stories out of him. Or have one of the others tell it wrong, forcing him to correct the record officially.

"Okay, changing direction slightly," Dan said instead. "Do we eventually build up our own naval fleet?"

Uly's eyes narrowed as he stared at her. Took her a moment to understand that it was shock on his part, not anger.

"A fleet?" he finally managed to ask.

Dan smiled. Uly really didn't understand his charisma. Probably just as well, at least for now. He could talk most folks into many things if he really wanted, though they had maintained a polite, formal relationship thus far.

"A fleet," she nodded back to him. "A lot of ex-pirates or folks interested in maybe doing something about pirates. Maybe keeping the Ononguli in their own Sector for once."

She turned in place to locate Katya, guarding the door but listening.

"No offense intended," Dan said.

"None taken, sir," Katya replied with a grin. "Not sure how you might manage it, since we can be a bit free-wheeling, but if anybody could, it would be Conductor Fortier."

Dan turned back fast enough to catch Uly's quick flush of embarrassment.

"I have enough things to worry about as it is," Uly said. Then his smile turned wicked. "In fact, I am hereby ordering you and Nasrin to start thinking about how we might form some larger political and military entity."

"Political?" Nasrin asked, surprise twisting her tentacles around.

"Logistics chains, sailor," he replied. "If we're not stealing shit from people, then we'll need to be manufacturing those things instead. That requires a home base, and an industrial capacity."

"And that's not *Z'Gosza*?" Nasrin asked.

Dan grinned in turn.

"Not just," Dan told the woman. "We don't want all our eggs in one basket. When I was a privateer with the *Batyr* navy, we had a half-dozen places where we might sail to, well beyond *Danumash* ports, to dispose of things or trade for other things. Mostly food and raw metal we could machine as needed. It let us stay away for up to six months at a time without having to worry about resupply from home."

"Ergo, you expect to conquer, capture, or negotiate with some world to become our home base that isn't *Z'Gosza*," Nasrin nodded.

"Negotiate," he said, smile growing. "You catch more flies with honey than vinegar. And since it looks like I'm stuck with all of you as crew, we're not worried that much about returning to Imperial Sector Seventeen any time soon."

"Thus, we need a base," Nasrin nodded. "I'll talk to the boys when we get back to the ship. I'm sure they will have some ideas."

"Yes, but you're in charge," Dan spoke forcefully. "Don't let Haydar off the hook. Or Ethir. Or any of the Ononguli. In fact, interview them all about all the places they might know of. If we're going into the pirate hunting business formally, either those are bases we need to consider attacking at some point, or the worlds that would appreciate us driving off the bandits."

For a moment, Dan saw how young Nasrin was. It was easy to forget, but she was younger than Uly, which made Dan feel like something of an old maid. At least many of the other Mazhin were her age or older, as well as about half the Ononguli.

A door chime interrupted them.

Dan rose like a hunting cat, aware of the pistol and the rod on her thighs. And the armed women behind her as she made her way to the door.

The screen showed a single, Khet male, dressed in a uniform of the hotel, but a nicer version than the bellboy who had delivered their trunk.

Dan unlocked the hatch and opened it.

The man smiled and bowed, then handed her an envelope that wasn't sealed.

"The favor of a reply is requested," he said simply.

Dan felt Uly step up behind her, so she slipped to the side and handed it to him, still watching the Khet.

He read it, then nodded to the messenger.

"We'll be in the lobby in one hundred minutes," Uly said.

The man bowed again and withdrew. Dan closed the door and locked it.

Uly smiled.

"You will need to take a shower and dress in your better uniform, First Officer," he grinned. "We're having dinner with Administrator Khadijan and his film crew."

Oh, shit.

# TWENTY-ONE

Uly didn't have his dress uniform, presumably in a storage trunk back aboard *Marshall Castillon* against the day he either returned or it was shipped to his parents when he was declared *Absent From Duty, Presumed Lost*. He didn't miss the uniform, but it would be nice to figure out how to let his parents know he was still alive.

Eventually.

Tonight, he had changed into the one nice uniform that Omid Adl and Nasrin had made for him from fabric they'd been able to dye a close enough to match the *Batyr* maroon. Dan had a similar outfit as his First Officer, and not *merely* a bodyguard.

Likewise, the other three women with him had changed into more formal outfits. Nobody was armed, but Uly also knew he had three close-combat experts handy. And he supposed that a female pirate like Katya, outnumbered roughly ten-to-one by gender when Sobol had been Conductor, would also know how to take care of herself in a pinch.

Unless the authorities had decided that he was a pirate that should be arrested on arrival, Uly figured that he ought to be safe.

All this put a smile on his face as Yanouk led him into the hotel's lobby, a vast space with a two-story ceiling and crystal chandeliers. Thick rugs underfoot.

And an exceptional number of folks standing around beyond rope lines over there. Far more than had been here when he'd checked in a few hours ago. Plus station guards keeping the crowds at a distance.

Uly noted that the original film crew was present and directed Yanouk to walk towards them. Administrator Khadijan emerged from a nearby group as well.

There were a lot of cameras pointed his way. Uly was glad everyone had dressed up for this.

"Conductor," Khadijan said as they came to rest at a polite distance. "Is everything to your liking?"

Uly noted that the hotel manager was nearby, watching nervously. Uly bowed to him first, then Khadijan.

"It has been lovely so far," Uly offered. "I'm looking forward to seeing what *Z'Gosza* has to offer in the way of entertainments."

Bright smile. Give nothing away. Let the beautiful women around him all be ogled by a nervous crowd. Make a good impression.

"I've made arrangements for a dinner here at the hotel," Khadijan said, gesturing to the manager, who stepped close now, precise fussiness itself.

"If you would care to follow me?" the manager said, turning in such a way that all the cameras were focused on him.

Uly supposed that the hotel might become a place of pilgrimage at some point if he managed to pull this off.

He was not surprised when the manager led the group up onto something of a platform at one end of the dining hall. Maybe a meter and a quarter above the deck, up six steps, to a long rectangle of a table. They'd even managed to find a chair large enough for Yanouk to sit comfortably.

Standing close to the table, Uly could see where the table itself had been subsequently raised on blocks, as had most of the chairs, leaving something of a pit where an Emro woman didn't loom so much. Or need to fold herself uncomfortably to dine.

Director Bukra sat at the head of the table. Administrator Khadijan led Uly to the man's immediate left, which was the honored seat for a guest, according to Ethir, with Dan on the man's right. He bowed to his host and kept his grin in place.

Several other Khet were spaced around the table. Uly caught all of their names, but from the job titles involved, it was obvious that each was a representative of some other Director. Either outside the primary department, or perhaps from another corporation entirely.

Spies, sent to see what Bukra had reeled in, perhaps? Witnesses, in any case.

And lower ranking, which meant that Uly and his team had guessed right.

Director Bukra wanted all the glory and money to flow from him. At the same time, there would undoubtedly be quiet, side conversations to go into those details.

Doing business on *Z'Gosza*.

Menus were in Standard Spacer. Or rather, Auga, though Uly hadn't known that in school when he'd learned it. Merely that it was the *lingua franca* of space. Certainly, it let him speak with a wide selection of people.

And his accent wasn't even all that bad, but he had a good ear and had been able to adapt as they traveled.

"Is there anything on the menu that is dangerous for Humans?" the manager asked, hovering even as several waitstaff poured water and still-steaming Khet savory breads were delivered.

"The Aquawyvern should be avoided," Nasrin spoke up crisply. "Minor contamination in the kitchen will not be a problem, but eating a meal of it will produce certain chemical reactions that might trigger a medical incident."

Uly wondered how she knew that, but realized that she and her clan had all been slaves of *Danumash* at one point. And for a reasonable amount of time.

She smiled at him, as if reading his confusion.

"Rigby Botterill," she said, referencing the Knight who had been Master of Arms on *King Hewitt II.*

Nobody from that crew, Mazhin or Human, had anything nice to say about the man, even dead, which was a truly impressive feat.

Nasrin's smile suggested how much she must have enjoyed that episode. He'd get the details later.

"Past that," she said, turning back to the manager, "less spice will generally be better than more. A broad selection of samples, perhaps from common dishes, would be best, as it would allow my Conductor and his First Officer to truly appreciate the range of your cooking."

Uly watched the way her tentacles seemed to mesmerize the Khet. She'd said that her kind weren't all that common in these Sectors. Apparently, that was true.

The manager was rocked back onto his heels.

"Also," Nasrin pounced on him before he got very far in his thinking. "Do you serve beverages with an ethyl alcohol content of ten to twenty percent by volume?"

Blinks. Lots of them from the Khet, but Uly supposed that an aquatic species like that hadn't necessarily evolved to drink the fermentations of various sugars accidentally produced when grains were stored in containers.

"Ten percent?" the Khet replied, utterly aghast. "Isn't that level poisonous?"

"Humans can metabolize much higher," Dan slipped in, like they'd planned this. *They hadn't, had they?* "Up to perhaps fifty percent, depending. We consume it recreationally."

Director Bukra looked like he'd swallowed a hornet. Uly kept his smile neutral when he really wanted to laugh.

Inappropriate.

"I would have to check, madam," the man said.

Nasrin and Dan nodded and the manager withdrew like they were chasing him with knives.

Uly focused on Director Bukra.

"Has your afternoon been fruitful, sir?" Uly asked blandly.

Technically, they were late into the local day, as kept by the sun cycles on the planet below, but ships and stations never truly slept.

"We have had a chance to complete a preliminary review of the document at a very high level," Bukra replied, suggesting that they and their lawyers had read it, but not really started to understand things.

Not yet. It might take them a while.

"Have you encountered any complications that would utterly forbid us moving forward at present?" Uly pressed.

Better if he was going to board a shuttle after dinner and look for some other system to approach, than to be strung out for months waiting.

"There is a great deal of complexity involved," Bukra offered cannily.

Uly nodded. There was. Intentionally. The oligarchs of *Z'Gosza* were businessfolk. Legal structures and money were their *forte*. He'd offered both.

Not a barbarian warlord, after all.

Not *just*, at least.

"Understood, Director," Uly smiled. "At the same time, if you believe that we can do business, then I've come to the right place, and we can make certain assumptions about the future."

"Such as?" The fellow was suddenly wary again.

"I'd like to turn over my prisoners to law enforcement," Uly said. "Currently, my officers back on the ship tell me that they might recruit a few based on reputation or personal connections from previous ventures, but the bulk will need rehabilitation in a manner best handled by planetary authorities such as yours. From there, I might inquire if there were other pirates out there that might be profitably brought to justice. Perhaps as a measure of my seriousness on the topic."

He left it at that, wondering if they would take the bait. Or rather, who they might set up, given such a gift horse.

Bukra was back to blinking too rapidly, but he recovered quickly. Probably aware of all the spies around him taking his measure.

One of them spoke up now. From the coloration and height of his headcrest, Uly assumed early middle-age. Between Bukra and Khadijan in years. Just past peak fitness for the male, starting into the far side.

"Are you really intending to attack only pirates?" the man asked. "And to get paid for it?"

"Indeed, sir," Dan spoke up. "Where we come from, that's an honorable way of conducting warfare. That, and preying on the shipping of our enemies, but the *Corsac Fox* doesn't have any formal enemies in this Sector, not counting the Auga Empire itself."

Gasps, at the thought of declaring war on the entire Auga.

Audacity itself.

"Pirates are the enemies of civilization," Uly added, drawing eyes and head crests back his direction. "How much more profit could you generate, without bribes, protection money, and ransoms that came out of your quarterly statements and annual bonuses?"

Ethir had provided that language. Uly thought it entirely insane to simply pay off such criminals instead of hunting them down. At the same time, Dan had agreed with the Thogin. She had belonged to a division of the *Batyr* fleet back home that had specifically undertaken such tasks.

Uly, and *Vanguard Lesauvage*, had been more directly confrontational with the Seven Kingdoms.

But, from the reactions of the various witnesses, Ethir had been right. They saw everything in terms of profit and loss. Quarterly reports. Formal Corporatism, civil law to the contrary be damned.

Uly kept his growl to himself. He was in Rome. They got to set the rules.

For now.

"Bukra, is he serious?" the man turned to his fellow, perhaps touching on rude, but Uly marked it down to surprise, rather than manners.

"Conductor Fortier has proposed a treaty exactly to those points," Bukra replied in a snide, superior tone. "The *Corsac Fox* suggests that it can be done. And done profitably, as he has said just now. Your organization has a copy of the contract."

Uly caught the reference, but now was not the moment to correct Bukra. Not when the fish had just scooped up all his little minnows in his hands.

The Director had called *him* the *Corsac Fox*, rather than the ship. That was entirely untrue.

Or was it?

He had a crew behind him, but hadn't Dan, Haydar, and everybody else said that he was the key to making this thing work? That without him, they'd all be pirates, prisoners, or slaves fairly quickly.

Did that make him **The** *Corsac Fox*?

Perhaps.

He smiled at the discomfort Director Bukra had inflicted on a group that the esteemed Khet undoubtedly saw as spies and flunkies.

The first spy turned back to Uly now, face hardening.

"According to my records, that ship is the *Iron Wasp*," he said simply.

"Was," Uly corrected him firmly. "Not anymore. The Auga took it away from Adrian Sobol and then I took both it and my second ship directly from them. When I arrived here, I captured two small-time pirate raiders. If there's enough profit in it, I'd like to take down more of them. You gentlemen will have to decide if the margins are sufficient, both on the positive and the negative ends of the ledger."

Again, Ethir had prepped him with the vocabulary to use here. Uly wondered how long that sneaky devil had dreamed of pulling one over on oligarchs such as this table represented.

Their reactions had Bukra and Khadijan practically preening, so Uly counted it as a win. He understood politics well enough to know that making Director Bukra look good in front of his peers and competitors would help Uly's crew down the line.

More questions were interrupted by the arrival of a convoy of waitstaff, all bearing trays and folding tables to rest them on. The manager had listened to Nasrin, and was delivering communal dinner, which was really more of what he was used to. Back on both of the cruisers where he'd served most of his career, the wardroom made troughs of it.

And on *Corsac Fox*, but Vahid was a far better chef than Uly'd been exposed to since he left home for military schools.

Maybe he needed to invite all the major players to one of Vahid's extravagances on the ship?

Politics.

For now, he listened to Nasrin explain each dish.

# TWENTY-TWO

Rabiu burped and covered his mouth, but it was just him and Director Bukra again, back in that worthy's inner sanctum, guarded by Deputies and locked doors.

"Remind me to eat there more frequently," Bukra nodded. "That was simply amazing."

"Agreed, sir," Rabiu offered. "What was your estimate of our outcome?"

"You were the one down at the far end of the table, being politely ignored," Bukra laughed. "You tell me what they thought. Everyone was busy looking politely at me."

Rabiu nodded.

In the scale of things, he'd been an Administrator of the lower ranks, a week ago before the *Corsac Fox* arrived to upset all their lives. Already, Director Bukra had put him in charge of several tasks and projects that normally would have gone to a more senior operative, so Rabiu presumed that he had moved up in the world.

The spies from other outfits hadn't understood that.

Yet.

"Most of them are well behind you on the knowledge and understanding curve, sir," Rabiu began. "They know the thing but haven't come to understand what our Fox implies."

"The concept of significant profit while minimizing loss plays well with them," Bukra noted.

"I got the impression that someone on Fortier's staff really understands business at a deeper level than a mere military officer should," Rabiu acknowledged. "He's got smart people behind him."

"Yes," Bukra said. "That means that he had plans within plans. Looking at that contract, they've been working on this plan for a while and it is a good one. Worse, we might take it at face value."

"Sir?" Rabiu jerked upright. "Really?"

"The structures he proposes can all be adapted from what we already do," the Director nodded. "And your suggestion about using Probate Court earned you a gold star from the Factor when I briefed him."

Rabiu felt his headcrest elevate in surprise. Factor Bitrus had heard? And approved it?

He could almost taste the bonus.

Bukra laughed.

"From here, we need to prove that this wasn't all some elaborate scam on the Fox's part," Bukra continued.

"A scam?"

"Set up some pirates he doesn't like," the Director nodded. "Use them to get in with us, so that he can set *Z'Gosza* up for some future pirate raid that hits all of our expensive shipping in harbor and ruins however many corporations with various bankruptcy proceedings."

"I didn't get that impression from him, sir," Rabiu said. "Or the women advising him. The other Human, Chastain, struck me as exceptionally sharp on the topic."

"Agreed, Rabiu," Bukra replied.

"So how do we go about determining if they are on the level, sir?" Rabiu asked.

"He suggested a demonstration raid, didn't he?" Bukra asked. "At the top, before things got serious?"

"He did, sir," Rabiu replied, nervous at the evil glint he saw in his boss's eyes. "To establish that he was serious, and to presumably utilize the new system that we're negotiating into place. Are you planning on taking him up on the offer?"

"Better," Director Bukra replied. "The Factor has suggested a specific target."

Rabiu perked up. Factor Bitrus was getting directly, personally involved? How did he make himself look good with the ultimate boss? At least ultimate until Lawal Bukra was a Factor himself?

Would Rabiu have to choose which boss to stay with? Would he get that choice, or would circumstances force it upon him?

And how filthy rich could he get along the way?

"Where, sir?" Rabiu asked, feeling like the straight fish in a comedy duo.

"*Lacium*," Director Bukra replied with an evil grin.

Rabiu blinked once.

Truly a terrible place, if even half of the rumors and legends were true.

"Oh, and Rabiu?" Bukra pressed.

"Sir?"

"You're going along as my personal observer," the Director said.

Well, shit.

But then, he'd wanted to get rich, hadn't he?

# TWENTY-THREE

Uly studied the little comm that Haydar and Roshan had come up with. Likely invented themselves, knowing those two.

According to Haydar, it encrypted a signal, scrambled that result, stuttered it across nearly a thousand frequency/wavelength combinations, and then reversed incoming messages just as quickly.

Supposedly, nobody in this system would be able to listen in. Considering that Haydar and Roshan tended to be in competition to push the margins of invention on a daily basis, Uly felt safe, at least for now.

He was back in his suite. Dan was sitting close. Nasrin, Yanouk, and Katya were listening, but also watching the door against surprises. It was early in planetary morning, but he'd slept well, as had the others from the smiles on faces this morning.

He keyed the line.

"*Corsac Fox* here," Sterling Huff replied immediately, though sounding a bit groggy.

"Sterling, it's Uly," he said. "I need you to gather up Ethir, Haydar, Piruz, and Suka Kuri. The four of you on this line, then wake Drew Roscoe up and loop him in as well."

It felt odd, not calling people by ranks and last names, but he really wasn't in the navy anymore. They were pirates. Volunteers, all of them. They would follow where he led, but he couldn't just issue orders and expect them to be followed.

"Stand by, sir," Sterling said.

Uly leaned back and studied the women who were his honor guard and part of his inner circle of decision making. Dan had literally been there from the beginning, with Nasrin coming along not too long after that. Yanouk was Moss School, rather than Sabre, but Suka Kuri had taught her how to think in ways that revealed Anari as still a lower rank.

Still, with Suka Kuri and Dan Chastain training her, he could only imagine where Anari might end up, when it was all said and done. Even Katya had grown a little more relaxed, in spite of being thrown into the mix merely for her gender and species.

He had a good team. All of them.

"Okay, sir, I've got everyone on the line, though none of us are in the same chamber at present," Sterling came back on the line.

"Excellent work, everyone," Uly announced. "I've got news here, but I wanted to check on your status first, because mine will derail a lot of topics. What's new at your end?"

"Sir, this is Roscoe," Drew said. "I've completed the list of materials we need for both ships, as well as updated the inventory of things we could trade with the locals. Nothing important, but you might want to review it sooner rather than later in case it gives you leverage."

"Understood, Drew," Uly acknowledged. "Thank you for handling all of *Wren* mostly by yourself. Hopefully, we can either get you more crew, or find a spot to park that ship long-term and bring you back to the *Fox*."

"Uly, it's Haydar. I also have an interesting update for you."

"Go ahead."

"Nils gave me several names from the captured twenty-four," Haydar continued. "Both females and three of the males turned out to be acceptable as recruits, after being rigorously interviewed by myself, Piruz, and Suka Kuri. That's an additional five crew, though currently they are in separate holding cells from the ones I didn't pass, or the rest."

"Training?" Uly asked.

"Engineers or boarding crew toughs," Piruz spoke up. "Nobody that's coming in cold and untrained, but we'll want to pair them with current crew for a while, until we trust them."

"Understood," Uly said. "Good job, all of you. I've also been chatting with Director Bukra but more with Administrator Khadijan. We might be able to recruit some sailors locally, so we'll need a solid vetting process to make sure we don't take aboard any Trojan horses. You figure that out. Now, my news."

Uly paused and took a breath. Dan smiled grimly. The others watched.

"First off, sometime this morning, the locals will contact you and send over a shuttle," Uly said. "That's for everyone you don't want to keep, so feed them breakfast, then prep them for transfer."

"I'll get on that one immediately," Piruz answered.

"Additionally, I have a note from Administrator Khadijan this morning," Uly began. "Negotiations are ongoing at present, but they've suggested that we attack a system called *Lacium* as proof of our seriousness. I've never heard of it, but that's not surprising. Have any of you?"

The Humans would be no better than him, for all the same reasons.

"Sir," Sterling spoke before anyone else. "Yuriy Kovalchuk is nodding and raising his hand. Shall I put him on the line?"

"Please do, Sterling."

"Conductor, this is Kovalchuk." Yuriy was there. He'd been there when they stole the ship initially, leading Uly and his team up that long flight of stairs, then sitting a bridge watch and helping get everything warmed up and ready to fly. "I've been to *Lacium*. With Conductor Sobol in the old days. Not as part of our more recent raid, though."

Meaning, not the one that had taken them across the inner edge of Sector Fifteen to the inner edge of Seventeen, at least as seen through those three Auga eyes. And had gotten them all captured, with a hold full of intended slaves.

"How well defended is *Lacium*, Kovalchuk?" Uly asked.

There was a pause. He could almost see the fellow scratching at the base of one of his horns, a nervous tic that didn't stop the Ononguli from being a good sailor.

"We was always the biggest dog, sir," Kovalchuk replied a moment later. "Partly, that was Sobol not taking any shit from anybody, but we was also the one with the biggest ground crew if'n folks got rowdy, ya know?"

Uly parsed that into something understandable, then nodded to himself and Dan. She nodded back.

"Understood, Kovalchuk," he said. "I want you to sit down with the officers and basically brain dump anything you know, plus bring in any other sailors who might be able to contribute more. If they want us to hit the place, I want to know if we can succeed. If this is too hard of a nut to crack, we'll walk away from the negotiations. I won't know that until I see what intelligence they're willing to supply, over and above what my amazing crew can come up with. Questions at present?"

"I'm also kinda familiar with *Lacium*," Ethir said. "Like Kovalchuk, we passed through there a while back. I'll have some thoughts."

"Excellent." Uly smiled. The others smiled back at him. "I'll check in after lunch, and then again after dinner. You have your orders, but do not hesitate to take action if something comes up, or to contact one of us here on the station with questions. And thank you."

They got signed off and he smiled at his *personal guard*.

"You think they're on the level?" Dan asked.

"Oh, I doubt it," Uly laughed.

"Why is that?" Nasrin probed.

"I got the impression last night that the folks joining us for dinner were close enough to allies of Director Bukra," Uly said. "I expect him to be sending us someplace where his enemies are, one way or the other."

"Attacking *Lacium* helps only his organization?" Katya asked. "Not all of *Z'Gosza*?"

"It helps the whole system, when you look at it in terms of money saved not fighting piracy," Uly offered. "At the same time, we're likely hitting ships that have relationships with other corporations here on *Z'Gosza*. What will be interesting is the operational security."

"What's that?" Nasrin asked.

"It's where somebody has a secret," Dan grimaced. "Can they keep it, or will spies in Bukra's organization ferret them out and send those pirates at *Lacium* a note? And will they reinforce the system, or flee before we get there, leaving a mess like a major riot, but no ships or pirates to settle up with?"

"Because they'll just turn right back around and maybe increase their attacks against Bukra later?" Nasrin pressed.

"You got it," Dan nodded. "In a way, we're starting something of a war here. A civil war between at least two sides, Bukra's friends and his enemies, with maybe a lot of folks perched on the fence watching, but not immediately joining in."

"When will they jump?" Katya asked.

"When they figure out who's going to win?" Uly offered. "I'd like that to be us, for a variety of reasons, but I'm not about to commit this ship and crew to any action until we know better what's really going on."

"How long, do you suppose?" Dan asked.

"I'm guessing that either we'll get a better briefing packet and a reply to the original treaty language later today or tomorrow, or they'll be weeks dithering, at which point somebody leaks."

"So we need to be prepared to hit fast and hard?" Dan pressed.

"Just as soon as we can nail them down," Uly agreed.

Then he rose and stretched.

"Right now, we've got a list of museums and tourist things that Khadijan provided," he said. "Let's take advantage of them and learn something more about *Z'Gosza* society than we might learn in a bar or brothel."

The women laughed. A lot of sailors spent their leaves in those sorts of places, as well as their ready cash. Uly had never been interested in getting blackout drunk and waking up with a complete stranger.

And since he was in charge, he could actually enjoy himself today.

Tomorrow might get rough.

# TWENTY-FOUR

Nasrin studied the crowd with her many senses beyond merely sight and hearing. Her tentacles let her taste their fishiness, which was a new thing, but she'd spent enough time around the Khet now to begin distinguishing emotional signatures.

Mostly surprise, layered over with curiosity. And much of that aimed at Uly and Dan, rather than her. Nasrin supposed that a few Mazhin must have made it this way, but *Z'Gosza* was a long ways from the home she'd known before being captured by *Danumash*.

Nobody had ever encountered Humans. They all wanted to see but were generally being polite about keeping their distance.

She'd wondered at Uly's choice of itinerary, but these museums and shops meant that he was aiming towards the middle classes around here. Educated. Probably willing to see Humans and the rest of them through a different lens than the sorts of narrow-mindedness you might get elsewhere.

Folks who would see a better life pretty quickly if the *Corsac Fox* was successful.

Weirdly, it was only after the point when they finished that first museum and were headed towards a souq where the locals could visit a variety of small shops that someone finally became cognizant that Uly was escorted by four females.

Administrator Khadijan had his Deputy with him. The film crew were male, as were the folks that occasionally joined them for various tasks. In fact, most of the folks she'd seen were male. It wasn't as bad as a harem, where the women were isolated, but she'd understood from Ethir that men radically dominated this society, relegating wives and such to a second-class citizenship that caused her tentacles to get a little spiky.

Worse, many of the men in the souq were ogling her in a manner she'd originally come to associate with the officers and midshipmen of *King Hewitt II*. None of them had ever been able to overcome their specist revulsion to actually approach her, but Nasrin also understood that they would have, eventually.

She let her face fall into a hard scowl as she stared back at one male Khet. His face lost the lascivious grin that he'd been aiming at Dan and went starkly neutral.

"Is everything okay?" Katya Zehlennko murmured from close by.

None of them had brought weapons, leaving those locked up in the hotel room, since they were supposed to be diplomats first. At least with the public.

At the same time, Nasrin had studied unarmed combat forms similar to the ones Dan had taught everyone.

"Fine," she replied, hedging her lies since the male hadn't propositioned anyone. Yet.

"Was he a threat?" Katya asked, so she'd seen the interaction.

"Only in his mind," Nasrin growled back.

Slavery had taught her a certain stubbornness that she hadn't had when she'd been young. Willful, certainly, but not as brutal in her approach to things.

Not as cynical, perhaps.

They continued through the souq. Watchers watched. Dan and Uly occasionally stopped to look at things, but as far as Nasrin knew, they didn't have any local currency. Just the Imperial Guilders that they'd found boxed up on *Wren* against emergencies. Lots of Guilders.

Would the locals take that?

She supposed so, given that the entire system seemed to be dedicated to galactic trade. *Batyr* supposedly used Cash, while *Danumash* did everything in Thalers. How long until merchants here could convert such currency while dealing?

Nasrin got the impression that it wouldn't be long. Humans would eventually travel beyond their tiny pocket of Sector Seventeen. Hopefully, they would be more like Uly and less like Captain Winter had been, back on *King Hewitt II*.

Uly paused at one point and turned to look directly at her. She stepped closer at his nod.

"I know Omid likes to sew," he said, gesturing towards the nearby shop, which seemed to hold bolts of fabric in many rainbows of colors. "Given the size of crew I think we'll need eventually, will she be offended if we pick out a uniform color for the crew, then order pallet loads of such uniforms, instead of her making them like she did for Dan and me?"

Nasrin paused to consider it. No other officer she'd dealt with, in any culture, had ever put that much thought into how someone as quiet as Omid Adl would feel about something like that. Yet another reason she liked Uly, and supported him as Speaker for the Conclave, as well as Conductor.

"She would probably enjoy making a few things," Nasrin replied. "But she will understand that we're better off getting them made in a factory."

"Good," Uly said. "I have money. Could you pick her out a couple of bolts to take home?"

"Me?" Nasrin asked, a bit surprised. What did she know about fabric?

"You," he nodded. "I can only see it with my eyes and touch it with my fingers. I'd like to get her something that will make her tentacles happy."

Though he didn't understand how they worked, Uly was willing to acknowledge how many other senses the Mazhin had. That was why Omid didn't let anyone else do laundry. Those *Danumash* punks had no sense of smell at all.

Most species didn't. Mazhin did.

"I can try," she offered.

"After you," Uly said, gesturing.

It took her a moment, then she nodded and entered the shop, trailed by her friends and a mob of interested strangers.

She would need to find Omid something special.

# TWENTY-FIVE

Rabiu was back with Director Bukra, exhausted after escorting and shepherding the *Corsac Fox* and his crew all day, but elated at how the aliens had been accepted by the crowds by mid-afternoon.

Fortier seemed to intuitively understand how to get the masses on his side, without even speaking. Just walking around, shopping, and chatting comfortably with people.

"You're already in for a third bonus," the Director announced quietly as Rabiu settled.

He looked up from snagging a sweet pastry off the sideboard.

"Sir?"

"You haven't seen the news, Rabiu." Bukra laughed heartily. "There were several other crews filming, and the aliens are everywhere tonight. Plus, the *Corsac Fox* anti-piracy rumors have started. Our stock is up nearly three hundred basis points today, merely from the potential that a new species to trade with represents. That's on top of them hitting those pirates in plain sight of the station and everyone recording it. We're looking good. Factor Bitrus has had nice things to say about the competent way you've been handling things."

"Sir, I'm making it all up as I go," Rabiu admitted, frightened at what other tasks might be dropped on his fins if they thought he was some sort of superfish.

He did grab two pastries, though. There had been a lot of walking today, though none of the aliens had understood the mister-gates until he'd explained the need to keep his skin and scales hydrated in the artificial atmosphere of a station.

"And that's why Factor Bitrus has approved your bonuses," Bukra smiled. "Plus an acceleration on your vesting schedule and a new block of stock options once we nail down a solid treaty with the *Corsac Fox*."

Rabiu hadn't taken a bite, so he didn't choke. Barely. Gasped pretty hard.

"Sir?"

Bukra smiled. Smiled more. Looked like a shark spying a wounded tuna in the water.

Rabiu hoped it was somebody else.

"Your instincts at the start were perfect, Rabiu," Director Bukra said. "And continue to be. We're going to ride your luck as far as it takes us."

Left unsaid was that they might dump him as soon as it turned, but that was corporate life on *Z'Gosza*. Bonuses and new options might help insulate him against that fall.

"Have we made an offer to Uly?" Rabiu asked.

"Who?"

Rabiu cursed himself internally. The women with him didn't call him the *Corsac Fox*. Or even Conductor Fortier. He was Uly. Rabiu had fallen into that same habit in only a few hours.

"The *Corsac Fox*, sir," Rabiu corrected himself. "He takes a relaxed tone with his underlings and strangers. That's part of his charm."

And it was. Infectious, even. Rabiu made a note to take a break at some point tonight and deep dive into the news for how they were slanting their coverage. Must be good, from the way the Director—*and even the Factor!*—were taking it.

"Ah, yes, the *Corsac Fox*," Bukra nodded. "Factor Bitrus is having his people take one more run through the counteroffer, then they will be sending it out."

"Should we make arrangements for him to return to his ship for now, then?" Rabiu asked.

Bukra looked confused.

"Why?"

"I'm certain he has other advisors there, sir," Rabiu noted. "The women are all smart, but none of them wrote that language on trade concessions, from what I gathered today."

"Ah, I see," Bukra replied. "What do your instincts say, right this moment?"

Talk about being put on the spot.

Rabiu willed his heart to not stop beating—or his gill slits to flap loudly—and instead quickly reviewed his day. The way Uly had handled docents in two museums with cogent questions that showed him rapidly absorbing *Z'Gosza* and Khet history. Chatting with shopkeepers, and even buying little presents for several crew members with Imperial Guilders.

"He mentioned the possibility of hosting us to a dinner on his ship," Rabiu replied. "Said that he had a Mazhin chef at least as good as the folks who made us dinner at the hotel, so he must be utterly amazing. What if we offered to transport him to the ship now, letting him have all night and tomorrow to work with his legal advisors, then maybe hint at some sort of state dinner aboard his vessel tomorrow to go over final details, assuming everything is acceptable in broad? Should we invite the Factor? Would he go?"

Director Bukra was staring blankly at him.

Rabiu took his chance and chomped on the first pastry, cramming it all into his mouth, both because he might not get another chance, and to buy time to think while chewing, depending on how his boss replied.

High-wire act. No other way to describe it. And the winds were not friendly at this altitude.

But there were bonuses on the line. Vesting schedules and extra block allotments.

"I cannot speak for the Factor," Bukra replied slowly. "But I will put it to him. You contact the *Corsac Fox* and see if he'll go for it. That's a whole other level of political invitations we might wedge open some other negotiations with, so make sure you get a count of acceptable invitees."

Rabiu blinked. Chewed. Swallowed.

Gambled.

"How soon should I reach out?" he asked.

"Now," Bukra said.

Rabiu rose, second pastry in hand.

"Where are you going?" Bukra asked, obviously expecting him to call.

"I think I need to do this in person, sir," he said. "After all, you're hoping to attach me to their operation. Best they grow even more comfortable with me."

"If you think it's wise," Bukra said.

"Playing the odds, sir," Rabiu said.

And he needed to stretch this run of luck out as far as he could.

# TWENTY-SIX

Dan answered the door when she looked at the screen and saw that it was just Rabiu Khadijan standing in the corridor. She holstered the Exoripper while working the lock, then smiled at the Khet.

"Administrator?" she asked, stepping sideways and gesturing him into the room.

Dan was used to dealing with nervous, captured enemy officers. She didn't know the Khet as a species all that well, but she'd spent six hours and lunch with him today, so she thought she had a pretty good read on him.

Not as good as Nasrin obviously, but good enough.

"First Officer Chastain," he said formally.

"Dan," she corrected him as she closed the door and locked it again.

Uly had mostly broken him of that level of formality by lunch, but he'd reverted. Must have just come from Director Bukra and whoever else.

"Dan," he agreed, blinking twice and seemingly resetting into the person he'd been earlier. "Is Uly available? My people have a proposal."

"He's relaxing in his chamber at the moment," she countered. "Downtime before dinner. What can I help you with?"

He paused. Studied her for a long moment, going so far as to run her up one side and down the other like most men did. Nasrin had mentioned the passive sexism she'd picked up, as had Yanouk and Katya.

Endemic. She kept her face professional. Uly rarely ogled her like that.

"First Officer," he said absently, as if reminding himself. Then he nodded and stared into her eyes. "The Director wonders if you might be better served by the chance to return to your ship this evening, either now or after dinner, allowing you to review the proposal Factor Bitrus will be sending shortly with the rest of your officers."

Dan nodded as a placeholder as she absorbed the words. Somebody had finally seen the hands of Ethir and Haydar in the paperwork and wanted Uly talking directly to them.

"That's a possibility I can explore with Uly," she countered. "Was there something else?"

He had that look, too. Expectancy, or something.

The Khet pressed his big, fishy lips together for a moment.

"I was prepared to ask Uly about maybe hosting a dinner similar to last night, aboard your ship, tomorrow or the next day," he said. "I think the Factor would wish to come, in order to take Uly's measure directly. The Director as well, plus a compact count of others that might owe favors, either now or as a result."

"I see," Dan said, smiling to relax the Khet. "The Factor believes that this offer will be acceptable?"

She watched him hem and haw for a moment.

"I got the impression that they might take most of the contract language as written," Rabiu replied. "Understanding that *Z'Gosza* courts will be the jurisdiction to sort out issues and complications later. Plus, I don't expect them to sign anything until you return from *Lacium*. Which brings me to a second point of possible contention that I wished to sort out in private in case it might lead to issues later."

"Oh?" Dan asked.

Out of the corner of her eyes, she saw Nasrin taking a few steps closer. Probably close enough to read his mind by his changing scent, but Dan kept that smile out of her eyes. Yanouk was in her room, also napping like Uly. Katya remained on the couch, where she'd been reading.

"In the matter of *Lacium*," he began, like this was a court case or a contract, which it probably was, knowing these folks. "Director Bukra has determined that he wishes to send a personal observer along on your mission, to report back their findings. Namely me, if Uly finds that acceptable."

"Do you want to come?" she asked, catching some hesitation.

He turned square to her when he'd been angled slightly before. Both eyes locked on her hard for a moment, but the emotion she sensed was fear. Certainly, Nasrin didn't rush the Khet and tackle him in that moment.

"It is a fantastic opportunity for my career," he said in the tiniest voice.

Ah. Profit.

And risk.

"Assuming Uly doesn't object, there will be certain operational secrets that you will be expected to keep," she said, reaching in her memory for the term Ethir had used. Ah, yes. "Non-disclosure agreements you will need to sign, with jurisdiction in a *Z'Gosza* Chancery Court."

Where all trade arguments were adjudicated on this planet.

Rabiu blinked again, even more rapidly. His breathing had grown shallow.

Dan smiled to help him relax, and to take some of the sting out of her words. Ethir had given them a dangerous set of tools. That Thogin miscreant was certainly smarter and sharper than he ever let on to outsiders. Probably saw all this as his way of getting back at the larger species who tended to prey on the small ones like his.

"Nothing bad, Rabiu," she assured him a moment later. "And probably a non-compete as well."

"You expect me to run off and join pirates?" he gasped. "Other pirates?"

"No," she smiled and shook her head. "We don't want you telling them how we operate. Trade secrets, and all that, that will make us more successful than those other pirates. Or other corporations that come into being once they realize how much better privateering can be over simpl piracy."

"Oh," he replied, like all that made perfect sense to him. Dan knew she'd owe Ethir something special for his next birthday for the way he'd set *Z'Gosza* up for them. "Yes, of course. All of that should be standard. Should I send over some contract language for you to review?"

"What are we reviewing?" Uly's voice suddenly broke in.

Dan had missed his hatch opening. And Yanouk's. Either the walls were thinner than she'd thought, or neither had been doing more than sitting in the quiet darkness and had heard the conversation.

"Non-disclosures, non-competes, and possibly hosting Rabiu's people for dinner tomorrow on the ship," Dan explained.

"You have it in hand?" he asked as he moved to a chair not far from Katya.

"I do," Dan said.

"Great," he said. "You tell me what our next steps are."

Dan smiled with her whole soul. Every time she got a chance to compare Uly to Lieutenant Dupuis, her former superior officer back on *Marshall Castillon*, the crevice separating the two got wider.

Uly assumed her competence and listened. Dupuis had assumed his superiority and ordered.

She nodded and turned back to Rabiu.

"Your people are sending a new packet?" she asked.

The Khet nodded warily, utterly shocked out of his fins that she was taking command and speaking in Uly's name. At the same time, she'd gotten the impression that Rabiu had been doing the same for Director Bukra.

The big difference was that Uly would back her. She'd understood that Rabiu's bosses would feed him to the other sharks if he screwed up.

Life, if he wanted to be rich.

"Since we're all awake at this point, why don't you join us for dinner?" she asked. "There was a diner off a back corridor of the souq that Yanouk wanted to try, just from the smell. We'll do a quiet dinner, being social instead of formal. You send a note to your people to prep a shuttle, then after dinner, we'll swing by here and pack, while you do the same, rendezvousing with us at the bay. We'll let the ship know what's up. And depending on the contract offer, set up Vahid to blow your folks away with dinner tomorrow."

More blinks. Poor guy had grown up in a culture and society that saw everything as business relationships.

Which meant that he'd owe her big for all this.

Dan couldn't wait to take him up on that.

# TWENTY-SEVEN

Uly closed his eyes and let his nose compare the food in front of him to a roast chicken in a yellow-brown curry over rice. The scent was amazingly close, but he'd never had a savory sauce that was blue.

At least naturally. Navy cooks could do all manner of things if they got bored and the Lead Specialist was willing to answer to snitty officers.

Hunks of meat grilled on thin metal spikes reminded him of home, but the taste was saltier. Everything was saltier, but he'd learned that the seas of the Khet homeworld were like that, and they needed to add salt to their diet to make up for places that didn't have the same chemistry.

Damned good food, though.

Midway through the third small course of communal plates, his comm beeped.

"Fortier," he said as he answered. "I'm at dinner in public."

"Ramezani, sir," Haydar replied, falling immediately into a more formal tone than he otherwise would have, if they were in the suite without outsiders around. "I have an update on the new contract language you forwarded, once the legal department had a chance to review it."

Namely Haydar, Ethir, and Suka Kuri, being their usual sneaky selves.

"What was their first level approximation?" Uly asked, also sounding formal and naval in ways that he really didn't miss so much these days.

"Sections Six, Fourteen, Nineteen, and Twenty-three had no significant changes from the original, sir," Haydar said. "There is one appendix discussing currency arbitrage rates that will need to be negotiated in finer detail, but that will require a bit of research on our part, to determine if we wish to accept the *Z'Gosza Interbank Overnight Rate* as a standard or propose something less regional."

Uly managed to stay perfectly still, and not even drop his chicken in curry as the implications hit him. Three of those sections were the ones that Ethir had expected to be massacred or even removed, once Rabiu's bosses' lawyers got into it.

They functionally made this an agreement between national actors, rather than a corporate services contract, which was what Uly had expected to end up with when it was all done. Never in his wildest dreams had he actually expected them to say yes.

It still would have been profitable, but if Factor Bitrus signed that document, or worse, convinced the Governor to, Uly would be a visiting Head of State, as far as legal affairs and extraterritoriality were concerned under Chancery law on this planet.

Haydar's droll, underhanded way of mentioning that told Uly that he and Ethir had probably screamed loud enough to be heard on the station when they'd looked at the new mark-up.

Yanouk perked up as well, then blushed when Uly glanced at her. But then, everyone tended to look at the big, green woman and mistake her for a Sabre School bully, instead of a Moss School artist in the process of being personally trained by an Exemplar of the Arts.

Lots of brains there. Uly smiled.

It was nice being surrounded by so much competence. And that they were all fairly attractive women was just icing on an awesome cake. He felt like he could take on the galaxy with this team backing him.

"Understood, Mr. Ramezani," Uly replied, modulating his voice to sound bored and dismissive, when he also wanted to scream and maybe dance. "I will await your recommendations on currency conversion standards. And remind Chef Siah that we'll be expecting eleven guests for dinner tomorrow night."

"Excellent news, sir," Haydar said. "We will have further updates after you board."

And he cut the line.

It all sounded perfectly reasonably and a bit dry. Technical minutiae and contract law. The women at the table all seemed to be vibrating at a higher pitch than before, even Katya, who hadn't been involved in the treaty language sections.

He turned and harpooned Rabiu with a stern look. The Khet quailed visibly, gulping nervously.

"Dan discussed non-disclosures earlier," Uly began simply. "And non-competes. As of now, I am willing to accept you as part of my crew, serving as a temporary observer with a rank equal to Cornet, or the lowest ranking officer as those things go. However, you will need to verbally acknowledge at this moment that you will be bound by certain things, even before I review the contracts that you will sign later."

He left it at that, images of a hungry cat and a scared mouse dancing in his head as he studied the Khet Administrator.

"Such as?" Rabiu managed breathily.

"You will be present as certain negotiations with your superiors are finalized, and thus privy to details that might radically alter the final document, Rabiu," Uly said simply. "If I can rely on you to not brief them on things until the document is signed, you can remain with us. Otherwise, I might need to leave you on the station until such time as I depart for *Lacium*, and then keep you isolated from some of my operational planning. I appreciate that I'm putting you in a complicated—if not impossible—situation, so this is your opportunity to have a lovely dinner now, then withdraw. Otherwise, I will expect you to keep your mouth shut. Is that clear?"

"Will this be anything negative for my organization, my superiors, or *Z'Gosza* in general, sir?" Rabiu asked, sounding like he was quoting a legal textbook.

"On the contrary, Rabiu," Uly smiled. "This will hopefully work out even better for everyone. But it will reshape the expected relationship between my ship and your organization and your government, depending on a few crucial details in the final document. It will be fair, all the way around."

"Oh," the Khet nodded. "As long as you aren't setting me up to commit any major felonies or treason, I should be able to give verbal assent now, presuming final contract language to be signed on review, sir."

Uly nodded. This was going to be one hell of a test of the Khet's loyalties and sensibilities, but Uly needed friends. If he didn't have a home base that was a safe harbor, he'd end up reverting to piracy. Maybe sailing to *Lacium* and operating out of there, instead of attacking the place.

Time to take a few risks. If nothing else, success would bind Rabiu more firmly to the *Corsac Fox*, and the apparent legend already forming, according to the news tonight, where he was The Fox, rather than the ship and crew.

"The sections Haydar quoted just now?" Uly said, waiting for Rabiu to nod before continuing. "Those establish that I represent a foreign government, rather than being an employee of your organization under contract to perform certain tasks."

"Yes," Rabiu nodded. "Plausible deniability later, when people grow angry that you're upsetting their way of life. Nobody can come back after Factor Bitrus for damages, whether real or imagined."

"Indeed," Uly agreed. "They also set me up as a foreign head of state under your laws, Rabiu. And interactions between us will take on elements of foreign policy. That's both good and bad. On the good side, myself and my crew will not necessarily be directly impacted by *Z'Gosza* law. On the bad side, that means that any office I open here will be an embassy, rather than corporate operations. I will need to establish a permanent base that becomes my capital world, somewhere else."

The Khet's eyes got huge and his mouth fell open.

"*Lacium*?" he whispered.

"Maybe," Uly acknowledged. "That depends on what intelligence your folks can supply, as well as what my team can dig out of our computers. But there is a strong possibility, yes. This is why you needed to be bound by confidentiality, Rabiu. This might be so much bigger than it was, even this morning."

"Aye," the Khet whispered. "Wow."

The others had all stopped eating as well, staring at the interaction with smiles or scowls, depending.

Uly took the opportunity to reach out and spoon more chicken and curry onto his plate, plus something close enough to naan to count for his purposes. That seemed to break the hypnosis holding the others, and they restarted with gusto.

Things were getting strange.

# TWENTY-EIGHT

Haydar had taken the opportunity to assemble a broader team on the bridge. There was space for it, and he had the most experience with this sort of thing, as long as he could keep Piruz from spilling the beans.

The Horse Thief was here, standing next to Sterling Huff, who was commanding and flying the ship at present, but who also happened to be a far more gifted stellar cartographer and geographer than anybody had given him credit for. Including himself.

Growing into the man he would be in a few more years, which was all the more impressive.

Drew Roscoe was tied into comm from *Wren*, listening.

Suka Kuri and Anari Supasei. Exemplar of the Arts and Sabre School student, though she was not yet even Yanouk's peer, to say nothing of Dan's. Still, combat had been her dream once and it was coming back. Haydar had already pulled her entirely out of engineering and assigned her to work for Beranger and Travers full time.

Ethir had all of his cousins, because while they hadn't been to *Lacium*, they knew that lifestyle.

Fortunately, he also had a bunch of former Ononguli pirates handy. Many of whom knew *Lacium* directly, or had heard a lot of stories. Nils

Shevchenko and Yuriy Kovalchuk would speak for them, at least for now.

"What do we know about the target that the locals propose?" Haydar asked, letting his tentacles sniff the air.

Nervous, but focused nervousness. Mission specific. Locked on.

Piruz stirred.

"You would not believe this," he said, which was frequently how his stories began. "It turns out that some idiot pirate took a film crew like the one that's been shadowing Uly and the crew on the station. The footage is old and outdated, but we all have an idea how lazy pirates can be."

Nods. The Mazhin did not technically commit piracy as a culture. Mostly. And then they took a much more professional view of it than other folks when they did.

"How long ago?" Ethir asked, sounding more like a university professor than a criminal delinquent.

"About forty years," Piruz said. "Found it as an entertainment vid when we logged in to the station. Oh, and do these people not know *anything* about computer security?"

"Everything's paper on this planet," Waltin Gysby spoke up. Probably the smartest of the four cousins, but not the leader by any stretch. He just wanted to read, most of the time. "Contracts are printed, signed, embossed, and filed. They don't trust electronic records because those are too easy to manipulate."

Haydar nodded. He'd poked a bit, but not tried to hack into any systems over there as he'd been too busy. Plus, he had a project that was only about three-quarters done at present. It would make slicing such systems almost child's play when he finished.

"Anyway, I have a vid," Piruz said. "Quick scanned it. Lots of lovely, establishing shots with orchestral music. I can map you most of close orbit as it was then. We'll need whatever others can provide, unless you want me committing computer felonies getting into systems we presume might be able to detect such an intrusion."

"Let's wait to see what Uly wants," Haydar temporized. He turned to the Ononguli representatives. "You'll identify anyone who has physically been in *Lacium* and forward them to Piruz. Nobody's old enough to have been there when that footage was shot, so they might be able to update any changes."

Both nodded.

"What did we get from the locals for data?" he asked.

He, Ethir, and Suka Kuri had been reading the treaty, not the attack data.

"Records suggest that *Corsac Fox* might be the biggest whale in the system when we arrive," Sterling Huff spoke up. "Upwards from seventy percent of all hulls that they expect are in the Seeker range, comparable to the two ships we captured here. A few Interceptors, but nothing as big or as heavily armed as us, due to our twin 6dm in a single turret. The rest are pure cargo haulers, from single-family tramp freighters up to commercial megacarriers, depending on what's been captured recently."

Haydar nodded. Sterling bore almost no resemblance to the young man who had been his captor before all this. Not the least of which was that he'd grown nearly twenty centimeters since Uly and Dan had arrived. And started to shave, which was simply unnatural, but apparently something Human males did.

"Orbital defenses?" he asked, looking around.

"Supposedly one big station in orbit, well armed," Piruz spoke. "Most of their chop shops and repair yards are close by, but independent. There is a colony of sorts, down on the surface, where the pirates go for R&R. Plus some farms and ranches that provide food, but almost nothing in the way of industry. Again, most of that's in orbit, what little of it there was in those days."

"It ain't changed since," Ethir and Shevchenko managed in almost perfect harmony.

"You talk," Ethir ordered when the Ononguli fell silent.

"If you need something, you either cut it out of a ship you've captured, or deal with some smugglers to bring you things," Nils continued. "Ships either get chopped down into spare parts quickly, or they get sold on someplace else that knows they're buying stolen goods. Conductor Sobol did that a few times in other places. We wouldn't have made it to *Lacium* unless that last raid had turned out way different, but there is supposedly a network of similar systems across a couple of Imperial Sectors, ranging all the way back to our old home in Twenty-One. As long as you stay over there, *Z'Gosza* can't impound you, and they don't have records from that far away to prove you might be in a stolen ship when you register it there."

"Lots of folks intentionally looking the other way, in the interests of trade?" Haydar asked.

"In the interests of profit, maybe," Ethir offered. "Remember, we're dealing with oligarchs, which is a fancy title for pirates in suits. They write the laws such that they don't have to follow them themselves."

Haydar nodded. On the one hand, recruiting more officers and crew would let him get back to his lab. On the other, he did have to admit—if only to himself—how much he was enjoying this sort of thing. Uly's fault, for bringing together such a fun and amazing crew of lunatics.

Including him.

"Okay," he said as everyone watched him. "Dig in and digest. Start assembling notes into something I can add to an executive summary. Piruz, tell Roshan to look passively at the computer security on the station. We don't need to alter records, but anything we might dig up helps Uly decide if he wants to do this. And how. Let's move it, people."

Bodies surged into motion.

"Huff, you come off duty for now and work on it as well," Haydar decided. "I haven't entirely forgotten how to fly a starship, so I'll relieve you for a long watch."

Huff nodded and stampeded after the others. Haydar wondered if he'd just loosed a fox into a henhouse, to use the Humanism he'd picked up.

He had, of course.

A *Corsac Fox*.

That put a smile on his face.

# CORSAC FOX

# TWENTY-NINE

Dan was looking forward to being home, which was even weirder, when she realized that she thought of a stolen pirate frignaught as home. The shuttle was close to docking, a monstrous vessel that wouldn't fit into one of the small flight bays, because it was big enough to haul back the remaining pirates when it left.

Inside, the entire volume of the shuttle was given over to seats like a commercial passenger liner, with two aisles. Dan had her folks by the forward hatch, with a group of guards diagonally opposite, across and back.

*And it wasn't that she didn't trust all the guards that had been sent along,* but she really didn't, so she and the ladies were on extra alert. That meant safeties off and Nasrin with a Firesphere loaded. Excessive damage if she had to fire it in here.

The guards had all stayed over in their corner of the passenger bay as a result. Uly didn't seem to notice, but Nasrin's tentacles were practically writhing.

"All hands, prepare to dock," the pilot announced over the intercom.

Dan drew her Heavy Exoripper and thumbed the safety off. Uly looked over quizzically.

She smiled. He nodded, but didn't speak.

She was in charge of his security, and he was letting her be. It was good.

Yanouk rose as soon as they docked, which could have been dangerous, but the big woman was nimble. And holding a monstrous ax in one hand. Again, intimidating, in case those boys over there had orders that might have involved rushing the ship.

Like she'd done from this same airlock, seemingly a lifetime ago.

Uly rose. The others did as well. Rabiu was only now catching on to how high tensions were, but he took his cue from Uly and stayed silent, falling in.

Dan picked out the senior enlisted Khet in the group, rather than the officer in charge of those dozen.

"We'll deliver your load shortly," she ordered simply. "You should prepare for them here."

As in, you will not be going aboard my ship and assisting, so don't ask.

Too many secrets. Rabiu would keep his mouth shut, or he'd find out the hard way that Dan played rough. Not that Uly needed to know. Uly had charmed the whole, damned station—maybe the planet— according to the local news.

Her job was Bad Cop. She was good at that. Especially with her three friends, all of them armed and primed for violence.

The guards nodded warily. And remained seated.

Dan turned to Uly and smiled.

"Anything I need to be prepared for?" he asked.

Again, awesome. He didn't demand explanations, unlike that punk Dupuis. Accepted her orders and listened.

"Hopefully not," Dan lilted merrily.

He nodded and moved to the aisle, then the forward hatch. It began to open quickly. Katya got into the tunnel ahead of him, because Dan had ordered her to. Uly shrugged and made sure that Rabiu stayed close and out of the way.

The far lock hatch opened and Dan spied Anari and Travers looming over the rest. And it was a mob over there.

Katya went through. Uly and Rabiu followed. Dan blew a kiss to the guards and went through, with Nasrin coming last.

The bay on the ship was full, but that was all of the pirates seated around the walls in chairs, guarded by a lot of her people, including armed Ononguli pirate engineers.

Dan walked to Anari, standing next to Wyndham. The Sabre School warrior-trainee wasn't as good as Beranger or Travers, but that was lack of experience. She had the makings of an officer in the same way that Solomon Wyndham would. And a lot more intimidating mass and height.

"Status?" she asked Anari pointedly, ignoring Wyndham next to her.

Training. Always training.

"All returning prisoners accounted for, sir," Anari replied crisply while Wyndham watched, also learning, but he was a Middie, so technically in charge of all security while she'd been gone. And sometimes while she was here. "They have undergone a basic medical and had boosters for common diseases based on cultural notes provided. There have been no disciplinary issues to date."

"Excellent work," Dan said, turning to include both of them.

Not that she doubted Beranger and Travers being able to handle things, but it was nice to see a staff forming, because Emil Beranger and Gennady Travers were not ever going to turn into Lead Specialists, let alone officers.

She'd been around those two long enough.

Dan rotated in place to eyeball all of the folks who Haydar hadn't kept.

"You will rise," she ordered in a voice brooking no nonsense.

And a Heavy Exoripper in one hand with the safety off.

These pirates did understand jail protocols. They were almost a choreographed dance troupe standing up. Then coming to rest.

She picked out the one closest to the hatch and nodded.

"All prisoners, right face!" she snapped. "Into the transport at a slow march."

Uly had dragged Rabiu off to one side, but the Khet would get to see this part of the performance, before discovering the truth about how thinly crewed the ship really was.

That was when things might get a little iffy.

The pirates left. Dan heard the guards on the far side of the airlock getting them settled and then locked down. Pity that they didn't have anyone like Marlowe Michaels to short-circuit the lock systems so that they might hijack that shuttle and make their escape.

But then, they didn't have Uly.

She did.

Dan turned to Solomon and nodded. He was technically in charge of security. She'd just wanted to leave an imprint on the pirates for later. And Rabiu Khadijan.

Solomon Wyndham walked to the airlock and looked through.

"Sealing the airlock now," he announced loudly, then pressed the button.

It beeped closed.

"Shuttle, I show solid seals at my end," Solomon continued a few moments later. "You will undock and back away."

"Acknowledged, *Corsac Fox*," the pilot replied over the line. "Detaching now."

Dan felt the locks thump through her feet.

Solomon and Anari had turned to her. As had everyone else, but those two were watching Rabiu carefully.

Outsider. *Was the performance over yet, sir?*

Dan smiled. Solomon Wyndham had the makings of an excellent officer, one of these days. Like Sterling Huff though, still a kid. Not even fifteen years Standard yet, at that.

Anari was an adult Emro. Trained as an engineer by fool Auga who had assumed she was too smart to be Sabre School, because they didn't understand the Moss or Sabre Schools at all.

Where might Dan be in five years, if she got this group trained the way she wanted them?

Ready to take on the galaxy.

"Solomon, Anari, this is Administrator Rabiu Khadijan," Dan introduced them. "Security Officer Solomon Wyndham. Sabre School student Anari Supasei. It's safe, he's been sworn to secrecy about everything he sees aboard."

Solomon blew out a heavy breath and slipped his Exoripper into a holster. Anari collapsed her boarding halberd into the basic ax form.

"Haydar kept a couple, obviously, sir," Solomon said. "But we're going to need a small army if we want to try something as crazy as what they're planning up on the bridge."

Dan liked the way Rabiu's eyes got big again. Shocks piled on shocks, but at least the Khet hadn't gone entirely cynical yet.

She turned to Uly.

He nodded. Then grinned and reminded her that while she wasn't old at twenty-nine, he was still five years her junior.

Then Conductor Fortier returned and he faced Rabiu.

"This is where it gets interesting," he said simply.

Dan wondered if the poor Khet might faint.

# THIRTY

Rabiu felt like the smallest tuna at a feeding frenzy, looking around at all the heavily armed aliens surrounding him. Mentally, he'd been prepared for it, but confronting Humans, Mazhin, Emro, Ononguli, and even Thogin in such a mix nearly caused him to stumble.

Then Uly suggesting it was about to get worse?

Dan turned to the group.

"All hands, back to normal duty, since our other guests are gone," she yelled.

Rabiu watched her unbuckle her weapons and hand them to a short, squat Human male.

"Put this in the armory," Dan ordered. "Rest of you do the same, except for whoever has Haydar's guests."

Rabiu focused on maintaining a calm exterior. The crew filed out with laughter and jokes, leaving him alone with Uly and Dan for the moment.

"This way," Uly grinned.

That turned out to be a long staircase up, broken regularly by airtight hatches, until they finally emerged at the bridge, about the time Rabiu was willing to surrender.

Didn't these people believe in lifts?

"No," Uly said. "Lifts often fail in battle, trapping you. Better to rely on ladders and stairs."

Rabiu shut his maw when he realized he'd been muttering with his outside voice instead of the inside one. And smiled, because the two Humans were smiling as well.

The bridge crew was also widely mixed. Two male Mazhin. Several male Ononguli. The oldest Emro woman Rabiu thought he'd ever seen, anywhere. Three Thogin, including the one who had been below earlier.

Uly moved to stand next to an older, more mature Mazhin at the Conductor's station, drawing Rabiu in his wake. The one Thogin stepped closer.

"Non-disclosures and non-competes," Uly reminded him, tying Rabiu's hands in a variety of ways and he really didn't even know what he'd gotten himself into.

Except that there were going to be accelerated vesting and extra option blocks if he didn't screw anything up.

Rabiu nodded when everyone turned to stare at him.

He was committed. For good or ill.

*I mean, how bad could it be?*

"Khet, you can keep your mouth shut?" the Thogin asked in a voice far more intimidating than his small size suggested.

"Within limits, yes," Rabiu replied. Careful, but nervous.

The Thogin turned to Uly.

"We're gonna need help," the small being said. "Like, lots. Not necessarily firepower, but raw crew to handle everything here. On top of that, someone will need to send along at least a battalion of troops, assuming we're successful in the first part."

"Talk to me," Uly ordered.

Just like that. Rabiu was still getting used to a commander so in control of things that he could turn major chunks of work over to underlings without constantly monitoring them.

How did these people get anything done?

Then he paused. His own Deputy, Kyauta Alhaji, was off handling all those tasks that Rabiu would have normally been doing, before he got sidetracked—promoted?—by the arrival of the pirates.

Was *Z'Gosza* too bureaucratic? Was such a thing possible?

Of course it was. Look at the Auga.

Until now, Rabiu had expected that *Z'Gosza* was at the other end of the spectrum from Auga in terms of paperwork.

Were they only in the middle somewhere? Worse, closer to Auga? Food for thought.

"So, we have a pretty good understanding of what we'd be facing over there," the Thogin said.

Rabiu noted that he hadn't been introduced yet. Merely dropped into the situation and expected to tread water successfully.

The Mazhin by the rail spoke up now. He seemed younger than the one currently in command, if that was what that chair meant.

"One station, not as heavily armed as this local one, but tough," that gentleman said. "It's all the little stations around it that will need an occupation force we aren't prepared to handle."

Rabiu wasn't prepared for Uly's laugh. Or the way the Conductor turned to face him now, sober but not scowling.

"When we stole this ship, Rabiu, I ended up with barely enough engineers to run it. Hardly enough to fight if anything went wrong," Uly said. "Then I stole *Wren*, so some of my folks are over there pulling impossible shifts right now while we sit here in orbit and pretend to be packed to the gills with crew."

"That was why you recruited some of the pirates, wasn't it?" Rabiu asked, understanding dawning.

"Correct," Uly nodded. "Not enough, but bodies at least known to someone on my crew and vouched for. That's also why I wanted to recruit here. I need sailors. This ship had a crew of over four hundred at one point. I have less than twenty percent of that."

"Oh," Rabiu managed.

Shit. Non-disclosure. This was going to be exactly the sort of thing such a document would cover.

He shrugged.

Smallest tuna in a feeding frenzy. And he needed to protect Director Bukra and Factor Bitrus.

And Uly and Dan.

"How many crew would you need, to fight other ships?" he asked.

Rabiu didn't know much about warships, but most of the crew of a starship was either command, engineers, or warm bodies handling day-to-day maintenance.

"If we could get twenty people with the right credentials, that would be sufficient," the older Mazhin interrupted. "For now."

"You certain?" Uly asked.

Asked. Director Bukra would have barked insults or orders. Uly was a better leader of beings. Simple as that.

"For now," the Mazhin nodded, his tentacles seemingly agreeing.

"We still need an army," the Thogin pointed out.

"I think we can negotiate for that part." Uly smiled at Rabiu. "It's in their interest for us to take a base we can hold later."

"Plus, you might be able to recruit folks from that army afterwards," Rabiu offered, aware of how close to stepping across certain lines he might be treading.

But Director Bukra had wanted *Lacium* eliminated as a pirate stronghold. Wouldn't a bigger hammer be better for that?

Everyone was staring at him. Rabiu kept his headcrest down and his gill slits closed, mostly by force of will.

"I am not violating any secrecies by suggesting that your success makes my bosses look good by reflection with the wider planetary system," Rabiu continued. "They wanted me here to see how we could pull it off, when others might not be interested in such an outcome."

"What do we need?" Uly asked the room.

"Six gun teams," the Mazhin in command said. "I've got a few folks that can fix it when something goes wrong, but only barely and they're slow. Full teams mean we can overwhelm someone with pretty good firepower. That also frees up a lot of my engineers to go back to their regular duties. Wyndham will need troops, but I doubt that he or Supasei are ready to lead them into battle."

"Correct," Dan interjected. "That will be my job, assuming we have an army I can lead."

Rabiu felt his mouth fall open. Then he remembered those four women on the way back from the station. She probably could.

Uly's smile was back.

"We'll need a few hours to review things here, Rabiu," Uly said. "Then I'll supply you with a stack-ranked list, from those things critical to our success down to wishes if money was no object. You can transmit that to your bosses, giving them things we can talk about over dinner tomorrow. That, or we'll just talk politics first, then retire with your Factor and your Director for the hard stuff. How does that sound?"

Like trouble brewing, but Rabiu didn't say that.

Uly and the others seemed convinced that they could pull it off. And Bukra had said that they were going to ride Rabiu's instincts and luck as long as it lasted.

Time to roll the dice.

"I'll see what I can do, Uly," he said.

# THIRTY-ONE

Uly had sent Administrator Khadijan off to settle, put for now in an empty officer's quarters. Uly had a lot of those, all cleaned within an inch of their lives by Omid, then set up for whoever would take them over later.

The whole ship was that way now. Everything pirate had been, at a dead minimum, taken down and cleaned. More than half had either gone into stores or simply been jettisoned in deep space.

He needed a couple hundred thousand liters of paint, but that wasn't critical. He'd need a hundred painters at that point. At least he had a Mazhin and Emro Arts Council to decide what colors, textures, and flavors to paint the walls.

Functional did not have to mean ugly.

A chime at the hatch. Uly rose from his seat, feeling decades older than he was, but that was stress. And carrying everything on his shoulders. Dan and the others were doing amazing work, but as Haydar had said, they needed somewhere between twenty and three hundred crew they could trust.

He opened the hatch to Haydar. Alone.

Uly stepped back and gestured the man in. Haydar moved to the couch that dominated this front room and Uly retook the chair that was warm.

He considered coffee or something, but it was late in his personal day and he needed to sleep.

"You look like hell," Haydar announced. Like it was a surprise or something.

Uly shrugged.

"Can we capture *Lacium*?" he countered. "You've seen what they transmitted, plus whatever Ethir and the others knew or were able to dig up."

"Capture?" Haydar asked. "Certainly. I think you called it a Trojan Horse. Or someone did and made me look it up at some point."

"Oh?" Uly asked.

"A case of mistaken identity." Haydar's smile included his eyes and his tentacles. "*Iron Wasp* sails in and folks assume Adrian Sobol is in command. We correct them. With guns."

"Do we expect that nobody from here has gotten there with the news?" Uly asked.

It was Haydar's turn to shrug, which was a Human thing he'd picked up at some point. Mazhin used their tentacles to semaphore a similar idea.

"If we don't wait around here for a few months, we ought to outrun spies," Haydar finally offered. "What I don't know is if you think such an assault is wise, or where it falls into your grander plan."

"You're assuming I have such a plan," Uly countered.

"You do," Haydar smiled. "I've gotten to know you well enough over the last year, Uly. Those plans aren't etched into stone. Maybe sketched with carbon graphite, easily erased or adapted as the situation evolves."

Uly grinned.

"I would say it is impossible to make concrete plans," he corrected. "But, like Vahid in his kitchen, you adapt as you have to."

"*Lacium*?" Haydar asked.

"You noted that they seem to be willing to accept certain sections of the proposed contract as is," Uly said. "Those sections that make this a treaty between nations instead of a business arrangement."

"We're going to be a nation?" Haydar pressed. "*Batyr*?"

"No, not *Batyr*," Uly shook his head. "Something new. Yet another something new, as it were. But if we can capture and hold *Lacium*, we could turn it into a place. A base for us, where trade and civilization occur, instead of a pirate truck stop, which I think Ethir called it first."

"What do we do with it?" Haydar asked.

"Build a new star-nation, I guess," Uly offered. "Dan and I have talked about it, and neither of us want to return to active duty or *Batyr* right now. Nor could we, with the various groups of people we have accumulated who also don't want to go anywhere. So we're here. That means we need to make the most of it."

"You'll need some sort of government," Haydar noted. "Unless you planned to retire from command already and become the new governor."

Uly felt his face grimace, then smoothed it out. Then he had an idea.

Haydar perked up, tentacles pointed toward Uly.

"Yes?" Haydar stirred.

"What if we treated *Lacium* the same way we intend *Z'Gosza*?" Uly asked.

"I'm not sure I follow, Uly."

"We have a contract between nations," Uly explained. "The *Corsac Fox* and *Z'Gosza*. What about the *Corsac Fox* and *Lacium* instead of merely capturing or conquering it? All in, and then some. We rearrange their current government, putting the farmers and ranchers on the ground in charge instead of the pirates. Then sign a similar treaty, including maybe protecting them like a mercenary navy. I can just as easily bring captured warships there for disposal as I would *Z'Gosza*. Maybe bring freighters and cargo here and warships there. They buy them cheap and have an immediate warfleet at hand. If they are structured as a freeport, then anyone who agrees to follow the rules can trade there. That means ex-pirates who want to go straight can sign on for duty, maybe with citizenship as the reward after five years."

"And no extraditions to other places that might remember them less fondly," Haydar mused.

"Exactly," Uly said. "Over the long term, *Lacium* might turn back into a pirate haven. Or a competitor to *Z'Gosza* for trade. I don't know, save that it puts them in control of their own destiny."

"And breaks up a zone of piracy that threatens civilization," Haydar nodded. Then he rose and moved to the hatch. "You're a dangerous being, Uly Fortier."

"Why's that?" Uly asked.

"Because I think it will work," Haydar laughed, keying the hatch.

Uly found himself alone as Haydar departed. The grimace was back, but he was alone, so he could indulge it.

All he'd ever wanted to do was serve in *Batyr*'s navy. Now, he didn't even want to return. At most, maybe he'd find a way to send a message home, letting them know he was alive and thriving.

What was he going to have to build out here, if he wanted to be happy?

# THIRTY-TWO

Rabiu had been given access to a comm system that was connected to the station. Unencrypted, but he didn't think he needed to say anything that would cause trouble.

With either side.

Director Bukra was on speaker on the other end.

"And that's the list as Conductor Fortier has transmitted it to me, sir," Rabiu said.

And it was. Let them figure out the implications that were already stirring uncomfortably under his headcrest. Plus, he'd told them that the Observer Mission came with non-disclosure agreements, so he was limited in what he could say.

Maybe more than strictly called for, especially since he hadn't actually signed anything yet, but Rabiu found himself warming more and more to the *Corsac Fox* and his crew. Good beings.

"They need an army?" Bukra asked. Demanded. Gasped. Something with a lot of pent-up emotions.

"A temporary occupation force, as I was given to understand it, sir," Rabiu replied. "And large enough that the locals would be emotionally overwhelmed before they could decide to resist."

At least that's what the Thogin had said. And seemed convinced.

"Administrator, this is Factor Bitrus," a new voice came over the line.

Rabiu was glad that he was alone in his quarters. Without a video link. So nobody saw him goggle in utter shock.

"Go ahead, sir," he managed, even sounding remarkably normal, regardless of the truth.

"The sailors requested should be available locally as recruits," the FACTOR HIMSELF said. "Or we could transfer them off of one of our armed vessels temporarily. What is the expected disposition of the ground forces?"

Rabiu paused to breathe. And control his voice. And his headcrest.

Riding his luck until it broke.

And he liked Uly.

"I was under the impression that they would like to recruit permanent crew if possible," he replied. "However, in the interests of speed, they might be willing to accept temporary transfers. At the same time, Conductor Fortier might attempt to recruit such sailors later, unless such will be strictly forbidden contractually."

There was a pause. Digesting one bite before the teeth came out to tear off another hunk of his hide?

"And the troops?" Factor Bitrus asked.

"Again, Conductor Fortier might be interested in building up his land forces against similar future needs, Factor," Rabiu replied. "Related to that, if you intend a long-term occupation of *Lacium*—assuming success—then it might be that the locals there would like to recruit or hire those troops themselves. Or have the opportunity to hire themselves a planetary defense militia that we might assist with from a technical and logistical standpoint. I presume we'd be interested in forming tighter trade alignment with the merchants and consumers of *Lacium* in that case, so it might be in our interests to limit our profit on the front, while playing for long-term lock-in on the back."

Somebody gasped on the other end of the line. He didn't know who. Rabiu still nearly wet himself in response anyway.

He was negotiating this deal like a Director at the minimum. Possibly a junior Factor, if there was such a thing. Factor-in-Training?

But they wanted *Lacium* broken. The only way to do that successfully was to put it back together again in a different pattern later.

Maybe one that had Uly's finprints on it.

"Lock-in, Administrator?" Director Bukra asked now, but Rabiu had the impression that he was repeating the Factor's words in order to draw all the feeding frenzy down on his own headcrest instead.

"If they want to be more than a pirate haven, that means trade and eventually local manufacturing to assist their development, Director," Rabiu said, nodding to himself alone in his chamber. "If we lock them in cheap now, they will be more likely to want to buy parts and service contracts from *Z'Gosza* over a longer profit horizon. Plus, the *Corsac Fox* might want to make that his permanent operating base. We want him as an ally and not necessarily a subordinate branch office, yes?"

Rabiu couldn't believe that he was actually negotiating with his own superiors on this topic. At the same time, they had specifically said they wanted Uly to succeed.

The *Corsac Fox* was sharp. And had a lot of smart and capable people around him. The women were also deadly, but the males Uly had left behind didn't strike Rabiu as fools.

Uly had created a persona for *Z'Goszan* society to consume. A good one, too, because Rabiu had taken Bukra's orders and found a friendly news crew and offered them what might turn into a much-longer-term mission to document the *Corsac Fox* for *Z'Goszan* viewers to fall in love with. Idolize.

Rabiu wondered if he was in the process of changing sides, but he was still following those original orders.

Nobody, however, had realized where it might take them. Even Rabiu only had a dim vision, as if through kelp beds.

He was riding his luck and trusting Uly. Much as the others were riding his.

"You have given us much to consider, Administrator," the Factor replied. "We shall be ready to meet with your *Corsac Fox* tomorrow over dinner and perhaps come to some preliminary agreements."

Rabiu nodded to himself.

"I understand," he stated.

He was doing what they had ordered him to do. And had put him in the position to understand the needs of all sides, that they might work out an agreement.

"Oh, and Rabiu?" Director Bukra spoke.

Rabiu held his breath.

"Good job."

And the line went dead.

Rabiu wondered if he might pass out, but there was still too much to do.

# THIRTY-THREE

Haydar was asleep. Had been asleep. The beeping was intruding and wouldn't go away until whoever it was on the other end was satisfied at having woken him up from a lovely dream.

He opened his eyes, cursing quietly that the Ononguli were a sight-based species. A Mazhin-designed ship would have let him read the display with his tentacles.

Piruz. A little past zero-dark-thirty.

Of course, the Horse Thief knew that. And laughed to himself.

"This had better be good," he growled anyway as he keyed the line open.

"Normal people have been up and working for a while now, old man," Piruz replied tartly.

Haydar doubted it. The sun was barely over the horizon on the planet below. Smart people were letting underlings work while they enjoyed their warm beds.

"What?" Haydar grumped.

"I took some of those tools that you've been working on," Piruz replied, his tone sobering enough that Haydar sat up in bed. "Found something."

Those tools were data analysis and decryption tools. For all of

Auga's vaunted bureaucracy, Haydar was beginning to wonder if the Mazhin had *forgotten* more about electronic security than the Auga Empire or anybody else ever knew. Certainly, the local computer systems they could access from the station hadn't impressed him with their boundary security.

"And?" Haydar asked, fully awake now.

There weren't many reasons to wake him up that didn't also involve alert sirens sounding.

"And I figured it might be worth rousting your silly, blue ass," Piruz said. "I'm standing on the threshold of what might be the top level data-core for the organization that Khadijan represents. Haven't knocked. Haven't done anything, because one mistake likely pisses those people off at the time when Uly is working a deal with them."

"Why are you waking me up, then?" Haydar pressed. "Back away. We can hit it later if we need."

"Sure," Piruz agreed. "But I thought you might want to look before we did. I just intercepted and decrypted a message from someone ordering a passenger liner be hired and brought close enough to the station to ferry troops aboard."

Haydar felt his tentacles go rigid, like he'd licked a hot battery.

"How many troops?" he asked.

"Dunno," Piruz replied, grinning from the tone. "That's the part inside I thought you might want to crack open softly for me."

Haydar was fully awake. And it wasn't that early. He'd been up late, coding and debugging things. Probably the same tools a Horse Thief had grabbed off the build machine this morning to use.

"Fix some coffee," Haydar said. "I'll be right there."

# THIRTY-FOUR

Dan was aft and down, running a training class for advanced students. The first class of the day was for the engineers who were still learning their right foot from their left, followed up by the folks who were past that.

Beranger and Travers weren't all that interested in moving up, so they'd stayed as senior students with the first group, then departed. Functionally, both of them were First Degree black belts, using one of the more common methods Humanity had come up with for ranking warriors over the course of Human civilization.

The Advanced Class was for folks intending to go beyond that. Both up and sideways.

Nasrin was present. Though she was more an artist, Mazhin dance forms had all evolved from or been infused with open hand/closed fist combat forms. Similarly, Suka Kuri had noted how many Moss School movements were shared with the Sabre School, though the old woman was merely sitting off to one side of the training floor watching today, like a Fleet Marshall conducting an inspection.

Both Yanouk and Anari were on the dance floor. Yanouk had more experience, having trained for dance under Suka Kuri before joining the

Humans to learn how to hit people. Anari had more potential, as yet underdeveloped because the Auga were bureaucratic fools.

Poor Solomon Wyndham was the only male, after the junior class had evacuated. He was just starting to grow, in the same way that Sterling Huff would be to her height soon.

Solomon wouldn't ever be a physical threat to the two Emro women, but he would be big for a Human when he'd reached his final height, then put on the bulk of adulthood in another decade. Not a lot of species besides Emro he couldn't threaten at that point.

Today, they were practicing a Mazhin form called *Sunflower Fist*. It was something Nasrin had taught Dan and her grunts at the same time Dan had taught the Mazhin woman various iterations of the Human *Tai Chi Chuan* styles she had learned from *Batyr* drill instructors in a previous life.

As Nasrin had noted at the time, many Human forms had started off with an assumption of someone grabbing one or both wrists. The response was to lift both arms and drive the attacker back.

For Dan, such opening movements generally taught a student to first move circularly in each of three axes of motion, as a preliminary to actual fighting, but she couldn't argue past that.

The Mazhin assumed that the first punch had been thrown in a bar fight, so one moved out of the way, then knocked the first attacker down. Then went after his friends as they decided to get stupid. Or any other fool deciding to throw a punch or swing a bottle.

*Not like Dan had* any *experience in bar fights...*

The Mazhin short form had twenty-four parts. Just enough for someone to engage all four walls offensively and defensively. The longer version tacked fifty-four more parts onto that, with several repetitions or variations designed to make certain responses automatic.

And, like the sunflower for which it was named, the form kept your head on a swivel, tracking opponents around you as you moved through the space.

Dan had studied a variety of deadly arts in her time. Boarding troopers in the *Batyr* navy might fight unarmed in a closet, all the way up to storming an empty cargo bay under fire while the defenders voided the ship's atmosphere.

She didn't expect anyone but Solomon to need that full curriculum. At the same time, Solomon would need that for as long as he wanted to be a Security Officer, and the other women had all wanted to learn.

All part of life in the navy. Plus, the possibility of an armed assault against one or more pirate stations in the near future.

They completed the long version of the form and Dan nodded.

"Weapons training next," Dan decided. "All of you start at the far end with boarding ax and work back and forth with cut and thrust."

Instead of joining them, Dan moved to where Suka Kuri had been watching. The old woman was Moss School, but Dan had the impression she could have gone Sabre just as easily. And likely just as far.

In the background, Dan's four students grabbed the training weapons and got to work. The two Emro women had the advantage there because the weapons could deploy to three meters long and be swung overhead. At the same time, very few ships had enough open volume overhead for an Emro in boarding armor to do that.

Instead, you had to keep it generally to two meters, then stab forward with the spike, or reverse the weapon to use the butt end to knock people down or stun them.

Solomon was the best student here, because he had the aggressiveness for the weapon, mixed with the size to stay contained in a normal starship corridor while moving forward. Anari was getting there. The other two were more pretty than lethal, though both were moving that direction as well.

"Uly is expecting an infantry assault?" Suka Kuri asked quietly as they watched the others practice.

"I think he's prepared to order one," Dan corrected the Exemplar. "We won't know until we get there what choice the defenders will make."

"Solomon will make a formidable warrior when he fully grows up," Suka Kuri noted.

"I agree," Dan said. "But that's probably eight Standard years away."

She saw Suka Kuri nod out of the corner of one eye.

"Nasrin moves with incredible grace," Suka Kuri continued. "Yanouk and Anari are both beginning to emulate her, though all of them move like you do."

Dan nodded. She'd had certain things pounded in pretty deep, to the point that her old *sensei*'s voice occasionally came out of her mouth when she spoke on the training floor.

"Should we locate a Sabre School Adept to help train Anari?" Dan asked the woman.

"Not yet," Suka Kuri replied. "She is but a Student today. When she reaches a level of expertise to be called a Seeker, it may be more appropriate. I have taken to teaching her certain things she will need to know, while you are her Adept at present."

"Me?" Dan asked, surprised. "I'm hardly an Adept of the Sabre School."

"Partly, you are correct," Suka Kuri acknowledged gravely. Then turned and grinned. "Thus, I am providing the history of the Emro arts that Anari will need. At the same time, the Sabre School requires a certain level of militant deadliness of its followers. Anari is in a space where she can learn Human and Mazhin forms, which no other Emro has likely ever seen."

"Aren't there Emro or Sabre School forms she should be acquiring?" Dan pressed.

She wasn't prepared for the old woman's bark of pure delight.

"Dan, there are only so many ways an erect biped can move in the process of striking, kicking, or blocking an opponent," Suka Kuri said with laughing eyes. "Every culture calls them something different. Every style assembles them into a different order, emphasizing some things and ignoring others. When you feel that Anari Supasei is qualified as a young boarding officer to your standards, I expect that she will be at least as good as the senior-most Sabre School Seekers. Perhaps a young Adept herself. Remember, both Moss and Sabre exist to learn. We are not put here to ossify old techniques and require our students to mimic our movements centuries after we're dead. We are charged to go out and discover, then bring that knowledge and wisdom to other seekers, that they might achieve a higher level of mastery in turn. I merely hope I live long enough to see Anari become an Exemplar herself. She has it in her. Already, she approaches Yanouk in some forms."

Dan nodded. The Auga had tested Anari and assigned her to engineering school, stating flatly that she must be Moss School because she was too smart for Sabre. Suka Kuri, a literal *Living Legend* of the Emro, disagreed with that conclusion.

Dan would listen to the expert here. Like Uly listened to her.

"I wonder what forms the Thogin have," Dan mused aloud.

Ethir and Ralphye showed up to the junior class occasionally enough to learn the form and then practice it, but had not mentioned anything they had studied elsewhere.

"I expect it will be fast," Suka Kuri replied. "Grapples intended to get a larger opponent to the ground where smaller, faster Thogin can keep that greater mass from being useful. The boys, however, are not the serious students that you and Anari will need."

"Agreed," Dan said. "I'll add that to the recruitment list."

"And, Dan?" Suka Kuri asked in a tone that caused Dan to ignore her four students and turn to the woman. "We'll want at least one female Thogin warrior."

Dan felt her face break into a huge grin. On the station, that had caused its own set of ripples, especially considering how outwardly sexist *Z'Gosza* society had come across to Dan.

Uly would have an entire, deadly team of women protecting him.

All part of the *Corsac Fox*'s legend.

# THIRTY-FIVE

Uly sat behind his desk with coffee in hand. And too many things up in the air to fully comprehend what Haydar and Piruz were telling him. Or what they'd done. Or why he was here.

"Back up," Uly interrupted the stream of words. "You did what?"

He watched two sets of tentacles fold and twist like two kids caught with their hands in a cookie jar by Mom.

"We broke into Factor Bitrus's main datacore and copied out significant chunks of his data in the form of downloading a wide variety of *Z'Gosza* historical romance vids," Piruz eventually replied with a grin.

Haydar had started to speak, but subsided. Uly looked at his favorite horse thief.

"Vids take up a LOT of volume," Piruz nodded enthusiastically. "Way more than raw data."

"And you found what?" Uly asked, turning to Haydar.

"Bitrus ordered a local passenger liner be hired for six months at above normal rates," Haydar said. "Suggesting that he's in the process of locating or hiring you a small army for the ground assault Ethir and the others think might be necessary at some point."

Uly drank some more coffee, letting the warmth and especially caffeine hit him. Wasn't actually coffee, but it was a seed pod that could be roasted to a similar taste, with a close enough chemical composition.

Once he found a planet that grew habanero peppers, he'd be set. No, Dan wanted chocolate or something similar. And Vahid had an order in for live chickens that could be bred, though that roast chicken dish he'd had on the station might get them close.

Piracy vids never stopped to consider logistics. You just took food from whoever you attacked. And those movies were always one, single species.

He had half of the species he knew of within the sound of his voice right now.

"How big is that ship?" he asked his two juvenile delinquents.

Both looked at him surprised from eyes and tentacles. Probably expected to get yelled at.

"In for a penny, in for a pound," he said, quoting the Mazhin currency they used on their ships.

They grinned like truants now.

"Crew plus up to two thousand passengers," Piruz nodded. "And a lot of food supplies, assuming a higher quality of passenger than armed soldiers. How many were you thinking you needed?"

"I have no idea," Uly replied. "Your notes are decades out of date, somewhat updated from Ethir and a few of the Ononguli who have only tangential experience at best. Two thousand is more than we need, but I'm not going to turn them away if Khadijan's folks want to supply us that. If anything, it might look like we captured a civilian liner and needed help dealing with a bunch of rich hostages we needed to ransom."

Both Mazhin's eyes got big. Tentacles got excited, for lack of a better word.

"More mistaken identity?" Haydar asked.

It was Uly's turn to grin.

"If they think we're *Iron Wasp* and associated prisoners, we can get a lot closer than an armed warship dropping out of warp on top of them," he said.

A chime at his door interrupted. Uly nodded to Piruz to open it, revealing Rabiu Khadijan.

"Come in," Uly told the Khet. "I was just going over some logistics planning with Haydar and Piruz. What can I help you with?"

In the back of his mind, he was trying to send scents to tell them to lie, but those two were pretty sharp already.

Rabiu seemed friendly, but nobody had forced him into a corner to choose sides yet. Nor did Uly want to.

Not yet.

"I have been going over the latest proposal from Factor Bitrus," Rabiu replied as he came to rest next to the others.

The office was larger than Uly normally wanted, so it didn't feel crowded. He could probably add three more on that side and still breathe.

"And?" Uly prompted when the Khet fell silent.

"Two options," Rabiu said, his headcrest telegraphing up and down in ways Uly recognized, but didn't know well enough to read. Not like Mazhin tentacles. "First, you can recruit thirty to forty crew with gunnery ratings from the general population. That might take some time, and I got the impression that you would prefer to move quickly?"

"That's right," Uly agreed. "The less time someone has to sell this information to the pirates, the better the odds that we can succeed. What was the alternative?"

"Factor Bitrus offered to transfer several crews from one of his other armed vessels," Rabiu said.

Uly held himself perfectly still. As did Piruz. A glance at Haydar for a subtle nod.

"That would be faster," Uly said. "What's the downside you see?"

"He might want them back later," Rabiu replied earnestly. "I told him I would see which way you leaned. He might forbid long-term recruitment, depending."

Uly leaned back and finished his coffee, already wishing he'd brought a whole carafe with him this morning. The day had that feel to it.

"Is there a risk to bringing in trained crews?" Uly asked, looking directly at Rabiu and hoping the two Mazhin wouldn't speak up.

"The possibility of divided loyalties," Rabiu replied. "I don't know your long-range plans well enough to judge outcomes, Uly."

Honest, which was interesting considering how short a time Uly had been here. He'd gotten the impression that everything around here was layered up in capitalist tendencies that put personal profit above the greater societal good, however dumb that was over generational scales.

Now, however, was not the time for a lecture on *Batyr* culture. Or even *Danumash*. Everybody approached civilization their own way. And the Khet of *Z'Gosza* treated contract law as the highest form of civilization.

*Whatever gets you through warp-space...*

"Would they be a problem over the short term?" Uly countered.

"No," Rabiu said. "Professionals with reputations to maintain. However..."

"Yes?"

"Factor Bitrus probably assumes that you have two or three times the crew you do, and are simply short-handed on the guns, rather than having escaped Auga control with basically only engineers and officers," Rabiu said. "I am concerned that such knowledge might tempt the Factor to reconsider his options. Especially if he thought that he could capture this ship with surprise."

"I don't think you folks truly understand Human violence," Haydar spoke up finally.

"Sir?" Rabiu turned to him.

Haydar smiled. To an outsider, it probably even looked warm.

Uly had known the man for the better part of a year in close quarters.

*Feral* was the term he'd have used.

"Humans are at least as violent as the Ononguli or the Auga, Administrator," Haydar growled.

"Rabiu," Uly interrupted. "He's Rabiu. We're all friends here."

Better to keep Haydar from frightening the poor Khet to death, especially if the subtle things Uly could see meant that the fellow was possibly changing sides, at least emotionally.

Rabiu grinned nervously. Haydar and Piruz nodded. Both relaxed some, but Uly doubted that Rabiu saw it.

"Rabiu," Haydar continued. "Humans are dangerous. Even with the few on this ship. Dan and Solomon are probably each worth four or six Khet sailors. The others that Dan is training are, also. An attempt at piracy by Khet mercenaries is likely to be short-circuited in a blaze of violence that will make your fins turn black watching."

"Really?" Rabiu asked.

"Really," Piruz assured him.

Both spoke from experience, mostly with the *Combined Crowns of Danumash*, but also with Uly's crew.

"So if we had an additional twenty-five to thirty gunners aboard for battle, and they tried something?" Rabiu asked.

"Anari Supasei is Sabre School," Haydar said sagely. "Dan Chastain is her teacher."

"Oh," Rabiu said.

Uly liked the way Haydar had finessed that. Rude, but essentially accurate. *Technically correct*, which was always the best kind.

Suggesting that Dan was a Sabre School Elder without ever coming out.

He'd never met one, so Uly couldn't be sure.

He was, however, exceptionally certain how dangerous Dan Chastain was if pressed.

And this crew had experience at that kind of piracy.

"We'll be prepared, just in case," Uly said to smooth things over. "For now, we'll assume that the Factor is dealing honestly with us, and that his interests stretch beyond a single attack on *Lacium* to the possibility of an entire campaign against piracy in this region."

Rabiu relaxed. As did the two Mazhin. They were closer to violence themselves.

"Also, I have the impression that Factor Bitrus is prepared to sign some sort of deal tonight," Rabiu continued. "You really want to move as fast as possible?"

"If they can load troops and deliver gunners, I'd be gone in the morning," Uly replied.

Rabiu nodded.

"Let me see what my contacts can tell me on that front then, sir," he nodded, immediately withdrawing.

Uly turned to Haydar and Piruz.

"Do not let him know until much, much later," Uly said. "After we're certain that it's not a trap."

"At the same time, I think I'd like to go deeper into those records myself and settle things in my own mind," Haydar replied.

"Just don't get caught," Uly reminded him. "We've got Rabiu as a channel. Exploit that as well."

"Will do," Piruz chirped.

They departed and Uly considered his empty coffee mug.

And wondered if he was ever going to get enough sleep again.

# THIRTY-SIX

Uly was back in the nice uniform. Cleaned and shaved and ready for company. Dan was next to him. Her warrior women were all close by and armed for effect, plus Suka Kuri in a gloriously blue, kimono-style robe she'd dug out or had made at some point.

Him, and females, with Haydar and Sterling watching things from up on the bridge.

Factor Bitrus was a shorter, plumper version of Rabiu Khadijan. Lawal Bukra fell in between them. Uly was one hundred and eighty-five centimeters tall. Nasrin was one hundred and seventy. Rabiu was almost Uly's height. The other two were closer to Nasrin's.

And Uly continued to be skinny, regardless of what Dan or Vahid had tried to put weight on him. The three Khet were simply squishy. Bureaucratically overweight.

Still, smiles and polite friendliness.

Other Khet accompanied Bitrus. Generally dressed in slacks and tunics comparable to Bukra, so Uly assumed Directors. Muted colors across the board that faded against his maroons. Most appeared to be either Bukra's peers, or spies for other Factors who were friendly enough to be included in a small dinner to plot a new foreign policy for *Z'Gosza*.

Or whatever this qualified as.

Rabiu stepped into the middle ground from Uly's side, turning sideways like a referee at a sporting event, though he seemed to be the most nervous person present.

"Factor Ahmadu Bitrus, I present to you Ulysses Fortier, the *Corsac Fox*," Rabiu said. "Conductor, Factor Ahmadu Bitrus."

Uly stepped forward and nodded deeply. *Z'Gosza* didn't shake hands like Human cultures still did, in order to show that one was not holding a sword or pistol.

The others got introduced as well. Mostly Directors, but Uly would need a complete corporate Table of Management in front of him for the Factor to be certain if all these people reported to the Khet.

They all feared him, that much was obvious.

Except Rabiu. What did that say?

"Factor and friends, welcome aboard my vessel," Uly said.

The camera crew had come along, shooting more footage from a corner. Uly would need to sort them out after he knew which direction dinner was going.

And he didn't call the ship *Corsac Fox*. Apparently, the Khet locals had fully embraced that as Uly, instead. Yet another case of mistaken identity, right up there with this no longer being the *Iron Wasp*.

He smiled. They smiled back.

"Our chef has worked all day to present a meal he believes is representative of the many species and cultures that have come together today," Uly continued. "If you would please join me, we'll break bread first, then have a long series of small courses over which we can discuss business."

That seemed to be the right thing to say. Rabiu had suggested it, business being the highest art form to these Khet.

He led. Rabiu escorted Bukra and the Factor. Dan and her team gathered up the guests like wayward sheep and kept them on track.

Vahid had recruited everybody not directly on duty somewhere, reporting to either him or Omid as they had baked, chopped, stirred, or even set tables. Everyone had showered and dressed nice as well. At least the ones who would be seen by company.

Uly was at the head of the table. Bitrus and Bukra on his left and right. Dan at the far end. Nasrin, Yanouk, Anari, Katya, and Suka Kuri along each side. Ethir too, though Uly had been told that was only because there weren't any female Thogin to sit at the table and mildly disrupt the sexist Khet.

No female Khet had accompanied the business leaders, after all. Dan and Suka Kuri were up to something, but his job was to be aloof and somewhat patriarchal here, regardless of his actual age.

Factor Bitrus's peer, when everyone else at the table was some manner of minion to someone.

Vahid started with a form of sourdough bread that wasn't Human wheat, but again served a similar purpose. Ononguli originally, but grown damned near everywhere these days.

Except on those backwards Human worlds in the far swamps of Imperial Sector Seventeen.

Idly, Uly wondered what sorts of trouble he might cause, just bringing all these alien plants or animals home, so that they could sample what the rest of the galaxy consumed.

Butter that wasn't from a terrestrial cow, but from a type of plant that produced an oil one could emulsify equally.

If it was pink, that was just too bad. Close your eyes and you'd be hard pressed to taste the difference.

There was not as much alcohol with dinner as a Human meal would have done. Especially the *Batyr* navy. Some wine for Dan, which just added a nervous edge to the Khet, who couldn't process ethyl alcohol in anywhere near the concentrations Uly and his kind could.

Vahid had been working from the depths of the Ononguli stores, supplemented originally by everything Adrian Sobol had captured from *King Hewitt II* in order to keep his Human prisoners alive. And The Spatula had learned how to cook for Humans, in addition to everyone else.

Small courses, served common style in larger bowls or on plates that people snagged samples from. A great way to tell people you weren't trying to poison them, not accounting for all the various species and exotic food allergies one might find at this table.

Bland, in terms of spice, but Vahid had risen above himself. And Uly utterly loved the look of pure joy on Dan's face when the stewards delivered fresh chocolate cake for dessert, plus options for fruit in cream, or sweet puddings. All simple. All exceptionally done.

He burped quietly and settled with a glass of port that would have cost him at least a month's wages, back when he'd been serving in the navy.

Captain Winter and his officers aboard *King Hewitt II* might have been assholes, especially from the stories the surviving crew told, but they'd had access to some top-notch booze. And with not nearly as many people interested in drinking it, Uly had his pick.

Mostly, he settled on one glass with dinner, and occasionally, like now, one glass as a treat over dessert. Gotta stretch the stuff. Or figure out where to find the right yeast to make more.

Factor Bitrus slumped equally, smiling. Bukra as well. Rabiu released a tiny sigh that most of the table missed, since they weren't paying attention to the Khet.

It was good.

Factor Bitrus was sipping a juice and cream drink. He studied Uly now. The table fell into one of those moments of extended silence when several side conversations all ended at the same instant.

Uly nodded to the Khet.

"I hope this was to your liking, Factor?" he asked.

"I'd hire your Mazhin if I thought I could," Bitrus smiled, offering one of the highest possible compliments *Z'Goszan* business knew.

He couldn't. The Twins were probably the last two that would leave, based on what Uly had heard. And he technically *Spoke* for their Conclave, which was just weird.

"To business?" Uly asked.

He didn't have Haydar's cunning handy, but he did have Ethir. And Dan. And Suka Kuri. And Nasrin. And the others. Uly was not worried on that score.

"You have exceedingly few counteroffers to our reply," Bitrus said simply, as if confused.

Or looking for the trap that wasn't really there.

Uly nodded.

"Our original offer, while detailed, was fairly straightforward, sir," he replied. "It built on existing structures and policies here, while opening the way to new types of commerce, previously unknown in this region. At the same time, you didn't offer many modifications yourself, understanding that it is all theoretical until the first time we actually arrived with captured ships, crews, and cargo that we need to dispose of. I imagine that to be the moment when addenda will become obvious and necessary."

He paused there and Bitrus nodded, still wary.

"From there, you have proposed a raid on a known pirate haven," Uly continued. "In order to undertake such an effort, my crew and I will need your material assistance, as Administrator Khadijan has spelled out. If we have a broad, general agreement on those terms, then we can nail down details now, and move to an operational tempo."

"How quickly could you attack?" Bukra asked, apparently speaking for Bitrus in such a way that he could be disowned later.

Rabiu had suggested such a pattern. After all, he'd been the sacrificial tuna on Day One, though Uly hadn't needed to consume him.

"Assuming you could provide both portions of my request, I could sail in four hours," Uly replied, drawing gasps all the way around the table. "Long enough for the crew to arrive and be bunked. Long enough for the second vessel to be loaded and a course plotted. Then we move, before the bad guys understand what's coming."

He stared at Bukra as he spoke, watching the Factor out of the corner of his eye.

"My only critical question at this point is if I would be allowed to recruit some or all of the folks you have provided, once this mission is complete," Uly said simply. "I'm somewhat thin on crew, as you are aware, and would rather work with folks that have been vouched for by others I know."

"Can you capture *Lacium*?" the Factor asked now, disrupting the usual social flow of his disposable minions.

"I can try," Uly replied, turning to look at the one Khet who really mattered.

The rest—including the film crew shooting all of this—were window dressing, at the end of the day. Factor Bitrus would provide what Uly needed, or he wouldn't.

"I will also remind you that the former *Iron Wasp* is desperately over-armed for an Interceptor," Uly continued. "And that most of the vessels one might expect to be in harbor will be smaller, Seeker-class boats. Plus, I doubt that the pirates will suddenly decide to organize themselves into a naval force under sharp discipline. If I do this right, I expect them to scatter like seeds in a wind. That is also acceptable on my part, as they are far less of a threat without a base from which to operate."

"Like yourself?" Bukra asked, apparently following some script. Or reading his boss's face.

"I have *Wren*," Uly said simply. "That ship gives me at least a year as a forward operating base, without selling off certain materials I don't need. I have that long to create this thing, if I don't capture *Lacium*, or at least enough tonnage there to continue to support my operational tempo."

"You did not answer the original question, Conductor," the Factor said. "Can you capture *Lacium*?"

"He can drive off or destroy many of the defenders," Dan interjected. "That leaves a main station we need to address, and however many other facilities will need to be physically assaulted. Based on the limited intelligence we have available, I need a minimum of six hundred professional soldiers. Eight hundred to one thousand would be even better. With anything less, I cannot be certain that I won't have to simply destroy any platforms that resist, instead of boarding them individually to neutralize."

"You won't have—?" The Factor stuttered off into nothingness.

"That's correct, sir," Dan said. "Uly will be in operational control of this vessel, filling the billet of a Fleet Captain, or possibly even an Echelon, which are senior naval command ranks—flag officers—where we come from. I will be leading my troops into battle, depending on the quality of the officer corps that they come with. If these are veterans with a good enlisted cadre, comfortable with taking orders and executing, then we might launch several attacks simultaneously, thereby greatly limiting the amount of damage we have to do. Assuming that you desire *Lacium* to remain a functional port when we're done."

"As opposed to?" the Factor asked slowly, even more lost than before.

Uly kept his face neutral. Dan was in charge of the ground assault. Nobody else he would trust to manage it.

"As opposed to simply annihilating everything in orbit with weapons fire and reducing the colony to whatever industrial base they have on the ground," Dan replied. "Assuming you don't want that subsequently destroyed by orbital bombardment."

It was the calm, professional, emotionless way she said all that that seemed to have the biggest impact on the Khet. All of them shuddered, but Haydar had said that they didn't understand violence. Not like Humans did it.

To the Factor, all this would be described in terms of profit and loss on quarterly statements. They didn't fathom Uly standing off with 6dm wavebolts to shatter things, either occupied or abandoned, while sipping coffee. He hoped it wouldn't come to that.

Which wasn't the same thing as not doing it, if necessary.

Khet heads rotated away from Dan in visible horror, turning to him like turrets. Uly smiled, but it wasn't particularly warm. That just made them recoil all the harder.

"You're serious," Factor Bitrus whispered in a terrible awe.

"You want the job done, Factor," Uly replied soberly. "That's what it looks like. Nobody has ever wanted it that badly before, obviously. And yes, I can capture *Lacium*, if you provide the resources I need. I can hold it, as well. After that, I hope to have need of a local, friendly Admiralty Court on *Z'Gosza* to dispose of former piratical hardware and personnel so I don't have to pick between letting them all go and hoping for the best, or killing them out of hand."

He left it at that. Hung it out there like bait on a long line, as Rabiu had mentioned while setting all this up.

A visibly frightened Factor Bitrus and Director Bukra turned to Rabiu next. Something silent but intent passed. Uly watched. Dan watched.

Rabiu nodded.

"He can do it, sir," Rabiu said simply. "If we provide him what he needs. Are you serious enough to succeed?"

Uly noted that Rabiu didn't say *we*. He'd said *you*.

Looked like the Khet had chosen sides anyway.

Now, they just had to go do it.

Factor Bitrus nodded at some internal commentary. Then turned his terrible gaze to Director Bukra.

"Director, I believe that we are close to a final agreement," the Khet said. "I will rely on you and Administrator Rabiu to work with the *Corsac Fox* and his staff on any last-minute details, but you should initiate your plans now."

Uly nodded.

Whatever was about to happen was why Haydar and Sterling had a full crew on the bridge, along with the rest of the crew aft in engineering.

Just in case this was a trap.

# THIRTY-SEVEN

Dan watched Bukra. The Director moved with great delicacy, noting, no doubt, the Emro woman on his far side from Uly, and how hyped up Yanouk was for violence.

It wasn't a natural thing for Yanouk. Not like Anari was turning into. At the same time, the Khet didn't know that.

He nodded to his boss. To Uly. To her. To the table.

Bukra pulled a communicator from his pocket with excessive care and visibility.

"Operations," a voice replied immediately when the Khet opened it.

"This is Director Bukra," he said. "We have approval for Phase Two and Phase Three. Begin loading the transport and send the gunnery teams to their shuttle to board Corsac Fox soonest."

"Which staffing level should I communicate to the transport, Director Bukra?" the man on the comm asked in the sort of bored, professional voice of a senior enlisted specialist working from a checklist in front of him.

As opposed, she hoped, to one slamming a fin down on an alert button with glee.

Bukra turned to the Factor who was making these decisions.

Khet had hands similar to Humans. Four fingers and a thumb, more or less. More webbing. Different bone shapes. Same pattern for tool using.

Factor Bitrus held up one index finger silently. Both Bukra and Rabiu beside her gasped quietly.

Bukra nodded and swallowed before responding.

"Fully loaded, Operations," Bukra said.

"Confirming eight operational combat teams from Apex Mechanical Security Solutions," the Operations clerk replied.

"That is correct," Bukra said. "Troops and personal gear as quickly as they can load. We'll follow up with a cargo carrier hauling additional supplies shortly."

"Acknowledged, Director Bukra," Operations said. "Sounding the alert for the teams now. Estimated twenty minutes on the shuttle. The transport should take roughly three hours to complete boarding and launch."

"Keep me posted if these numbers change," Bukra said, then cut the line and turned to face her down the long table. "That will be fourteen hundred troops, ninety percent of which will be Khet, with a broad mix of others."

"Eight security groups?" Dan asked. "Did I have that right? And he called them combat teams?"

"You are correct," the Khet nodded to her as he put away the comm unit. "They are normally used in similar operations, when we wish to rescue important hostages if we can locate them. Or to storm pirates when we can sail a harmless-looking cargo carrier and induce them to attack. Presumably, they will be adequate in a similar role here. We've employed this company closely for more than a generation at this point."

Dan nodded. Smiled even.

"How will they react to having my ladies put in command of them?" she asked, gesturing to her team. Solomon wasn't here, but he'd be in command of a team as well.

They didn't need to know that. Yet.

Bitrus and Bukra didn't flinch as hard as the others, but Dan didn't think the strangers worked for the Factor. None of this group had been at the previous dinner. New favors being traded. Or new spies watching what Factor Bitrus and his organization were up to.

Something.

Hell, even the camera crew was surprised, though the one holding the camera itself moved like he was gyroscopically stabilized.

"They will follow orders, sir," Director Bukra replied carefully.

"Then we should be in good shape," she said, smiling to take some of the sting out of her earlier words.

If Uly had stepped up to something like a Fleet Captain or even a flag officer Echelon, she supposed she should be executing as a Commander, with Solomon and the ladies all needing to be at least Lieutenants.

More things to sort out as Uly's Second-in-Command.

Uly lifted his glass. Dan did the same.

"Factor, I believe we have enough of an agreement to start changing the galaxy?" he asked.

The others lifted glasses as well, the toast at dinner being something that had spanned many cultures.

"I believe you are correct, *Corsac Fox*," the Factor said.

"Friends and comrades, I give you victory," Uly said.

Dan drank with the others.

Hopefully, they could even pull it off.

# COMPASS ROSE

# THIRTY-EIGHT

Tuesday.

Not that it mattered in deep space. And not this far from home in Sector Twenty-One. The locals were mostly Khet and Ugotha.

Lukyan and his crew were Ononguli. *Compass Rose* was an Ononguli ship.

Lukyan kept his ship's time and calendar set to Rayzian, the Ononguli capital. Even way the hell over here. Reminded him of home, not that he was headed back that way anytime soon.

It was late in the day, regardless of what the local yahoos thought. He didn't care what *Lacium* thought the time was. He was keeping Ononguli time and they could just deal with it.

Lukyan sipped his tea and considered Tuesdays in general.

Bit of a yawn. Not much interesting happening, but that was acceptable. The most recent patrol hadn't been all that impressive.

He wondered if there were simply too many pirates operating in the immediate region these days and had starting spooking the little fish. The Khet were merchants, after all, not warriors.

Not bad-asses, like him and his boys.

The tea was even a little thin. Not rousing him.

He looked around the bridge. All horns and backs of heads, but he didn't have any outsiders on this ship. Ononguli crew, bowsprit to aftlights.

The screen on the wall in front of him was set to a god's eye view from above, so he had *Lacium* and the main station over in the northwest corner, plus all the ships and factories in lower orbit.

*Compass Rose* was getting ready to head out for another sweep. Maybe find themselves a fat Khet tuna swimming lazily along. Something.

Tuesday was definitely dragging on him today.

Lukyan studied the readouts of the argosy around him. *Compass Rose* frequently sailed with two other ships as something more than a mob and less than a squadron. The Armed Probe *Legend of Ymnan* could haul a lot of cargo once the *Rose* nailed somebody. That crew was all Khet, most of them from farther out in the Sector. The Seeker *Spirit of Iniquity* had the best sensors, being an old scout ship that had been demobilized a generation ago and saved from the wrecker at the last minute.

Still, the ship always smelled weird. Ugotha were masters of biochemistry, and could even communicate by smell, so the ship was heavy with strange scents, every time he'd gone aboard to talk to Conductor Zorion Aldana. Didn't matter that two-thirds of the ship's crew wasn't Ugotha. The Conductor and senior staff mostly were.

On the other hand, Lukyan supposed that *Compass Rose* smelled funky to the Ugotha or the Khet. Whatever. As long as *Spirit of Iniquity* could find them, and *Legend of Ymnan* could haul away cargo when they didn't want the whole vessel, it had been a pretty profitable team.

Tuesdays just wore on him occasionally.

"Hey, that's weird," a voice intruded on his musing.

Lukyan stirred and looked around. Dmytro was Piloting today. He reached out a hand to tap the screen between himself and the Gunner's station, currently unoccupied because they were safe at harbor in *Lacium*.

Nobody would bother them here.

"What's weird?" Lukyan asked, feeling like the straight man in some strange comedy routine.

Tuesdays, ya know?

"Two ships just dropped out of warp bubble, high and kinda lateral to us," Dmytro replied.

"And?" The comedy was going to write itself today, wasn't it?

"And I'm pretty sure that the smaller one is *Iron Wasp*, boss," Dmytro said, again tapping.

Lukyan grumbled and dialed up the screen on his own console. Wasn't as big as the main, but he wasn't supposed to be flying the ship or fighting it. Merely commanding.

Not that his crew of troublemakers needed him for a kick in the ass to get moving all that often. Usually a hard jerk on the chain to back them off.

Hmmm. Yup, two ships. One heavy Interceptor by size. One cargo carrier. No, that's a passenger liner. Huh.

Lukyan found the button he wanted and pushed it.

"Sobol here," his First Officer replied a moment later.

"Your cousin supposed to be in this region of space?" Lukyan asked.

"Huh?"

Yup, comedy day. And possibly catching. Lukyan hoped that his shots were enough up to date. Hate to have to go see a doc for this. They might never stop laughing if he caught a case of the Tuesdays.

"*Iron Wasp*," Lukyan spelled it out. "Adrian Sobol. Your famous cousin."

Well, sort of famous. And not always in a great way. Kinda a hothead with a reputation for shooting before he aimed. Aggressive, though, which was what you really wanted in an Ononguli commander.

Lukyan wondered if that pirate had ever had a case of the Tuesdays sneak up on him.

"Not following, Lukyan," Maks Sobol replied.

"Haul your ass up the bridge then and see," Lukyan said.

*Iron Wasp* shouldn't be over here. Adrian usually worked closer to the Ononguli Sphere. Lukyan wondered if the boy had decided to go all in on one of those grand, epic voyages that the bards talked about, centuries later.

*Compass Rose* was fine over here, making them all a polite living.

Still, if that was a passenger liner, then good old Adrian must have hit the motherload. Maybe he needed help? For a small fee?

"Dmytro, what are those two doing now?" Lukyan asked. "And plot a course to slip over, in case Maks wants to see his cousin, or *Iron Wasp* wants some help. But don't execute it yet."

"Yeah, I don't want those crazy yahoos firing warning shots at me, either, Lukyan," Dmytro laughed.

Sour, black comedy was still comedy, right? And Adrian Sobol had a rep.

Crazy git.

Still, distant kin and all that. Might have news from home. Lords of the Endless Plains knew that Lukyan hadn't been back to the Ononguli Sphere in years at this point. Safer. Hopefully, Nadiya's parents had gotten over that one situation and weren't mad at him anymore. It had been long enough, hadn't it?

Tuesdays...

"Oh, shit!" Dmytro suddenly exclaimed.

"WHAT?" Lukyan demanded.

About that moment, Maks came through the main hatch, stuttering to a halt as he heard Dmytro.

"*Iron Wasp* just opened fire on the station!"

# THIRTY-NINE

Uly had made sure to set up a rendezvous with the Khet transport vessel and *Wren* in a place Ethir and Haydar had assured him no smart pirate would look to hide or hunt. Middle of nowhere, off any trade lanes.

Quiet.

Dan and her folks had transferred over for the operation. Eight combat teams. Dan. Solomon. Nasrin. Yanouk. Anari. Katya. Beranger. Travers. The last three didn't have much experience commanding troops. Hell, nobody but Dan did, but she had put someone she trusted with each of those eight teams.

If nothing else, it let her relay commands and information quickly. And she'd said that the team's lieutenants were all adequate to her needs in the short term.

Uly looked around his bridge. They'd rearranged sleep patterns again. And parked *Wren* where only this group could find it, though Drew Roscoe had had his folks disable the Variable Pulse Spatial Generator by removing certain parts and carrying them with him.

Uly had a base. Hopefully nobody else would stumble across it and loot it behind his back, because he needed everybody aboard the *Corsac Fox*.

Bitrus had been true to his word. Six gunnery teams for the turrets, all experienced and used to working as individual units. He and Haydar had gotten them aboard and kept them from mentioning to anyone that they'd just added nearly a third to the overall crew before he sailed.

The gunners hadn't complained. Several of them had even laughed at the realization. That was good, at least for now.

Dan had still worked with Haydar and Piruz to functionally lock three quarters of the ship off-limits from the outsiders. Their quarters, the mess hall, and the guns was about all they could get to.

Uly understood that he was a little paranoid, but he'd been a prisoner. And all of his Mazhin friends had been slaves at one point.

So, he was armed on his bridge. As was everyone he could see.

Just in case.

"*Swift Passage*, this is *Corsac Fox*," Drew announced.

Sterling Huff had the makings of a great officer, one of these days. And a gift for stellar cartography.

Drew was a Sailing Master as good as any Uly had ever met, and better than most.

Having everybody in one place aboard *Corsac Fox* was nice. Plus, Sterling was acting as Gunner today, which mostly meant telling those six teams of newcomers who to shoot at.

"Go ahead, *Corsac Fox*," a voice replied. *Z'Gosza* accent, presumably Khet.

By sheer numbers, this was technically a Khet operation. The important bits were alien, though.

"*Swift Passage*, I have plotted your course and transmitting now," Drew said. "We'll be going in first, so try not to get blipped out of warp by any pirates along the way, okay?"

Chuckles, both here and over the comm. Some fool pirate would rue that mistake for the rest of his days. Factor Bitrus had said that he normally sent one team as a Q-ship surprise, a cargo vessel of passenger liner waddling along to be attacked.

Even *Iron Wasp* when it had been captured had only had about three hundred boarding troops, about two teams, aboard.

Eight was overwhelming force.

Useful today.

"Course plot received, *Corsac Fox*," the pilot over there replied. "We are two seconds behind you and off your starboard when you depart."

"Counting down," Drew said, looking around. "Four. Three. Two. One. Initiating."

He cut the line and concentrated on his console. *Corsac Fox* was now operating in a tiny bubble of space that had been pinched by the generators. Outside that, space was being brutally warped in such a way that *Corsac Fox* was a seed being squeezed between two fingers, flying out along a calculated line at a medium FTL speed.

Fantastic way to get around, except that you left a wake behind you. The better tuned the engines, the smaller that wake and the quicker it faded, but it was still there. A faster ship could come up behind you and get close enough to bounce you out, leaving a situation with an attacker and a victim in close proximity.

And that blade cut both ways.

"Estimated time to arrival?" Uly asked, mostly to confirm.

"Twenty-four minutes, sir," Drew replied.

"Sterling, you go take a potty break now," Uly ordered. "And have the wardroom send you up a pot of whatever you want to drink. You'll be at the tip of the spear pretty quickly and I'll need you focused."

"Aye, sir," Sterling said, locking his board and rising.

They had no idea how long this would take. The system might surrender quickly. They might fight to the death. It could be over in minutes. Or hours.

Or even days, but he'd deal with that issue when he got there. If it turned into a siege, he had other problems in front of him.

"Haydar, how are our guests?" Uly asked.

"A year ago, I'd have said primed and violent, Uly," Haydar replied. Then he shrugged. "For Khet, they seem dangerous enough. No offense, Rabiu."

"None taken," the Khet ambassador replied.

Uly had made sure that Rabiu spent an afternoon with Dan in the two training classes, first watching amateurs go through their motions before sitting in as the Advanced Students put on a performance.

It had been worth it, to watch Rabiu's face freeze when he caught a glimpse of real violence. Twenty-eight gunners, all of them Khet, were not a threat while Dan and the ladies were aboard.

Or after Uly got them all back.

"Keep an eye on them anyway," Uly ordered. "Lock everything for now but understand that if we get into a damage-control situation, that might change. I don't think Bitrus is about to double-deal, but I'm also not taking it at face value today. Later, when we win, it will be different."

Rabiu nodded, as did Haydar.

One by one, everyone cycled out for a quick break, including Uly, though he hoped to do nothing but issue top-level orders today. Drew and Sterling knew what to do. Haydar had been in more space battles than *everyone else* put together, he'd finally admitted quietly, so he could watch the flow of ships and see things Uly would probably miss.

Dan was set to unleash a horde of angry locusts on a local pirate truck stop.

He studied his coffee but decided that he didn't need more. Not yet.

"All hands, this is your Sailing Master," Drew announced. "Stand by to emerge at *Lacium*."

# FORTY

Haydar really did like Uly, to have finally told that young man that much about his own youth. At the same time, Uly *Spoke* for the Clan. And the Conclave would have to listen to him, if they ever found another Mazhin ship. Unlikely, but what were the odds of accomplishing all the other crazy shit that Uly had managed so far?

So, today he was keeping strategic overwatch when they emerged. Sniffing out all the folks that might decide to get sneaky or stupid.

Not hard to do if you have a lot of ships maneuvering in close proximity in three dimensions. Fortunately, Mazhin tended to be exceptional at that sort of thing. All those tentacles.

He turned to look at Uly. Conductor. Speaker.

*Hero.*

Vahid had summed it all up when talking about the importance of Uly's luck. Hopefully, it held today. With a little help from his friends.

"All hands, this is your Sailing Master," Drew Roscoe said. "Stand by to emerge at *Lacium*."

And then the warp bubble was gone and they were back in real space.

*Lacium.* Below and slightly off to one side. Big station in orbit, closer. Drew Roscoe had been able to plot them down tight, knowing that it maintained a geo-synchronous orbit. Same place in the sky, all the time, visible at night as a star with a bit of a disk. Really small moon.

Still freaking huge.

Haydar turned his scanners on the station and pinged it hard enough that any Mazhin over there would have their tentacles stand on end. Then a ping on the ships and stations around them.

Nothing big, save for three monstrous cargo carriers. The big, bulk cruisers that carried gigatons of grains or raw materials from point to point, rather than the small ones hauling priority cargo. Several of those as well, but only one ship in the Interceptor mass-range, and that down at the bottom. Maybe an old patrol corvette that someone had stolen or salvaged.

Not a threat to the *Corsac Fox*.

Either of them.

"Haydar, how are we doing?" Uly asked.

"Twenty-eight ships that might be dangerous," Haydar replied, tagging them on everyone's display. "No cohesion beyond three sets flying in something close enough to a formation to maybe qualify. *Swift Passage* is right behind us where Drew plotted them. We might have surprise."

He heard Uly's soft sigh of relief. Well, tasted it more than anything. Anybody without tentacles probably missed it, but they already lived in such a poor sensory environment that Haydar frequently felt pity for them.

Then something caught his eye.

Haydar started typing.

"Drew, has anybody hailed us yet?" Uly asked in the background.

Haydar ignored it. Them. Everything.

Data nerd had just awoken and grabbed a tentacle to drag his head around.

"Negative, sir," Drew was replying in some other realm. "No, strike that. Somebody just called us *Iron Wasp*. On channel six."

Haydar typed.

"Son of a bitch," he muttered, then reached over and cut off channel six just as Uly started to talk.

He turned to his lucky Conductor and wondered just how many gods liked that boy.

Most of them?

"Talk to me," Uly said calmly. Expectantly.

Haydar drew a breath and considered his next words.

Somebody had fucked up so amazingly that it felt like it absolutely had to be a trap, didn't it? Was anybody that stupid? Could you be, and survive in this business?

He rotated to look at Uly with his eyes, instead of just his tentacles. Humans were an eye-contact species.

"I scanned the station when we arrived," Haydar said, committing himself to the stupidity of believing that the metaphorical ice under his feet was thick enough to hold him up.

"And?"

"And there are a metric shit-ton of wavebolt mounts visible, as one would expect with a station this size in a lawless place like *Lacium*," Haydar started walking across that frozen pond in his head.

"However, they all look like 1dm and 2dm mounts, Uly. I'm scanning only two 6dm on this entire facing, and Drew could dive us down below them and maybe block one of those."

"What are you saying, Haydar?" Uly asked, but Haydar could see the knowledge already in Uly's eyes.

He was talking for everyone else present. Sterling and Roscoe. Yuriy Kovalchuk. Rabiu Khadijan.

Haydar stilled his tentacles by force of will.

"I think we out-gun them, Uly," he said.

Hopefully, the ice would hold.

# FORTY-ONE

Uly studied Haydar Ramezani. Roshan had pretty much built up an insurmountable leap in inventing things by now, using the arcane scoring system those two had developed over however long.

At the same time, Haydar had been willing to step out of his lab at least half the time and be a fantastic Data Officer when Uly needed him.

Like now.

The man had committed himself to the job, too.

Uly considered the nature of the wavebolt as a weapon. A small plasma weapon, contained in a magnetic ball by means of a set of control circuits. By bleeding off tiny amounts of plasma, the torpedo moved at high speeds towards a target. When it got there, the detonating circuits could either shape it into a fist that punched, or a plasma lance designed to pierce a ship's electroshield array like an ice pick.

*King Hewitt II* had been caught unaware by Uly's Forward Cruiser *Marshall Castillon*, back in a previous life. They hadn't even gotten up their array, so a plasma spike had punched a hole from side to side through the ship's bridge, killing everyone forward.

*Mistress of Sail* Hylda Hobbs had been the only one of those folks that anybody missed.

Uly *considered*.

A lot of 1dm and 2dm wavebolts. Useful defensively, because you could always fire one of your own at an incoming bolt to destroy both. On *Corsac Fox*, he had four such 1dm mounts, functionally on the corners.

In piracy, they were both offensive and defensive. It was the turret forward with twin 6dm that made the ship a threat to anything smaller than a Striker, what he would have called a cruiser back home.

If he had more sixes than they did, he could stand off and bombard the station. They could probably intercept incoming bolts, though he wasn't even sure about that if their armaments were that badly thought out. He might actually score a few hits, without getting badly mauled in the process.

"Haydar, what about Neutron Omnipulsars?" Uly asked

"I see two mounts, Uly," Haydar said. "Hemispheric right and left as we sail, with the left one lined up and the right low on the far horizon to us."

"And we could sail below it as well?" Uly confirmed.

Simply confirmed. It would be his decision, but Haydar had just handed him a big hammer to use on that station.

"We could," Haydar said. "It puts us a lot closer to some of the factory stations, and I don't know how those are armed. Shouldn't have anything, but I'm not willing to trust that until we do get closer and I can rattle their frames with the scanners."

Uly nodded.

"Drew, work with Haydar to find us a blind spot on that station and maneuver as close to it as you can get," Uly ordered.

He drew a breath and turned to the young man on whose shoulders it would come to rest.

"Sterling, open fire with the sixes."

# FORTY-TWO

Sterling heard the words and it was like an electric current ran into his soul from the keyboard under his fingertips.

He didn't feel like a veteran, but he supposed that he was. After all, he'd been in command of the entire vessel that first time, while Mr. Ramezani had fired the wavebolts.

Today, it was Sterling's turn.

He'd heard the conversation around him while plotting firing solutions. He could do that for the first two or three salvos, before the gunners in their turrets had to manage most of the work.

Mr. Ramezani was correct. None of those tubes pointed back looked like they were big. Defensive guns only.

Hadn't anybody ever tried something like this before?

Of course not. If you were going to be a pirate, you attacked innocent civilians, not other pirates.

That was what the Captain was for. What he was about.

What was about to happen today.

Sterling locked in his target for the first salvo and pressed the button to launch. Left, then right.

"Turret crews, reload for rapid fire," he said into his dedicated line.

"Defensive batteries, stand by. Neutron Omnipulsars, keep your heads on swivels. We aren't surrounded but might be as everyone maneuvers."

He nodded to himself. Caught others looking at him with a little surprise but Sterling didn't understand why.

This was almost word for word how the training videos did it. But then he realized that Drew was technically a civilian. Mr. Ramezani and Mr. Kossari were supposedly formerly pirates like Kovalchuk, but hadn't served in uniform.

Only the Captain and him, weird as that was to think. And they'd been enemies at the time.

"Bolt one tracking true, sir," Sterling announced, not looking up.

Around him, Drew was starting to push buttons and slide things around with greater force in his fingers. Not that it mattered with this sort of equipment, but Sterling understood that the adrenaline sometimes got to be too much.

Like now.

"Bolt two also tracking true," he said to the room.

Two massive balls of angry energy, racing madly across the planetary orbit towards the big station. They'd finally woken up enough to energize their electroshield array but hadn't brought their Neutron Omnipulsars in line. Or rather, the one that could bear over there.

Sterling had to adjust his scanner lock as the ship started to rotate, bow down on the gyros and the Navigation Displacer thrusters.

Pretty soon, they'd start firing back.

Then Sterling would see how good those training videos had prepared him.

# FORTY-THREE

Drew let his backbrain fly the ship today. Automatic movements after this long, though it had taken him a while to get used to how the Ononguli built their control systems.

Alien. Weird. Not impossible, but every once in a while he still turned his entire console backlighting blue instead of tapping the thruster controller array.

Were they left-handed or something? Maybe. He'd try to remember to ask.

*Corsac Fox* nosed over under his expert guidance, sliding downwards almost like riding a wave, but that was just to keep the narrowest part of the ship pointed at the station. Harder to hit that way.

And to let Sterling's guns stay locked in place. Way easier to hit someone that way, and it looked like Haydar was right about the defensive array.

Wasn't Drew's problem. He had to drift the ship across an icy parking lot and into a space without rubbing up against anyone as he went.

Drew studied the horizon. And the vector plot of other stations and ships. Most of the factories were moving in perfect unison with the main station. Little sheep staying close to the dog, as it were. Safer for everyone that way.

It was all the ships around here that could turn into a pain in his ass. None of them had gotten up this morning expecting to be in the middle of a firefight, that much was obvious. Folks were lighting their thrusters on whatever line they'd been sailing.

Nobody could spin up a warp bubble with *Corsac Fox* and the station both generating fields. Not quite overlapped, but it made a double bubble, here, like a pair of women's breasts straining against a shirt that was too small.

In a good way.

Drew smiled and chuckled to himself, glad that Mazhin tentacles only gave the impression of reading your mind. They didn't actually allow it, or he'd probably be in trouble.

Wasn't like Captain Fortier hadn't managed to find a whole team of beautiful women or anything. And they were all deadly, too, which just made his *Danumash* upbringing flinch even more unconsciously. Throw in whip-smart and it was utterly awesome.

The old coots back home usually didn't think women should even own shoes, let alone wear them. Keep them indoors, tending the house, the kitchen, and the young'uns.

Dumbasses had never met a woman like Dan Chastain. Or the rest. Wouldn't know what hit them if they did.

Kinda like Captain was about to do to these yahoos.

Drew maneuvered some more. That one baby Interceptor wasn't awake. Might be pulling maintenance with systems shut down from the way they were hanging in space. Drew still let his drift run a little long and wide, such that those folks would be trying to fire a wavebolt past a smaller cargo ship in between if they wanted to fire.

Not impossible, but trying would be like walking into a bar fight and trying to hit some jackass, only to punch somebody else who'd stepped into your way.

Not that Drew had ever been in that situation before.

"Sterling, target seven will be eclipsed shortly," Drew said. "They might still try to fire at us, so make sure somebody on your team is watching scanners."

"I've got that arc covered," Haydar said instead. "They will have to try for a lock on us. I'll see that happening if they do."

Drew supposed that he would. He'd watched Haydar do impossible things with the scanner suite on this ship. And then the results, dumping it all into some weird-ass data grid, then massaging it into magical information faster than about anybody Drew had ever seen.

A sudden warning on his screen caused Drew to adjust the view.

"I got a ship blue-shifting on us," he called, in case Haydar had missed that. "Somebody talk to me. What's he doing? Why is he coming this way?"

Wasn't Drew's job to address them. Might be someone happened to be pointed this way and was accelerating before they came about to run.

Or they might be charging over to rescue the station.

Uly, Sterling, or Haydar would give him flying instructions.

Then Drew would work his magic.

But still, what the hell was *Compass Rose* up to over there?

# FORTY-FOUR

Lukyan watched a pair of *Iron Wasp*'s heavy sixes start chasing the station.

What the ever-loving fuck was going on?

"Any response to hail?" he demanded, but nobody responded.

So Lukyan paused and opened the cage to uncover his favorite button on the entire ship.

He mashed it and the alert sirens wound up. That ought to burn out the Tuesdays around here. Assuming folks didn't piss themselves in surprise. *Lacium* was supposed to be a safe harbor.

Folks were knitting, or whatever they did off duty. Better not to ask, as long as nobody was bleeding.

"Somebody get me a gunner," Lukyan yelled, uncertain who had the roster today.

It had been a Tuesday, five minutes ago. Technically still was, but apparently the Lords of the Endless Plains had seen fit to answer his request for a little excitement.

Never tempt the gods.

"Negative on hail, Lukyan," Dmytro answered. "They just settled in, looked around, and opened up on the station. We at war with the locals?"

Shit, anything was possible. And that was *Iron Wasp*. Nobody else that size had a twin six turret.

Hell, even *Compass Rose* only mounted a single 3dm in a full-arc turret forward.

But if *Iron Wasp* had decided to blow up *Lacium*, was this a Clan call that he needed to answer? Ononguli this far from home were usually a lot more slack about that shit, but Adrian might not realize he had cousins in harbor when he attacked.

What the ever-loving fuck was going on?

"Dmytro, engage your course," Lukyan decided. "Slowly. Get us headed in that direction in case we're supposed to help. Somebody hail them. Find out what the hell Sobol's up to. Maks, you do that. Maybe he'll talk to you."

Oskar finally appeared and slid into the gunner's chair, taking a moment to latch himself in before bringing things live.

Not a lot *Compass Rose* could do in a mess like this, and Lukyan didn't figure that *Legend of Ymnan* or *Spirit of Iniquity* would necessarily jump in to help. Not if this was Ononguli politics suddenly erupting all over the place.

But Lukyan had had to sign all those agreements with the elders, way back when he'd taken command of *Compass Rose*. If that meant that he was at war with the locals, that was the cost of the job.

What the ever-loving fuck was going on?

# FORTY-FIVE

Uly studied the boards. Fox in the henhouse. Literally, in his case, being the *Corsac Fox* himself according to the Z'Goszans.

Around them, ships were starting to wake up. Most of them were red-shifting according to Haydar's read. Moving away from the scene of battle, possibly as rapidly as they could get.

Except for one. Flying an Ononguli flag like the supposed *Iron Wasp*.

*Compass Rose.*

Did that Conductor think that Adrian Sobol was still in command?

Weirder things had happened. Look at where Uly found himself.

"Haydar, are they still hailing us?" Uly asked.

Pause. Buttons clicked. Switches flipped. Tentacles moving like a shoal of fish.

"Affirmative, Uly," Haydar finally said. "One Maks Sobol, attempting to get in touch with Adrian. Claims to be a cousin of some sort, like he expects the name to mean something and thought he got some simpleton on the text line that doesn't know any better."

"Is he helping or moving to attack?" Uly asked.

"Stand by," Haydar replied. "I'm guessing that he's maneuvering to get closer, but it doesn't look like he'd setting up to attack us. Not bow on to us or the station at the moment."

"Sidling over in case?" Uly asked.

Haydar glanced up sharply, then shrugged.

"Maybe," he said definitively.

Uly nodded.

"Ignore him, but watch where he goes," Uly decided. "Sterling, have one of your gun teams take primary responsibility for overwatch on that vector. Keep your attention on the station. Are they returning fire yet?"

"Aye, sir," Sterling said. "One Six has arc. Weirdly, about half of the Ones and Twos have not fired yet."

"Repeat that?" Uly said.

"I have a number of defensive tubes with arc to engage us sir," Sterling clarified. "By bore size, 1dm and 2dm mounts. Eight of them have not fired at all, while the other nine have. At this range, a 2dm will exceed their effective range and impact on our electroshield array with about as much force as a newborn puppy. Sir."

Uly nodded to the youngster. No, young man. Sterling Huff was turning into an excellent officer. Uly made a mental note to start promoting his midshipmen to formal ranks. Wouldn't matter what the Party apparatus back home said, since he wasn't in the *Batyr* navy anymore.

At the same time, he needed a solid core of officers running things, and Sterling was turning out even better than Uly had imagined when he'd first captured the young man.

"Sterling, they are only able to range and arc on us with that one 6dm?" Uly confirmed.

"That is correct, Captain," Sterling nodded. "Currently, they are using their 1dm tubes defensively, but my grandmother might be a better shot, since I doubt she needs three 'bolts to score a hit in counter-battery fire."

Uly let himself grin. Three was exceptionally bad shooting. Or panic, if they didn't think that a single 1dm would hit accurately enough to kill an incoming 6dm.

Had they never been attacked by a warship? Ever?

But then, *Z'Gosza* didn't maintain a navy. They had armed cargo vessels and things down in the Seeker range as both patrol craft and search-and-rescue.

Nothing about engaging in fleet actions against a hostile squadron. Or attacking pirate strongholds to break them up.

What kind of silly world had he stumbled into?

On the one hand, these species generally weren't as violent or dangerous as Humans tended to take for granted, the odd Ononguli notwithstanding. He had that as an advantage, for at least as long as no more Humans emerged from those distant swamps.

Or until the locals got pushed into a corner and came out like rats. There was always that.

He lived in a part of the galaxy where merchants sailed armed freighters and hoped that pirates didn't see them slip by. That, or weren't armed enough to challenge.

*Iron Wasp* was over-armed. Over-gunned.

A warship in the true sense of the word. At least as far as these folks would see it.

"Continue fire with the 6dm," Uly ordered. "Stay with general bolts, but slip in the occasional plasma lance shot, just in case you do get through, as I suspect that you might paralyze or even disable a portion of the station in that case. Haydar, any other threats?"

"*Compass Rose*, Uly," Haydar replied. "Intentions unknown, at least as long as I ignore this Maks Sobol fellow. He's getting a little frustrated, from the way his percentage of profanities per sentence keeps going up."

Uly chuckled. Only Haydar would track that sort of thing.

Uly marked a spot on his screen, then transmitted it to Haydar.

"Let me know if he crosses that line," Uly said,

"We destroying him if he does?" Sterling asked, obviously tracking more than just his targeting systems.

"We'll see, Mister Huff," Uly replied. "We'll see."

# FORTY-SIX

Lukyan was at least happy that he was having a better day than Maks, Tuesday or not. Low bar, since Maks was getting pretty colorful and a bit out of hand with whoever was playing with him on the other end.

"Maks," Lukyan said. Nothing. "MAKS!"

"WHAT?"

"Drink some tea," Lukyan offered.

"I don't HAVE any tea!"

"Exactly," Lukyan nodded.

Maks sat there dumbfounded for a few moments, then his face cleared.

"Right," the dork said. "Gotcha. Wardroom, send a pot of fresh tea forward."

Lukyan approved. He was out. Hadn't planned on getting more, but that had been a terrible case of *ennui* and Tuesdays.

Shit had gotten a little out of hand.

"Oh, SHIT!" Oskar announced. "Station hit! Pretty bad one, too."

"How bad?" Lukyan and Maks said in harmony.

Crap, they were back to comedy improv, weren't they? Even in the middle of a pitched starship battle. How bad was this day going to get?

"I'm reading power fluctuations and local overloads in several spots," Oskar replied. "Something broke. Not bad, but they might have just run out of oomph to fight with."

"What do you mean, *out*?" Lukyan demanded.

"Boss, they were firing with two 6dm at the top, then only one of them because *Iron Wasp* slipped below their weapon horizon," Oskar said. "Right now, I'm reading nothing but a long handful of point-defense stuff. Ones and Twos. That's it."

Lukyan goggled. Boggled. Stuttered in his mind.

What the ever-loving fuck was going on?

"Is *Iron Wasp* still shooting?" he asked.

"Affirmative, Lukyan," Oskar nodded. "Like they're going for the throat over there."

"Do they need any help from us?" Lukyan asked.

"Not that anybody has said," Oskar replied.

"Is that even Adrian?" Maks suddenly asked, causing Lukyan to nearly fall out of his chair whipping his head around.

There was a reason the first thing you did when you sat down was buckle yourself in.

"WHAT?" he demanded.

"Are we sure that's Adrian?" Maks repeated.

"Sensors showed it as *Iron Wasp*," Dmytro spoke up.

"Yes, sure," Maks nodded, calmness now. "But what if Adrian's no longer in command of that vessel?"

"Who then?" Lukyan demanded. "You know the kinds of rules we all live by. They'd still know who your cousin was."

"Assuming that they were Ononguli, yes," Maks said carefully.

Lukyan felt everything go utterly cold.

*Tuesday* fled screaming into the night, leaving *Ononguli Pirate Warship Commander* behind to hold the barricades. Pretty good option, all things considered.

"You think somebody captured the vessel and are using it Q-ship style to attack *Lacium*?" Lukyan asked.

"I got no idea, boss," Maks said, ceding that top rung on the ladder since Maks was only Second-in-Command around here.

Lukyan made the decisions. For good or ill.

"Would the Auga stomp in here and open fire like that?" he asked.

"I'd expect a Striker or three if they wanted to nail all our hides to the wall like trophies."

"Agreed," Dmytro added. "They don't do subtle."

Everyone nodded. Auga used a hammer. If it broke, they went back for a bigger hammer. That was why piracy was generally so successful.

That, and the number of light-centuries between here and the nearest Auga imperial naval base of any note.

"So not Ononguli, and not Auga?" Lukyan asked his top crew. "Who could it be?"

"Everybody else," Oskar laughed. "Shit, could be anybody."

Lukyan watched the grimace of pain flash across Maks's face, but that was family. If *Iron Wasp* was in somebody else's control, Adrian Sobol was probably dead. Or in an Auga prison. Somebody's prison.

Not here.

"Dmytro, hold our distance," Lukyan decided.

"Maintaining distance, aye," Dmytro said.

"Oh, SHIT!" Oskar barked.

Lukyan was going to have to break the boy of that habit, one of these days. Get him to use complete sentences instead of those sorts of utterances.

"WHAT?"

"*Iron Wasp* just accelerated towards the station, boss," Oskar said. "And that passenger liner is launching assault shuttles!"

Well, crap.

# FORTY-SEVEN

Dan had made the most of the force that Factor Bitrus had supplied. About a third of the troops, evenly mixed, had experience boarding enemy ships under combat situations like this. And she had four big assault shuttles. Larger than Seekers or Ultra-Bombers. Not as fast. No Variable Pulse Spatial Generator for a star drive, so you could cram a lot of other things inside.

In this case, a single 1dm wavebolt launcher, intended for defensive purposes, or to kick in doors, plus a Neutron Omnipulsar on a universal forward mount.

Given the ships at her disposal, she'd assigned two teams to each, and put Solomon, Beranger, and Travers in command of the double groupings, with each of them having one of her women as the other commander.

Right now, those three men had more experience at this sort of thing, and it wasn't something you could train on easily. Much easier in the doing.

Helped that she'd brought Nasrin with her. Strongest at this sort of thing today. Give Anari and Solomon another year, and they'd probably pass the Mazhin woman, but Dan was working with where they were today.

"Assault Command, this is *Corsac Fox*," Uly said over the common line that all of her troopers could listen to.

Better for morale, since they were all crammed into the passenger liner, then crammed into their boarding armor and stuffed into shuttles with barely room to turn around.

It was almost like taking a shower with three hundred of your closest friends. Hell, the medical list this morning had only had six people on it, which was lower than she'd been expecting.

And those six had been ordered by doctors to stay in bed, or they might have joined anyway.

Nobody wanted to miss this.

"This is Assault Command," Dan replied evenly, glancing over at Nasrin.

They both had helmets off, so Nasrin could taste the air around her. Almost entirely male, with less than two percent female troopers across the fourteen hundred she'd brought with her.

"Assault Command, we appear to have at least temporarily disabled the defensive battery on the main system," Uly said. "Per Drew and Sterling, you can launch into a region of 1dm and 2dm fire, but *Corsac Fox* will be flying with you to provide defensive fire and cover your backs. Prepare to launch all of your vessels. Designated landing points have not changed. Stand by to assume command, Dan."

She took a deep breath and nodded to herself.

They'd gamed it out many different ways, and none of them had been especially good. Nor especially bad, but there was too much unknown, even with what Piruz and the others had managed to dig up.

Uly would get them as close as he could, but it would be up to her force to carry things.

Assuming that they could land this many troopers safely, when the defenders would probably start shitting bricks and ignore *Corsac Fox* to blow the assault shuttles up.

"Acknowledged, *Corsac Fox*," Dan said, willing calmness into her voice and body language. "All troopers, lock your helmets and confirm readiness for vacuum combat. Assault Transport Force, stand by to launch. Bring all defensive systems to maximum and prepare to overload and burn out your systems."

And they would. They'd be dead too if something got through. "Assault Transport Force: Launch!"

225

# FORTY-EIGHT

Sterling had his new teams running pretty tight. As long as he kept up a fire of 6dm wavebolts inward, that station would be concentrating on using smaller bores to kill his attacks.

One had still gotten through, but that was Captain and Mr. Ramezani pointing out a weird quirk in the way the defensive tubes had been arrayed. Not exactly a blind spot, but somebody had messed up when building the station. Or adding weapons mounts later.

Enfilading fire was the term Captain Fortier had used.

It had worked. At least a quarter of the station had gone dark. And had lost a big chunk of their electroshield array on this facing.

He could probably hammer them with a couple of plasma lances right now and cut the station into pieces.

Captain wanted them intact.

"Forward turret, stand by for a change of targeting," Sterling announced.

On his screen, he shifted the big, purple cross from the damaged 6dm launcher to a spot low and left where four smaller wavebolts were mounted. Again, he considered a plasma lance, but a fist would probably work better, because it might jar things.

That station didn't feel all that tough, though Sterling couldn't say what it was that told him that.

It still felt right.

"Forward turret, give me two on this vector, rapid fire," Sterling said, leaning back enough to break his concentration. "Any 1dm teams, I need three of you ready to rapid-fire engage anything the station or anybody else wants to throw at us. *Compass Rose* team, stay with your target until otherwise notified. Neutron Omnipulsar teams, eyes forward please."

He paused and looked up. Captain gave him a warm smile and a thumbs up, so he must be doing something right.

He had a lot of friends about to charge across the no-man's-land when the bad guys were only slightly stunned.

Not out of action.

He needed to fix that.

# FORTY-NINE

Uly watched as *Swift Passage* fired four seed pods into the darkness, including Dan.

He knew that he could survive and continue on this mission without her, but he had no idea how he might go about it. Better if she outlived him.

"Drew, bring us closer," Uly ordered.

Drew looked up, then nodded. Haydar's hands took on an extra level of sharpness as he tapped his keys.

Sterling was extremely close to achieving the sort of flowstate where everything was perfectly correct and automatic.

This was the day for that to happen.

"Uly, *Compass Rose* just veered off," Haydar announced.

Uly brought his personal display screen around and studied it. Blue-shift gone. Slight red-shift at present, but nothing worth writing home about.

Somebody over there had decided that he'd gotten close enough, for now.

Uly didn't mind. One less wild card on the table. Hell, it would be even better if *Compass Rose* turned and started racing after all the other pirate ships that were fleeing, but his telepathic powers seemed to be insufficient to his needs.

He smiled wryly instead.

Sterling and his teams had pounded the station. Haydar had seen a spot where somebody had built the station with a square corner, then mounted the 6dm launcher too close to it. And the smaller ones too far away.

A blind spot.

Sterling had put a 6dm into it like threading a needle. With a ten-kilo sledgehammer from the effects on the station.

"Forward defense, engage left to right," Sterling suddenly called. "Assault Transports, start on your right and work inwards. All Neutron Omnipulsar teams start in the middle. Fire as you bear."

It took Uly a moment, but he saw the logic. *Corsac Fox* was closer, but not moving as quickly as the shuttles. Nor would he get as close to the station, at least for now. Sterling was laying down standard lanes for everyone, so that they didn't have to worry about their own flanks, since the four shuttles were to starboard as they closed.

A mass of 1dm wavebolts crashed out and raced downrange, impacting quickly on 1dm and 2dm from the station.

"One more salvo and you should be in their myopic range, Assault Transports," Sterling said. "Everybody stand by for it."

For a long moment, the space between the station and Uly's ships was clear, then one of the *Fox's* 6dm bolts got home with a fluorescent explosion of colors and lights that would have probably been deafening if it had happened in an atmosphere.

Pretty. And useful.

Somebody over there had lost track of targets. Or tried to do too many things at once. Or were more frightened of the assault shuttles than a torpedo coming at them.

As they should be.

# FIFTY

Dan had a read-out from the shuttle's bridge on the side of her Heads-Up Display. Not quite like the *Batyr* navy had done it, back in the day, but close enough for her, Beranger, and Travers. Solomon was getting there as well.

Uly or someone had spoofed the station. No other way to say it. Those folks had fired wavebolts at the shuttles, and forgotten that there were two 6dm bolts coming in.

One had hit.

A lot of the fire from the station had tapered off. Sterling Huff was sounding like a senior Gunnery Officer back home, in spite of the way his voice still cracked occasionally.

"This is Shuttle Three," a male voice came over the line. "I have a problem. We've lost the Omnipulsar. Dropping out of fire."

"Three, do you still have wavebolts?" Uly asked over the line, the Fleet Captain commanding the squadron.

"Affirmative, but we're suffering some power issues here."

"Understood, Three," Uly said. "Maintain formation and rate of fire. Those are your orders."

Dan sucked in a breath and ground her teeth together. Risky, but all things were risky when you were assaulting a hostile platform. That ship might not be able to fire back. Or cover someone else.

"Battery Two, there's a bolt tracking Shuttle Three. Somebody cross over and engage it."

"Battery Four, I am out of position to fire."

"Omnipulsar One, engaging, but that's the edge of my envelope. One of the shuttles needs to get involved."

"Shuttle Two, somebody get my 2dm so I can shield Three."

"Shuttle Four. Go ahead Two."

"*Corsac Fox*, moving to closer range," Drew Roscoe called over the line. "Everybody focus on this salvo and I'll draw them to me."

Dan flexed her hands, clenching and unclenching them. Nothing at all you could do in this situation as the warships around you engaged in a battle of the titans. And it never got any easier, regardless of the number of times she'd done it.

Worse, she was in command today, instead of some punk-ass lieutenant on *Marshal Castillon* who had connections and a four-year degree in military studies.

Dan had a decade as a grunt, a lot of that as a Senior Specialist or a Lead, but that wasn't the same as being Ground Forces Commander.

On the job learning.

Dan watched that 1dm bolt waver under the fire of several Omnipulsars. At the same time, not all of them, because you couldn't just ignore the rest to protect your friends.

"Stand by, Shuttle Two, I don't think we're going to get him."

"Partial Hit. Partial HIT!"

The screen flashed once then cleared. Shuttle Three still showed on her screen, but that didn't mean anything. It might be a holed carcass starting to tumble through space. Or it might only need a new paint job.

"Shuttle Three, what is your status?" Uly asked, calm and collected in a way Dan didn't think she could manage.

Not with Beranger and Yanouk over there.

"Shuttle Three, what is your status?"

Nothing.

Dan was certain that the bolt had punched through-and-through, like *Marshal Castillon* had done to *King Hewitt II*.

"Command, this is Shuttle Three," a different voice came on the line. "Internal damage and casualties sustained. Status unknown at present, but I've got flight power and the wavebolt seems to be intact. We'll board that bitch and sort it out. You can count on us."

"Assault Command, this is Trooper Miyoshi." Yanouk. "Trooper Beranger has been injured but not badly. I am assuming command of this force."

Dan blew out a breath. Emil Beranger was one of the toughest, meanest sailors she'd ever worked with. If he was down, that was either a broken leg or a concussion. But not dead. She hadn't just lost one of her oldest friends in the galaxy.

"Trooper Miyoshi, this is Assault Command," Dan replied, forcing herself to sound professional and aloof, in spite of everything. "The change of command is acknowledged. Stand by for boarding. All teams, stand by."

On her side screen, the icon for her force of shuttles was merging with the station. There was a crunch as the shuttle entered a flight bay and landed hard on the magnets holding it to the deck, followed by an ugly screech as the pilot had too much forward velocity and was gouging channels in the deck to scrub it off.

You used up equipment quickly doing that, but it also probably saved twenty seconds of flying politely.

"This is Shuttle One," the pilot announced. "We are landed."

Dan switched to the local channel to talk with the three-hundred-odd maniacs she had brought with her.

"Team One, open the hatch and charge."

# FIFTY-ONE

Yanouk looked around at the sea of faces looking back and her.

Up at her.

She was used to that. There weren't that many Emro around, and Anari was on Shuttle Four, which hadn't just come that close to being blown up.

Yanouk could see through a hole in the hull that had been high enough to not hit anyone directly.

Still, they were looking at her. Up at her.

Expecting orders.

Emil was at least teaching her a whole new vocabulary of Human swear words, but hopefully most of them wouldn't be necessary or appropriate today.

"Emil, I need the channel," Yanouk said sharply.

He tapered off quickly. Mostly muttering under his breath now, but that was fine. Yanouk expected that he was angrier that he had to stay behind than anything.

Still, she was in command.

And not even Sabre School, like Anari.

Moss was for scholars and artists, but Dan and Nasrin had shared with her the one tiny bit of information that bridged the two into a single entity.

Sabre School were Scholars of Violence.

And Yanouk had been studying under Dan for more than half a year now.

"Force Three, sort yourselves into able sailors and walking wounded," she announced. "Wounded and half of the medics will remain here as Base Three. The remaining able sailors will exit the shuttle and scout the immediate vicinity. Specialists and Senior Specialists, take command of your troops and establish a perimeter."

There wasn't time to ask Dan what to do. Or rely on Emil, since a medic was inserting a needle through the medical vent in his armor and hitting him with enough pain killers to stun an Emro.

Emil, apparently, ignored lesser doses, according to what Yanouk had seen and been told previously.

She was near the middle of the shuttle bay. Half the force was out before she emerged.

The bay was a place where a small Interceptor could land if they were careful. And shaped appropriately. Huge enough for sporting events or concerts, but the flat, squared-off ceiling overhead would be horrible for acoustics.

Not today's issue.

Yanouk confirmed that her weapon was charged. Being Emro, she'd picked up a Squad Exoripper to go with the ax slung on her back. If it came down to melee, there were probably more issues than she wanted to think about right now.

Taking a moment, she also confirmed that she was on the right channel. Her troopers could hear her. Dan could listen in, or issue orders depending.

Still, she was on her own right now, with something less than three hundred Khet, Ononguli, and Ugotha around her.

"Forward," she called, gesturing to the cargo lock that would get them inside.

Yanouk doubted that the station would be willing to close the outer bay doors and pressurize the space, but the airlock looked big enough to get half of her force in there at once.

More than half, with about twenty percent remaining behind, dead or too injured to continue.

Dan had warned all of them that it might happen. That shit went sideways when people started shooting at each other.

Yanouk was certainly seeing and doing things that most Moss School scholars didn't experience.

She got to the group who had been scouting.

"Can you force it to cycle us through?" she asked.

"Affirmative, sir," the Khet replied, looking up at her like a shark coming at him for a bite.

Unfortunate, but it helped when they were kind of sexist punks the rest of the time.

Nobody had patted her on the bottom, though she'd steeled herself that the Khet might think a woman wasn't tough enough to serve with them. Let alone lead them.

Yanouk considered it an even break, as she hadn't had to punch anybody into sick bay, either.

And she would have.

"Sir, should we blow it instead of just transitioning?" the Khet asked.

Yanouk had already had that argument with herself while walking this way.

"Negative," she replied. "The *Corsac Fox* wants the station as intact as possible when we're done. Blowing it apart doesn't do anybody any good. All heavy weapon gunners, separate from your current squads and join me in the cargo airlock."

Calculated risk. The locals might open side hatches and attack, but they'd be looking at a whole bunch of troopers with Exorippers and Painspheres in that case.

And the station wasn't supposed to have an army protecting it. Mostly rent-a-cops with truncheons to deal with unruly drunks.

Nothing at all like she had.

"All hands, stand by for airlock," the Khet leading her scouts said. "Everybody stay clear of the lines."

"And everybody point guns forward," Yanouk added.

Uly and Dan wanted the locals overwhelmed. She supposed that one hundred guns pointed at you might do the trick.
She hoped.

# FIFTY-TWO

Dan had read the backgrounds on the eight teams assigned to this mission and gone ahead and picked the two with the most veterans for herself. She'd compensated by assigning herself the roughest portion of the mission.

Main Bay, not that far from the space that was the equivalent of the station's bridge. And the spot most likely to be heavily defended against a rampaging pirate horde.

"Nasrin, I want your team to work to the left through airlocks and corridors," Dan said. "Not necessarily a pincer movement, but the more alarms you can cause to go off, the more we can distract and destabilize things while I move forward."

"Understood," Nasrin replied. "Team Two, form on me and rotate to port. Scout teams locate all the secondary airlocks and maintenance access out of here on that side."

Dan nodded. There was a reason she'd grabbed Nasrin, of the four she could have picked after putting her male veterans on other shuttles with other missions.

Nasrin didn't talk about her past any more than Haydar ever wanted to, but Dan had the impression by now that all Mazhin ships at least occasionally engaged in piratical escapades.

Haydar had been all in as a pirate at Nasrin's age. Nasrin had been a teenage student, but she'd also been a beautiful young woman as Mazhin—and other species—measured such things. As a result, she'd learned the art called Sunflower Fist. And others. Then spent time with Dan and her boys learning even deadlier things.

The two Emro women would both be amazing, one of these days, but they were starting so much farther back that it would take them years to catch up. Katya might never get there, but she'd thrown herself in wholeheartedly, given that the alternative had been to be one of a few female engineers on a deck dominated by males of several species.

Dan had a goal.

Today, that involved taking this station. Intact. Mostly not even ruffled if she could manage it.

"Team One, into the airlock and squeeze," Dan ordered. "Weapons live and prepared to fire. Omnibow troopers, load your Painspheres and prepare to suppress any defenders that try to hold this line."

Grunts, barks, and laughter were her reply. It was good. Seasoned troops, though surprised to have females in charge.

They'd get over themselves. Or Dan would ship the ones home who couldn't while recruiting the best of what remained.

Uly needed an army. And a nation. Dan was responsible for finding him both right at the moment.

"Assault Command, this is *Corsac Fox*," Uly came over the line. "We have suppressed most hostile fire from the station and are in the process of withdrawing to a safer engagement range. All four shuttles have landed and initiated their missions. Good luck."

Dan smiled. Just smiled.

He had put her in charge of this. And just reminded everyone that she was in overall command until he said otherwise.

Because he was **The** *Corsac Fox*.

At least she'd convinced Uly to let her dragoon the camera team into this. Or rather, she'd functionally kidnapped Shehu Okorie, the camerakhet, while Sani, Bello, and Adedayo—respectively the Producer, On-Air Talent, and Tech that had been added later—had stayed on the *Fox*. Not a lot they could do from there but watch and take notes.

Shehu was staying as close to her shadow as he could, filming and recording audio.

Because doesn't everybody take a film crew with them when assaulting an enemy stronghold?

She laughed. Her faceshield was polarized, or she'd have turned to the camera and winked right now.

"Assault Force, this is Assault Command," Dan called over the general comm line. "Let's do this thing."

# FIFTY-THREE

"Are you kidding me?" Lukyan asked.

Who he was asking was probably better left vague. Maks, Oskar, and Dmytro were generally ignoring his muttering. Lukyan hoped that the Lords of the Endless Plains weren't paying much attention either.

His Tuesday had kinda exploded on him.

"Oskar, confirm these numbers," he ordered, highlighting a section of the readout.

"I did, boss," Oskar replied. "Twice, before I sent them to you."

Lukyan subsided and grumbled.

Not only was that a troop transport instead of a passenger liner filled with pretty hostages to ransom, somebody had brought a freaking army with them to this dance.

Fourteen hundred sailors?

What the ever-loving fuck?

Lukyan paused and realized just how far out of whack things had gotten.

The Lords of the Endless Plains were up to something. That much was as obvious as the horns on his head.

And that was *Iron Wasp* over there, attacking the station without any warning.

Worse, they hadn't even fired a few shots then demanded the stationmaster surrender, like good, little pirates normally did in these situations.

Nope, land and start blasting. Worse yet, they'd hammered the shit out of the place, then backed off once all four of their shuttles landed, though Lukyan was surprised that the damaged one made it.

Hell of a wing shot. Not quite close enough, though.

That, or *Iron Wasp*'s new Conductor had brought a pack of rabid furlou with him who weren't about to let something as easy as a blown-up shuttle stop them from hunting down some lame orkac on the open steppes.

"Maks, they still ignoring you?" Lukyan asked his Second-in-Command.

"That's right, Lukyan," Maks replied.

Lukyan sighed.

Station was done, unless something utterly weird happened in the next thirty minutes. Too many damned guns. Rabid furlou. Something.

"Oskar, what are the other warships around here doing?" he asked.

"I've got traffic that suggests a few are planning to make a run at *Iron Wasp*," Oskar replied sourly. "Little boats, but they think that maybe they've got enough wavebolts combined across all of them to drive him off."

Lukyan laughed at that image. Somebody over there on *Iron Wasp* had a professional Gunner who made an expert pirate like Oskar look like a rank amateur by comparison.

"What's *Khile Heavy* doing?" he asked.

That Light Interceptor had been the biggest ship that regularly called on *Lacium*. None of the Ultra-Bombers or smaller Seeker-class boats around here were really a threat, including *Compass Rose*.

*Khile Heavy* would get his ass handed to him by *Iron Wasp*. Maybe with help.

"Looks like they were caught with their horns in a fence, Lukyan," Oskar laughed now. "I know that a chunk of crew had shore leave, and I'm guessing from power outputs right now that they'd pulled a lot of things apart on the wrong day."

"They any threat to *Iron Wasp*?" Lukyan pressed.

"Boss, they might not be a threat to us, if you were feeling frisky," Oskar replied.

Lukyan considered his options. And the fact that one *Conductor Elemér Petőfi* of the fabled pirate warship *Khile Heavy* was an asshole.

"Maks, you take command right now," Lukyan ordered. "I need to do something probably about as stupid as they come and can't keep watch on the yahoos over there while I'm doing it."

He waited for Maks to nod, then got to work.

Lukyan clicked a couple of buttons. Typed in a code that even Maks didn't know. Wouldn't unless and until he got into Lukyan's cabin and his safe to read that packet from the Clan Elders.

"*Iron Wasp*, this is Conductor Lukyan Chayka, aboard *Compass Rose*," he said simply, knowing that the message would get through on that end. Period. "I need to talk to your Conductor, right now."

# FIFTY-FOUR

Uly listened intently as Haydar snarled obscenities under his breath.

"Do you know what he did?" Uly asked as Haydar's tentacles nearly wound themselves into a ball.

"Yes," Haydar growled with an insulted grouch. Something about data nerds. "Shortly, I'll also know *how* he did it, as well. Then he won't be able to do it again."

Uly fought to keep the grin off his face. Someone had just challenged his Data Officer with a previously unknown network security flaw.

That was going to trigger an ugly war at some level. At least until Haydar and Roshan rewired or reprogrammed certain elements of the system to their liking.

Uly assumed he'd have to referee things before they got out of hand.

Right now, however, the Conductor of the Ononguli heavy Ultra-Bomber *Compass Rose* wanted to chat.

Uly studied the stats displayed, comparing them to the vessel that had attacked him right after their second escape, the one from Zhoralong.

Not a lot of similarity. *Compass Rose* was much larger, though it displayed the same curves of a slightly flattened tube with cantilevered wings across the top where several wavebolts could be held in single-shot launchers, though there was nothing there currently.

Instead, *Compass Rose* had a forward 3dm from the looks of it, plus a pair of Neutron Omnipulsars, top and bottom aft.

Pirate warship. The other two it had been near to when all this started looked like a simple Probe-class tramp freighter, probably armed, and a Seeker that looked sleek but only mounted a pair of 1dm in external launchers on the flanks.

Still, three of them might be enough to overwhelm the average Khet freighter.

Which was why Uly was here.

"*Compass Rose*, this is Conductor Ulysses Fortier," he replied on the line that had been *forced open* by this Chayka gentleman, much to Haydar's ongoing, muttering disgust.

He'd also opened the video line to let this Ononguli Conductor see what he was dealing with.

The being on the other end of the line looked like many of the Ononguli in Uly's crew. Felt roughly Human sized, plus that pair of horns that twisted outward and went up and then back from the forehead. Brown hair almost dark enough to be black in some lights, straight and medium length. Clean-shaven and a square jaw. Dark red skin, like a tomato.

Those same black eyeballs with red irises that seemed to glow in the dark.

Cunning eyes.

They stared at each other for a long moment.

Interestingly, the first question wasn't the one Uly always expected.

"Where's Adrian Sobol?" Chayka asked gruffly.

"Probably in an Auga prison somewhere," Uly replied. "That was the last place I saw him, before I broke out and stole his ship."

He left it at that as Chayka's eyes got big with surprise. Then he asked the other question.

"What species are you?" Chayka asked.

"Human," Uly said.

He didn't bother explaining Imperial Sector Seventeen. Or *Danumash* and *Batyr* and the various wars being fought over there.

If Chayka had never met a Human, and most Ononguli hadn't, then Uly saw no reason to enlighten him.

"What about Sobol's crew?" Chayka asked.

"A group of them came with me," Uly said. "Yuriy, come over here and say hello."

Yuriy Kovalchuk looked like he'd found himself in that one dream where you were walking naked into a classroom, facing a test you hadn't studied for. Uly smiled and nodded to put him at ease.

Kovalchuk rose and walked over around behind Uly's shoulder, where the camera would pick him up.

"Do you know Conductor Chayka or *Compass Rose*, Kovalchuk?" Uly asked, twisting around to look at his sailor.

"Negative, sir," Yuriy replied. "But we rarely came this direction when Sobol was in charge."

"Thank you, Yuriy," Uly nodded.

Kovalchuk skedaddled back to his station.

Uly turned his attention to the screen again.

"I'm about to capture *Lacium* Station, Conductor," he said simply. "Will that present a problem for you?"

"Me?" Chayka replied. "Not necessarily. However, I'm transmitting you some data about a group of ships over there that might be. *Khile Heavy*, however, probably isn't a threat right now. Hell, if you had any more sailors you could fly over and capture it."

"Why are you telling me this, Conductor Chayka?" Uly asked.

"Because you are flying an Ononguli hull, Conductor Fortier," the being replied. "With at least a partial Ononguli crew. That technically makes you a ship of the Ononguli Sphere, depending on how the clan elders want to look at things. Not a lot of us out this far, so technically I was required to come to your aid by the sorts of agreements that bind all Ononguli commanders. Still a bit iffy if that extends to you, since Humans are strangers around here, presumably from some periphery I've never been. At the same time, it looks an awful lot like a revolution just occurred in *Lacium*, and I'd rather be on the winning side, all things considered."

Uly considered that statement. And everything it implied. None of his Ononguli crew had mentioned anything like that, but they were all of them junior engineering and damage control qualified sailors. The officers and assault troopers had been sectioned off with Sobol at the beginning.

Uly didn't suppose that they would have known anything, to have been included as the runts in the litter when it came time to put them in cells with the Humans and the rest of Uly's people.

Still, Chayka was trying to be friendly. Haydar was nodding and gesturing at his screen with a thumbs up, so the data must meet his high standards.

"Conductor, I'm obviously a little busy at the moment," Uly offered. "Let's talk after I'm fully in control of this system."

"Understood, Conductor," Chayka replied. "I'll stand by over here."

Uly was about to cut the line when Sterling interrupted.

"Alert," he yelled sharply. "Pilot, bring us around to starboard immediately. Gun teams, stand by to engage enemy squadron except Battery Four, which will keep the station off our backs."

Uly dialed his screen around. The four vessels that Chayka had indicated might be trouble had all gone blue-shift in the last few seconds.

Fools were charging.

# FIFTY-FIVE

Dan was used to leading assaults as one of the senior-most enlisted sailors, back when she'd been doing this sort of thing on *Marshal Castillon*. Today, she was management.

Commander Sheridan Chastain, and all that implied.

She looked around the remains of the cargo lounge that her team had just cleared. Not badly damaged, at least by the standards of nearly two hundred armed hooligans. The Painspheres had done most of the work for her, but the goons around her had still opened fire with mostly stun weaponry on anything that moved, didn't move, might move, or was the wrong color.

Fortunately, nothing had caught fire, or the automated systems would have likely dropped vacuum locks everywhere and she'd have to blow bulkheads to get where she was going.

"Scout team. Tech team. Heavy team," she yelled, pointing and watching three groups coalesce around her.

Dan pointed at the main hatch out of the lounge.

"I need that opened immediately," she ordered, trusting that the right techs would get the job done. Possibly by blowing something up, since she hadn't said not to. Not yet. "Scouts through first, then heavy. Rest of the force through in squad numbers."

She'd also learned that the teams were assembled a certain way, then numbered. The team normally at the back was trained to hold a rear-guard against pirates slipping around behind a main assault, either to hold them or launch a pincer attack of their own.

Here, it meant that she just needed to stay with Team Four and let her experts speed-run the station as fast as they could. She didn't need to clear every deck and every cabin. Merely take over the bridge. One of the teams was tasked with engineering and life support. The other two were intended to hit the local police/security barracks from two directions.

Nasrin's group was to keep folks off Dan's back as she got to the stationmaster.

As expected, a small explosion announced a five-meters-wide hatch sliding back into the bulkhead, revealing a corridor wide enough for ground vehicles to be driven right off a shuttle and into a cargo hold without unloading first. Civilian station, designed to make cargo movements easy, rather than a military outpost where defenses were paramount.

Thirty troopers took off at nearly a dead run, while Dan started to jog with her remaining Khet.

Dan left her helmet on, but checked the local atmosphere and decided that it was good enough for now. The louvers would slam shut if the corridor lost pressure and opening them now let her run on station air instead of her bottle.

More importantly, it let her hear the first shots as her scouts encountered resistance.

Followed several seconds later by that particular, dull thump you got when somebody started firing Painspheres into crowds. Some screaming. More shots.

"Force One to Command," a male voice came laconically over the line. "We have secured a major intersection."

"Do you have signs pointing you to the bridge?" Dan asked.

She wasn't sure who was talking, because she had one hundred and seventy-five strangers under her command today.

"Affirmative, Command," he replied. "Looks like a nearby stairwell and up two levels."

She could see the cluster of troopers up ahead, down straight corridors.

"Force One, take the stairs and continue your assault," Dan ordered. "We'll hold the crossroads behind you."

She turned to one of her Lead Specialists, a career non-com type except that he was a civilian.

"Shuttle, intersection, bridge," she said. "Nail those down as our strongpoints for now."

"Gotcha, ma'am," he nodded. "Backstop, you'll have the intersection. Two other teams hold with them as mobile reserve. Everyone else in behind Force One."

It helped that she was taller than most of the Khet she'd met so far. They all tended to all be roughly the same height, with variances in mass and squish.

Dan understood the assignments, but not the vocabulary. Back home, the orders would have sounded entirely different, but accomplished the same thing.

She'd need to train a new army while she was at it. At least the *Fox* had space for a large battalion of troopers. Not fourteen hundred, but she didn't need that many.

Now, to see how good the security troopers around here were.

And how well they'd reacted to a pirate raid.

# FIFTY-SIX

Nasrin liked the Ononguli helmets they'd found for her and the others. It let her tentacles breathe.

Those punks in *Danumash* had always just forced her and the others to cram their tentacles into Human bowl helmets that were claustrophobia-inducing.

She'd opened vents as soon as they were sure they had good air, which let her absorb the fishiness of this many Khet, plus traces of Ugotha, Ononguli, Zuath, and many others.

Not a lot of smoke. Not a lot of cooking oils. Just beings moving around, doing their everyday mundane things.

Except that she was here.

Nasrin had been born on a ship. Most Mazhin were. Before *Danumash*, she'd only been on the surface of a planet four times.

Stations like this were second nature.

She turned to the Khet with the most stripes on the outside of his armor.

"I need controlled chaos on our left," she said. "Noise and panic, without destruction or death if we can avoid it. The Commander and the *Corsac Fox* are counting on us to be the distraction here."

The man studied her for a long moment.

"No fire. No vacuum," he said simply. "Got it."

"And keep the force in groups large enough that they don't get over-run," she reminded him. "The defenders will want to have an opinion about what we're doing, and they might get pissy."

He nodded.

"Force, no fires, and no vacuum," he repeated on a wider channel. "Hit the next intersection and see where we are. Be ready to break into squads that will maintain line-of-sight to at least one other squad."

Nasrin nodded.

"Also," she added a moment later. "Stun is good if they give you problems, but I'd rather you let unarmed civilians flee in a panic. That will infect others we can't get to. Remember, we're only holding the left flank for Assault Command. We don't have to capture and hold terrain or corridors."

A growl from the men under her command. Bodies in motion. Somebody, probably having always wanted to do so, bowled a single Painsphere down a corridor like a child's ball.

"Corridors are perfectly flat, top," a voice announced. "Gravity is also stable."

Sure, call it a physics experiment. Nasrin understood the troopers around her, though none of them had tentacles.

A few seconds later, the Painsphere hit something hard enough to rupture it with a distant boom.

Her Omnibow didn't have that sort of range in gravity. She'd been waiting for someone to cut the generators.

Nobody had.

Yet.

# FIFTY-SEVEN

It helped Yanouk to think of them all as a giant dance troupe of toddlers, mostly performing the same dance, though hardly anyone was on the beat. The height difference helped.

She remembered those years, both being that squirt as well as being one of the older kids trying to corral the younger ones somewhere close to harmonized.

Nobody had had guns then, though.

"Yanouk, this is Gennady," Travers said on the command line. "Somebody got their shit together on my side. Lots of them, dug in like ticks. It's going to take me a while to get through them or drive them back. I'm sending you my location and theirs. See what you can do from over there?"

"Understood, Gennady," Yanouk replied. "Stand by."

She turned to her top team leaders. The casualties on the shuttle had meant that they were a mix of folks not used to working with each other, though they were about two-thirds hers and one-third from the team Emil was supposed to be commanding.

One of the team leads brought out a tablet computer from a pocket and brought a rough map live. Yanouk was used to such things, though not in the same way that these men were.

She committed art, not violence. Moss School instead of Sabre.

Today, she was Sabre School.

"Where would you stage a reserve force to protect both the barracks and the point of contact with Gennady's team?" she asked when they all looked up, looking around.

Some of these men had been doing this job since before she was born. Only a fool would assume that they knew better that the professionals.

Three of them reached out and tapped various spots on the screen. They didn't have the exact layout of corridors and levels, but there were only so many ways to build a space station this size.

She nodded.

"Two-dimensional thinking," Yanouk told them, harking back to lessons from Suka Kuri.

Yanouk had always been told that she was bright and exceptional when she was young, but it wasn't until an Exemplar of the Arts chose her as a personal student that Yanouk had begun to understand.

It wasn't necessarily brains or intellectual firepower, so much as the ability to think outside boxes or warehouses.

"Sir?" the lead asked, head tilted back to look up at her.

Otherwise, he was about eyeball level with her breasts, which had caused more than one of them to be uncomfortable or distracted.

"They are holding a single level, top," she said. "What if we worked up a deck, then across? Can you access some sort of maintenance tunnels or corridors that would let us drop out of the ceiling on them?"

"Which group should we target?" he asked.

"If we can hit the barracks itself, do that," Yanouk replied. "That puts us in command of their armory and their escape route. Otherwise, between barracks and reserve force, so we can drive them into Gennady. He'll be dug in as well. We outnumber them, but the cramped quarters prevent us from bringing all those numbers to bear directly. We need to surprise and panic them. Then we rout them entirely."

The men nodded and started issuing orders and instructions to the larger group around her.

Helpfully, Yanouk had been making sure to listen when Suka Kuri taught Anari about the history of the Sabre School. She could sound like one of them today.

They probably needed that.

She certainly did.

# FIFTY-EIGHT

Uly studied the plot. *Khile Heavy* was not a threat. Conductor Chayka's note suggested that they were already extremely short of crew and had pulled generators apart to fix things while in harbor.

They could still shoot at him if he sailed too close to them.

It was the other force that was intending to be a pain in the ass.

Two medium-sized Ultra-Bombers. Both smaller than *Compass Rose*, but dangerous, purpose-built warships. One large Seeker that looked like a Systems Guard vessel that had been stolen or purchased out of a salvage yard late in its life, with an extra turret welded on aft and painted an entirely different color scheme. Most people put them forward, like a rhinoceros, so that Seeker must have had a need. Or a quirk of their architecture.

The last one was a tiny Ultra-Bomber that some maniac had modified to add wings as large as *Compass Rose* had. Then they had added hardpoints on those wings. Haydar's scan had revealed six boxes, three to a side, with an estimate of a 6dm or maybe even an 8dm launcher on the innermost pair, plus two pairs of 4dm outward from there.

Overwhelming firepower on a tin can he might need to crush

Assuming they didn't crush *Corsac Fox* with a wall of wavebolts when they got close.

"Sterling, what's the station doing?" Uly asked.

"Occasional potshots, sir," Sterling replied. "I'm guessing most of the gunners have given up because we're out of range, but somebody over there is pissed enough to try anyway."

"Make a note to find out who, when we're done here," Uly acknowledged. "Not sure if I want to punch him or hire him. Depends on what he has to say for himself."

Several of the folks around the bridge laughed at that.

Nobody got up in the morning and decided to be a pirate. Well, not counting psychopaths, who didn't count.

At the same time, that gunner might see himself as a defender of the helpless on this station.

Regardless of the truth of the situation.

"Drew, is there a sailing line we can take that doesn't let them all come down to optimum range and unleash hell on us?"

"Yes, but then *Khile Heavy* might be able to put a shot into our flank," Drew replied. "Dunno if he's playing possum over there or hoping that we ignore him because he's naked and defenseless. Not sure I want to risk finding out, either."

Uly nodded.

Shitty situation, no two ways about it. Worse, if he did move off far enough, ships trapped by the warp bubbles he and the station were emitting could escape.

Or was that the thing he needed?

His comm beeped. Instead of opening to let Chayka talk. Apparently Haydar had already started reprogramming the comm computer, in the middle of a space battle.

But then, that Mazhin was *pissed*.

"Conductor?" Uly asked Chayka as the Ononguli's face appeared.

"What are your orders, sir?" Chayka asked.

Uly blinked. Couldn't help it.

"My orders?" Uly asked.

"Ononguli vessel and crew," Chayka replied with a slight shrug, his serious face cracking into a grin as he talked. "Under attack by outsiders. And maybe by people I don't like all that much."

Uly considered it. Considered his other idea.

It would probably only work once, but he only needed it to work once. At least for now.

"*Compass Rose*, they are going to be sailing a line like this," Uly said, transmitting Drew's best guess. "I want you to sail a reciprocal of that but stay where you are. Well clear, going the other way. Then I want you diving down and out as fast as you can go, like you were about to head off and rendezvous with your other two cohorts."

"Fellow travelers, *Iron Wasp*," Chayka said. "Nothing more. Not folks I would trust right now with everything up in the air."

"Understood, *Compass Rose*," Uly said. "Be prepared to come about hard to port and ride your Navigation Displacer thrusters at max to come to rest, then begin accelerating onto a different line that will be obvious shortly."

"What are you doing during that time, *Iron Wasp*?" Chayka asked.

"Running away, *Compass Rose*," Uly said, catching all the surprised faces on his own bridge, as well as the Ononguli Conductor. "Oh, and I want to correct a case of mistaken identity, *Compass Rose*. This ship is now known as *Corsac Fox*."

He cut the line and turned to Drew.

"Bring us around, Drew," Uly ordered. "Straight up. Maximum acceleration. I don't really care about the line. Get me clearance from the planet and the station that you can transition to warp."

Haydar caught it first. The others were surprised or angry, depending, thinking he was running away from the fight.

And Dan and the others.

Only the Mazhin had caught the orders to *Compass Rose*.

Drew paused, then shook himself and started typing.

"Sterling, load the Sixes but hold them. Use the Ones and the Omnipulsar as necessary."

"Where are we going, sir?" Sterling asked.

"To surprise someone."

# FIFTY-NINE

Dan paused in the stairwell to check in with everyone.

Beranger was out cold but stable with a medic working on him. Yanouk was leading that force. Gennady had gotten a little too aggressive and run headlong into a blocking force and a major firefight.

Not that Gennady Travers had ever done *that* before.

"Repeat that, Solomon," she said as she listened to the line.

"Minor casualties in engineering, sir," Solomon said. "Apparently, nobody ever expected someone to try to raid via the life support generator section, even though it's right next to the shuttle bay. We were able to roll up about a dozen guards here, while suffering two dead and six wounded."

"And you are in control of both life support and engineering at this point?" Dan asked.

"Affirmative, sir," he said.

She could hear the smile in his voice.

One of these days, that boy was going to be a fully-grown man, and have size and mass to go with brains and experience.

Lord help the rest of the galaxy on that day.

"Should I do anything from here, sir?" he asked.

Dan considered it. Cut life support to various sections of the station? Or power? Gravity?

All terribly juvenile delinquent moves, but Uly wanted the place intact. And the locals at least somewhat friendly.

Too many people were likely to get seriously hurt if Solomon did anything at all.

"You draw all your forces back and hold your zone for now, Solomon," she ordered. "Do not patrol outside your immediate vicinity, and keep all locks and hatches sealed as tight as you can get. We ought to be able to take the other sections shortly, so they'll surrender."

"On it, sir," Solomon said.

Dan cut the line and shook her head.

They were so close she could taste it. Travers and Yanouk should be able to control that section. That left...

"Nasrin, how are your troops doing?" Dan asked.

"I've got a thin cloak ranging across about a third of the station on this level," Nasrin replied instantly. "Won't stop enemy fire, but it should keep the water off your back."

Dan nodded. That was really what she needed. Travers and Yanouk had most of the security forces on the station either bogged down or bottled up, down four levels from where Dan was about to launch her attack.

Dan switched back to her local channel.

"Scout team, report," she ordered.

The stairwell was crowded. The three teams she'd put on point were out in the main corridor, but local guards had managed to hold things well enough. And, unlike below, the bridge existed inside a contained box. Cutting bulkheads or routing troops through air ducts and back corridors was a good way to run up her own casualties.

Or was it?

"Scout team here," the man replied. "I have eyes on the main hatch to the bridge. It has automated defensive systems in place. Stun currently, but they hit us pretty hard before I was able to pull people back. Every time one of my people stirs, he gets zapped again. Heavy weapons haven't been able to damage things, unless you want us to blow shit to hell and damn the casualties on the far side of the bulkhead."

"Acknowledged, Scout team," Dan said. "Pull your immediate group back now. Team one replaces them. Team two as reserve against a counter-attack. Other teams stand by."

She switched channels.

"Yanouk, talk to me about back corridors," she said.

# SIXTY

Yanouk was forward. Not quite leading, but close enough to fire her Squad Exoripper over the heads of the shorter troopers in front of her. That weapon had been useful a few times, when a spray of sparks and hot metal had caused defenders to flinch back or run. Someone tucked in against a bulkhead was almost impossible to hit directly unless you got dead lucky.

"Dan, my lead people were able to get us into the maintenance systems," she replied. "It's almost a second set of corridors, behind things and not as well kept. Same number of bulkheads and hatches for my tech folks to crack, but not nearly as many people to argue with. I took it because we're maneuvering to surprise the folks bothering Gennady."

"Stay on that," Dan said. "Are your options multi-level?"

Are they what? Oh.

"Affirmative, Dan," Yanouk said. "Ladders rather than stairs. Places where a winch or block and tackle can be attached. Don't get caught in the open. I've been sending through individual squads, then hopping over them. Slow, but it let us not get ambushed too badly, the two times they tried it."

"Understood," Dan replied. "Out."

Yanouk sighed and focused. This almost felt like a backstage area. Or the service corridors in a shopping arcade, where the tourists were up front and didn't know about the loading docks.

She came to a corner where two groups were currently watching three ways.

"What do you have?" Yanouk asked the senior man.

"I think we are just about on top of our targets now," he said, then turned to point. "According to Force Two, that ladder over there should let us appear almost directly behind them. Dunno if we can get enough people into that small of a space to really hammer anybody, or if we're feeding folks into a meat grinder and hoping it breaks quickly."

Yanouk nodded. Not a particularly nice image. And it might be correct.

"Show me the crawlspace," she said, following as he moved to where another group of techs and scouts were all pointing guns down at a hatch that was currently closed.

"Show her," the Khet ordered.

One of the techs had a screen. From the image, he had opened the hatch long enough to slip a camera through, then closed it.

She could see an alcove off of a hallway, and occasionally hints of leg as folks jogged by at the edge of visibility.

"That's it," the tech said. "Space for maybe three if they were crammed in tight, but zero cover and no place to hide if the bad guys come at you. As the Lead said, meat-grinder."

Yanouk nodded. Then considered something Nasrin had mentioned earlier. That physics experiment. Flat decks and stable gravity, especially if Wyndham wasn't going to do anything rude.

She looked down at her leaders.

"I need four crazy people," she said. "Two armed with pistols. Then every Painsphere they can carry. Two more with Omnibows. Past that, the team most willing to charge an enemy base without cover while I lead."

Blinks.

Took her a moment, then Yanouk understood. Male chauvinist pigs, for the most part. Didn't think a female was as tough as them. As mean as them.

They had no understanding of Sabre School at all. Probably only bad vids that had no relationship with the truth.

One of the leads nodded.

"I've got the folks you need," he said.

Yanouk smiled at him.

"Pick your four," she said.

"Me and him," the Khet said, pointing to a nearby Specialist. Then he turned to another Khet. "Get me two bow gunners and tell the rest to rotate forward."

Yanouk issued a set of orders for the others. She was in charge.

And there was probably a better than even chance that she was about to do something that got her hurt or possibly even killed.

At the same time, it needed doing, and this was too much of a scratch force to flow smoothly, with parts of two larger groups cammed together awkwardly.

But there had been no doubts about their aggression and their skills.

Quickly, the forty folks she needed gathered. The lead and his side-kick got every pocket filled with Painspheres, then swapped larger weapons for Exoripper pistols.

Yanouk moved to the hatch in the deck down.

"I'm going down first," she said simply. "You two down next. When we attack, I need everyone else feeding in as quickly as they can drop a deck and get into the fray. Either we surprise them from a flank, or pinch them hard in the process of getting mauled, and hopefully Gennady's team can push before we get wiped out. Questions?"

"Full frontal assault, sir?" the Lead asked.

"That's right," she nodded.

He nodded.

"Let's do this thing."

She turned to the tech at the hatch.

"Open it," Yanouk ordered.

Khet-sized hole. Cramped for a full-grown Emro, which was why she had to go first. The others could move quicker without her bottle-necking things.

Yanouk slipped the big weapon onto her back and sat on the edge, legs dangling. Three-meter ceilings generally meant that she was fine if she paid attention in three dimensions.

Softly down, like the dancer she'd been in a different life.

Yesterday.

Yanouk drew the Squad Exoripper around front and held it vertical, putting her back against the left and prepared to lunge at someone coming from the right.

A moment later, the Lead dropped silently, squatting with his head at her knees. The other trooper arrived a moment after that.

Yanouk confirmed one trooper at the opening overhead, like a jumpmaster organizing drop-troopers. The tip of an Omnibow, unloaded because the Khet carrying it had to get down, and while the chances of an accidental discharge were low, it would debilitate her force if it happened here.

She looked down at the two craziest ones with her.

"Arm the Painspheres on the deck," she said, pointing. "Then roll them that way as hard as you can until you run out. I'll be firing over your head. Once they detonate, I'll lead. One of you follows, one of you pivots to protect our rear. Feed two-thirds of the force after me, while one-third holds this against anything coming from the other direction. Are you ready?"

The two Khet grinned wildly. The sidekick even cackled a little.

Troopers, about to commit juvenile delinquency.

Yanouk nodded.

"Go," she said, turning and sliding out just enough to present that long arm of a Squad Exoripper.

Normally, it was fired while the trooper was lying flat, with a bipod on the front, but Yanouk was tall enough to hold it like a normal rifle. And strong enough.

She wasn't looking at anything in particular as she pulled the trigger. Instead, she let movement draw the eye and fired as rapidly as the charging circuits would cycle.

There was some fire echoing down the corridor from even farther away. Gennady's people, holding their spot and keeping attention on them.

Then the first Painsphere erupted, a flash of blinding light and a dull whump, like someone trying to bash a wooden door down from outside.

Then three more in rapid sequence, a triphammer of noise and pressure that overrode the sudden screams of surprise and pain.

Yanouk stepped out and charged. Because she was Sabre School today, she howled as she went, imagining the image of a green, female giant suddenly attacking them from the rear.

Painspheres didn't generate much smoke, but there was a solid curtain of haze in the air. A taste of ozone and fear.

Some quiet part of her mind tracked footsteps behind her as the Lead or the sidekick followed. Hopefully, there would be more, but she was committed.

Heads had started to turn, but not as many as she'd expected. A great many bodies either slumped to the deck or on their hands and knees puking, depending on how much of the shock wave they'd absorbed.

Nasty weapons, Painspheres.

She fired from the hip, trying to be more terrifying than dangerous, understanding one of the key lessons Suka Kuri had taught Anari.

And her.

*Surprise occurs in the enemy's mind.*

She had surprised them.

Yanouk got to the first trooper, ducking as he fired a shot into the ceiling overhead and tapping the man in the chest with the butt of her weapon.

They were Khet. Fragile, as they had more cartilage than bone. If she used all her strength, she'd probably crush the being.

Instead, she bounced him off the bulkhead hard. The trooper behind her fired a shot and stunned the Khet sufficiently.

Yanouk shuffled as she got into the mob, using shins and feet to again thump but not break people. They weren't her enemy, except when they tried to shoot her. She shot anyone with a weapon looking her way, as did the trooper behind her.

Then a second trooper appeared.

"Duck, sir!" that one yelled, slipping to the side and firing his

Omnibow down the hallway. Then the trooper behind *him* did the same.

More detonations down there. More screams.

Yanouk stepped to one side and fired her big gun into the haze, again more worried about speed than accuracy. Painspheres were the weapon she would be needing today.

That, and fear.

A hatch opened and a Khet stepped out, goggling in shock as he looked up at her.

Older. Looked like an officer from the rank tabs on his shoulder and the pudginess around his middle that looked more like Rabiu Khadijan than anything.

Yanouk reached out and grabbed the fellow by his neck, using the being's jawbones as anchors to lift him up. Emro were strong naturally, and she might be wound a little too tight.

The Khet squealed, audible even over the sound of Yanouk's troops firing and howling as they stomped past her down the corridor. More explosions. More screaming.

"Order your men to surrender!" she snapped, shaking him just a little bit. "Otherwise, we might have to kill them all."

Adrenaline was a wonderful thing. Yanouk was holding a Khet aloft with one hand, while firing the Squad Exoripper at arm's length with the other, over the heads of her assault force.

The Khet officer blinked, coherence finally coming back into his eyes.

"Yes!" he screamed. "We surrender!"

Yanouk had unconsciously tracked her Lead trooper as he'd stayed by her side. That one pulled a comm from the officer's belt and held it up to the Khet's mouth.

"This is Joshusa," the Khet said. "All security forces surrender. Immediately. Right away. Now. Do it! Stop shooting!"

Yanouk didn't think the fellow had any idea what he was saying, but the sound of beam fire around her tapered off quickly.

"We surrender!" she heard. "Ransom!"

Ah, ransom. The ancient call that someone was worth more alive than dead. That was how pirates communicated with each other, and these folks thought that she and hers were pirates.

As opposed to the law.

"Gennady, what's your status?" Yanouk asked on the command line.

"They are giving up here," he replied. "Whatever you did, it seems to have worked."

"Start rounding them up and disarming them!" she yelled to her own troops.

Around her, the smell of the battle was exceptionally thick, so Yanouk sealed up her suit and went back to filtered air.

As she set the Khet down again, her Lead took charge of the man and she went into his office.

Looking down, she had been almost knee deep in bodies.

Part of her wanted to puke, but she was in a suit, and didn't feel like taking her helmet off.

Instead, she sat down on the top of the desk and focused on her breathing exercises.

The Lead appeared a few moments later.

"You okay, sir?" he asked.

"I will be," Yanouk replied. "I will be."

He nodded and ducked out again, all sounds of battle gone.

She would be. Just not yet.

## SIXTY-ONE

Dan was all set to have her folks blow four hatches or air ducts when something happened. She'd been following Yanouk's preparations, and the sounds of battle that her microphone had picked up.

Yanouk had a lovely singing voice. It was pretty good when howling profanities as well.

"Assault Command, the main hatch to the bridge just opened and a guy stepped out," someone called over the line. "Looks like he wants to surrender or something."

Dan turned to the tech with his hands all set to override the hatch in front of her.

"Open it exactly one decimeter," she said. "Enough to look in and shoot, but not one bit more."

He nodded and fiddled, then the hatch slid sideways.

Dan put her Heavy Exoripper and her eyeball to the gap. Inside, Khet and others had their hands up and weapons were on the deck.

"Force One, the locals appear to be surrendering," Dan said. "Rush them and round them up. Do not fire, but get ugly if anyone resists at this point."

Piracy was a polite sport, when managed by professionals. As she'd been, once upon a time. Folks fought back until they couldn't, if you were a professional. It was only against slavers that people were willing to fight you to the death.

She got in as soon as the hatch in front of her was wide enough.

Twenty crew. All previously armed. Many turning her direction with jaws dropped as Dan's other troopers began to spill in from the rear and sides.

"Everyone against that wall," Dan ordered, pointing.

The defenders moved as in a daze, fins in the air.

Dan located the one with the prettiest uniform and stomped over to him.

"Stand up," she snapped.

He was up like an ejection charge had gone off under his bureaucrat's bottom.

"We surrender!" he cried.

"Tell everyone," she replied.

"I have!"

Dan turned to one of the techs that had followed her into the bridge, pausing to look at the space.

Vaulted where they'd chopped out the deck overhead to create a mezzanine. Stations all around the walls, facing out, on both decks, with places where officers could walk around and look over shoulders.

At the center of the lower deck, a smaller ring of stations, all currently on but unoccupied as Khet and others moved over to the side wall.

Dan's team was filling the room from all directions.

"Set up a perimeter," she ordered. "Here and all the places we came in, so nobody does it to us in turn."

Bodies flew into motion.

"Oh, and keep most of these folks here until we know what the situation is," she added.

Her techs were all close.

"Take charge of station and communications," she said. "Get them to stop shooting at the *Corsac Fox*. Make sure that Wyndham's team is good, as well as all the prisoners that Travers and Miyoshi will have."

Nods. More bodies in motion.

"Commander, we have a problem," one of them said quickly.

Dan stretched her legs to look over a shoulder. It was a scan of local space, 3D projected and centered on the planet.

"What's up?" she asked, counting all the tiny stars orbiting the larger one that was this station.

"We're missing two, sir," the Khet said, eyes big.

"What?" Dan asked, not grasping the view.

"Our transport, sir," he said earnestly. "*Swift Passage* and *Corsac Fox*. They're both gone!"

# SIXTY-TWO

Uly keyed a line to *Swift Passage* and got that ship's Conductor quickly. Khet, like so many of the rest of the people with him today. Older. Professional enough for Uly's needs.

"You will transition to warp immediately," Uly ordered. "Only travel out a light-minute or three. Just enough to remain clear of everything down here. From the sounds on the station, we're winning, but I need all eyes rotated up and away so nobody decides to try to counter-attack that force. Am I clear?"

"Aye, Conductor," the Khet replied. "What will you be doing?"

"Attacking the enemy fleet, *Swift Passage*," Uly said.

He cut the line and looked over at Drew and Sterling. Both had finally caught on to what he had planned, and smiled back at him.

"Drew, I need a circular pattern of flight," Uly said. "The tightest loop you can cut to get us up, out, around, and back down. We'll come out behind that group at short range. Sterling, I want you to put a 6dm into that psycho, pixie Ultra-Bomber, then the second one into the Systems Guard ship."

"Acknowledged, sir," Sterling replied crisply. "First bolt into *Were-shark*. Second into *Scavenger Angel*. Do you want the reloads into *Host Tau* and *Dawn Assembly*?"

Uly studied the scan. Two medium Ultra-Bombers. Both a little smaller than *Compass Rose*. Not as heavily armed as *Scavenger Angel*, to say nothing of that tiny beast, *Wereshark*.

"See what things look like," Uly said. "Use your best judgment if I don't override."

Sterling smiled. Uly smiled back. After a couple of battles and a lot of training, Sterling Huff was getting pretty good at this.

"*Compass Rose*," Uly said, opening the line to the ship that had changed sides. Or sided with his Ononguli crew. "Execute your flight plan now."

Uly turned to Drew and got a nod.

"Pilot, take us out," he ordered.

Normally, the transition to the Variable Pulse Spatial Generator was done farther away from any planet, because they dimpled space/time with their gravity. Additionally, the station was running a small generator. Not enough to move the station, but enough to keep other ships from getting too close under warp. Especially when attacking.

Today, *Corsac Fox* had needed to get some distance from everyone, so that they could run. Or appear to run.

*Corsac Fox* slipped into their own pocket of warped space, one that lasted long enough to make it look like they'd fled.

Less than a minute later, Drew had snapped them up and around.

*Corsac Fox* came out of warp and all the scanners reset with new images. It helped that they'd functionally teleported to a different square on the same game board, so everything moved but he had all the data already needed.

"Firing one," Sterling announced. Long pause. "Firing two."

Uly watched the first 6dm wavebolt chasing after a greatly surprised *Wereshark*. As with that other patrol craft that had surprised them when they'd first stolen *Wren*, *Wereshark* had a single Neutron Omnipulsar mounted aft.

*Corsac Fox* had come out too close for them to do much about it. And all six of their hardpoints faced forward, so they couldn't fire any defensive wavebolts, either.

All aggression.

The 6dm impacted and *Wereshark* came apart, cantilevered wing going one way while most of the hull, minus the bow quarter went another. The front end had simply vanished in a flare of blinding light.

Given how Ultra-Bombers were designed and built, Uly presumed that the Conductor and his senior crew had been in that part. He wondered if Sterling's team had been able to aim that accurately.

*Scavenger Angel* managed a 2dm defensive shot from that odd rear turret that mostly disrupted the 6dm coming for their souls before it hit, but the torpedo still had enough power to rock the smaller vessel off its line of sail when it exploded.

"*Scavenger Angel*, this is *Corsac Fox*," Sterling suddenly called over an open line. "That was your only warning shot. Surrender right now or I'll do to you what I just did to *Wereshark*."

Uly caught himself short of interrupting. Sterling had done what he thought was correct, being aggressive with heavy weapons.

*Host Tau* had turned and was starting to run when *Compass Rose* fired a 3dm at them from short range, then rolled in place to present a ventral turret with a 1dm for defensive purposes, in case anybody else fired at them.

*Dawn Assembly* struck their flags without bothering to do anything. Probably saw the writing on the wall and decided that living through today was the better option.

Dying was the alternative.

Drew had left his warp generators online, so nobody could escape by jumping away in the way *Corsac Fox* had just done. Nor circle back.

They were all trapped under his guns.

*Host Tau* fired a 1dm into *Compass Rose*'s torpedo. At that small size, the two neutralized each other in a burst of energy probably visible from the ground if you were looking up.

"This is *Host Tau*," a voice came on the comm. "We're done here. What are your conditions?"

"*Iron Wasp*, this is *Scavenger Angel*, we give up!"

"All enemy ships, cut your engines and electroshield arrays," Uly ordered over an unsecured comm channel. "Anyone not doing so in twenty seconds will be presumed hostile and destroyed without mercy."

He muted the line and leaned back.

Haydar looked up.

"What are the rest doing?" Uly asked his Data Officer.

"The ones that could, sailed away as hard and fast as possible when we cut our generators," Haydar nodded. "Or got far enough from us that they could slip away. Mostly cargo ships, but a few that looked armed. It was the warships that mostly stayed around to play. I'm reading surrenders all over the place now that *Wereshark* is dead."

"Keep a few tentacles on them," Uly nodded. "I don't trust anyone at the moment. Some we might let escape later. A few, like *Khile Heavy*, will get captured as prizes or destroyed if they resist. Let everyone wind down, then have them shut their ships down and transfer all their crews to the station. Or to *Swift Passage,* once you can get a signal to them that it is safe to return."

Haydar nodded.

Uly blew out a huge breath.

Then he dialed a different line.

"Dan, this is Uly. What's your status?"

# SIXTY-THREE

Dan had the stationmaster seated with two of her troopers watching him. Most of his staff were also seated in chairs pulled away from any consoles, where they could be comfortable, but not do anything.

Solomon held engineering and life support systems. Yanouk's force was in pretty good shape, considering the casualties they'd had before the battle even started. Gennady was holding all the local security people in their own barracks, disarmed and no longer a problem. Nasrin was rounding up strays and collecting self-important folks who were demanding to know what was going on.

Anyone still doing that after she pointed an Omnibow in their face was either going to be an asshole, or someone Uly needed to talk to later.

Probably both.

"Dan, this is Uly. What's your status?" he asked.

"I think we won," she replied. "Casualties have been a little better than predicted, with perhaps six percent dead on my side and about fifteen percent wounded to some degree. I expect to get more than half of those back by tomorrow, after medics check them out or heavy stun wears off like a bad hangover."

"Excellent news, then," Uly said. "Except for the dead folks. We'll need to make sure that we set up some sort of benefits package for their families, over and above whatever Apex Mechanical Security Solutions does."

"I'll handle that," she said. "We're in good shape for an Admiralty Court from what my scanners show."

"Affirmative there," Uly said. "You'll be taking charge of a lot more prisoners shortly, though I expect a few ships will try to run. I might even let them go, depending, as I have other problems I need to deal with."

"*Compass Rose*?" she asked.

That one had suddenly opened fire and helped Uly box in that last group of diehards.

"Ononguli ship," Uly confirmed. "Said we were also such a vessel, so he was *required* to side with us. I need to get to the bottom of that."

"Required?" Dan asked.

"His words," Uly said. "Did you find *Khile Heavy*'s crew?"

"We've started pulling them and others out of bars and brothels," Dan replied. "A lot of sailors ignored the alerts. Or decided that they'd have shorter lines to some of the entertainment around here."

There was a pause.

She didn't think Uly was one of those moralist officers, intent on preventing their sailors from enjoying themselves off-duty, but it hadn't really come up, either. From the point that they'd gone after *King Hewitt II*, they hadn't either of them stopped running.

Nor had he expressed any interest in any of the crew members, her or others. Not that kind, anyway.

Lonely at the top, perhaps?

She made a note to remind him that they were pirates now, rather than sailors. And possibly rich, or at least stable enough to relax some.

"I think," Uly finally replied, "that you should look at putting all the captured sailors on the surface of the planet as soon as we can make arrangements for those folks to keep and house them. That keeps them from bothering you or me as we make our own arrangements."

"What are we thinking?" Dan asked.

"We've started a revolution here, Dan," he told her. "But I'm not done yet."

She nodded.

"I've got your back," she reminded him.

"That's the only reason I could ever think I'd pull it off," he replied. "Talk to you shortly."

He cut the line and Dan smiled at the stationmaster of this formerly piratical haven.

"I need you to connect me with the locals who are in charge," Dan said.

"I'm in command of this facility," he replied angrily, starting to stand up before a heavy green hand landed on his shoulder and slammed him back down.

"Not anymore," Dan reminded the fellow. "The *Corsac Fox* is in charge now."

# SIXTY-FOUR

Lukyan looked at the remains of his Tuesday.

*Wereshark* broken into pieces and the crew—the surviving crew—being rounded up by search-and-rescue tugs. *Legend of Ymnan* and *Spirit of Iniquity* had both bugged out as soon as trouble had started, running away fast when *Compass Rose* had moved into battle.

Of course, that wasn't entirely a new thing with Kyauta Bukar or Zorion Aldana.

Good riddance, if they'd decided to pick up stakes and move on.

*Khile Heavy* had wisely accepted *force majeure* when *Corsac Fox* had sailed over with an assault shuttle full of freshly victorious marines.

This Ulysses Fortier fellow owned orbital space above *Lacium*.

And was calling him on that private channel Ononguli vessels maintained.

"*Compass Rose*," Lukyan replied.

"Conductor Chayka, I think you and I should have a meeting aboard my ship," Fortier said. "Where we don't have to worry about our signals encryption paradigms."

It took Lukyan a few seconds to translate into something he could understand. Then he nodded.

"Agreed, Conductor," Lukyan said. "Normally, I'd leave my Second-in-Command in charge here, but he's a cousin of Adrian Sobol."

"I gathered as much from the way my Data Officer was handling him," Fortier said. "And I have all of the personal effects of the former crew aboard, if you wanted to take those crates back with you later. How soon will you be returning to the Ononguli Sphere?"

And that was the bitch of it right there, wasn't it?

But Lukyan was under the *Corsac Fox*'s guns. And bound by things that he didn't think Fortier fully understood.

Not yet, anyway.

"We have a lot to talk about, *Corsac Fox*," Lukyan replied. "Permission to come aboard?"

"Granted, *Compass Rose*," Fortier said. "Bring Maks and a shuttle with a lot of cargo volume. You might have to make several trips."

"Understood, *Corsac Fox*," Lukyan said. "Expect updates as we get organized here."

He cut the line and looked around.

Maks, Dmytro, and Oskar stared back at him.

"Dmytro, you're in charge until Maks and I get back," he ordered. "Oskar, you go off duty now and spell Dmytro later. I have no idea how long this will take. Nor how Fortier will react to the things I have to tell him. If something happens to us, there is a package in the safe in my cabin. Break the seal and read it for instructions from the clan elders back home. Then follow them if you ever want to see the Endless Plains again. Am I clear?"

Dmytro and Oskar both gulped and nodded, horns waving.

Lukyan rose and gestured to his Second-in-Command.

"Let's go, Maks," he said simply. "Dmytro, tell those yahoos aft to warm up the shuttle. And get all the junk out of it."

He exited the bridge. *Compass Rose* had two decks, being at the top end of the Ultra-Bomber design. Enough space for a crew of forty if everyone was cramped, though he usually flew with about thirty. Not a lot of cargo capacity, since he had a shuttle instead, but that was why he'd traveled with *Legend of Ymnan*, since they had a lot of cargo volume.

Aft, bodies were lugging junk and boxes out of the shuttle.

"Where do you want it, Lukyan?" one of them asked.

Lukyan considered his options. If they still had everything from *Iron Wasp*, he might be crammed to the horns with shit, but Lukyan also figured that he'd be making a speed-run home to Krilic, since it was the closest system in the Ononguli Sphere.

Of course, with the news he had, Lukyan was pretty sure that he'd end up having to go to Rayzian eventually.

Apparently, he'd tempted the Lords of the Endless Plains by complaining about his Tuesday.

"Pack everything tight," Lukyan replied. "Junk what you don't need in the short term. Expect that we're bringing home a lot more cargo that we have to transport as well, so a lot of you have to go back to doubling up and hot-bunking for a while. Work with Dmytro once I know the accumulated volume."

"Do we know who this *Corsac Fox* is, Lukyan?" the fellow asked. "Somebody said a new species or something."

"Yes," Lukyan nodded, drawing Maks off to one side so folks could get by with carts. "New species. New troubles around here."

Then they were past and he and Maks were alone for a moment.

"What about the Sphere?" Maks asked as they were alone.

"We've got to tell them, Maks," Lukyan said. "Just like I have to talk to this *Corsac Fox*."

"They aren't going to like it," Maks observed.

Lukyan grimaced.

"One of these days, you'll be a Conductor, Maks," he said. "You ain't seen nothing yet."

# SIXTY-FIVE

Haydar had gone ahead and told every ship that could to land on the planet below, picking out the couple of small starports that he could see. That would get the smallest ones out of his way for now. And give him a lot of warning if someone suddenly took off to be a problem.

Larger vessels had been told to evacuate all of their crew on shuttles. Dan had started hauling them to the ground as well, keeping only the officers up on the station.

Good way to control the situation, since the muscle and the brains were going to be at two different locations. That was the way his folks had done it in the old days, too.

Now, the bad part was about to slip up and bite him on the ass. Somehow. He just knew it.

*Khile Heavy*. Conductor Elemér Petőfi, though he'd been on the station and gotten dragged out of a Khet brothel by one of Nasrin's teams, trapped away from his ship when it had become clear that there was nothing he could do about the situation.

Haydar had half expected the being to jump in an escape pod and try his luck on the planet below. Assuming that he didn't have any enemies down there.

Not always a safe bet with pirates, even at a pirate truck stop like *Lacium*.

For now, Haydar sighed. Uly had put him in charge of interviewing some of the more important prisoners. Like Elemér Petőfi.

At least they were separated, with the Conductor on the station still and Haydar in one of the offices just behind the bridge of *Corsac Fox*.

From the view on the camera, it had taken Anari and Yanouk to finally convince the fellow to behave.

Khet, but a big one. At least as tall as Dan, with all the usual breadth and bulk of the species. Muscles. According to the notes from *Compass Rose*, something of an asshole, over and above the rest of the pirates around here.

*Wereshark*'s Conductor and crew had just been aggressive psychopaths, but they'd gotten that all knocked out of themselves by Huff's wavebolt.

Sterling had set out to kill *Wereshark*. Haydar had spent enough time around his Human friends now to understand that the young man might not have been kidding when he threatened to annihilate the rest of the ships in orbit after that.

Humans were like that. Had the locals any organization or discipline, the pirates might have been able to resist, but then they wouldn't have been pirates, would they?

Elemér Petőfi was seated in a chair, scowling angrily at the camera and screen. Haydar could see the thighs of the two Emro women who had put him there, and the big, green hands on his shoulders reminding him that each of them outweighed him. And were stronger.

Dan's idea. Haydar agreed fully.

Made his life easier.

"Conductor, my name is Haydar Ramezani," he introduced himself. "I represent the *Corsac Fox*, who has just captured this system, your vessel, and your crew."

Petőfi started to rise.

"We'll see about—" and Anari slammed him back down into the chair hard enough to knock all the wind out of the big Khet.

"This is not up for discussion, Petőfi," Haydar continued implacably. "The *Corsac Fox* has captured *Lacium*. Your vessel is one that has been designated as a prize. It will be sailed by a prize crew to *Z'Gosza*, where an Admiralty Court will adjudicate ownership in favor of the *Corsac Fox*, who will then put said vessel up for sale to the highest bidder. It is my understanding that his intention is to either have the *Z'Goszan* government buy it as a warship they induct into service, or locate a consortium of investors who will acquire it to participate in the same pirate-hunting that *Corsac Fox* is doing."

"You can't do this!" Petőfi raged, careful not to move. Or maybe unable to, with Anari leaning on him.

"I can and have, Conductor," Haydar replied. "This conversation was a courtesy, not a requirement. As you have a list of open warrants and indictments in other systems, according to my records, I would suggest that you not return to *Z'Gosza* to contest the Court, unless you think you can avoid being arrested in the process."

He paused. Smiled at the dumb-ass Khet who was still a pirate when grown-ups had given up on invisible friends and religious aspirations to make something useful of their lives.

"At present, the *Corsac Fox* has no reason to make things personal with you, Conductor," Haydar concluded. "Nor have you given me any reason to change his mind. You will be transported to the surface when we depart, and thereafter have the opportunity to pursue gainful employment. Good day."

He went ahead and cut the line before that jackass could say anything. All of this could have been done with printed memos that folks handed out, but Uly had wanted several of the conductors to have it personally rammed home.

There was a new sheriff in town, as Dan had explained the future.

His name was Ulysses Fortier, but already people had stopped calling the ship by that given name, and transferred it to Uly.

**He** was the *Corsac Fox*.

# SIXTY-SIX

Uly had remained on the bridge and sent Sterling down to greet his guests when they arrived, once he knew that the shuttle docking had a pilot and two passengers, all Ononguli. With the station taken and under control, he'd brought back enough security folks to protect himself, though Emil Beranger was still in a medically induced coma while medics and Khet surgeons worked on saving his leg, plus all the things that had been broken, ruptured, or singed.

The man had been lucky to be alive when the shuttle docked. The Khets treating him were still shocked that he hadn't died, but they'd never met a Human before.

And among Humans, Uly didn't know many people more stubborn than Beranger. Maybe himself and Dan. Maybe.

Haydar and Piruz entered the bridge. Armed, because everybody else was.

"Time?" he asked.

Haydar nodded.

Uly reached into a drawer under his chair and pulled out a pistol and holster that he attached as he stood up. Only for looks, because he wasn't that good of a shot, and Dan was over on the station supervising with about half of her force.

"Kovalchuk, you and Drew keep the shop," Uly told them. "I'll be close by with Sterling, but don't hesitate to shoot first and then sound the alarms. Am I understood?"

The Ononguli engineer who sat bridge watches paled, then nodded. Drew did the same.

"Ethir, you ready?" Uly asked.

"No, but that won't stop us," the tiny fellow replied with a laugh. "Let's go be big and bad."

Uly shook his head chuckling, but moved aft to the bigger conference room, where folks could stretch out their arms and breathe. Chayka's request to chat had felt larger than Uly's usual office, even when it could hold two Emro women and half a dozen others.

He sat off-center of the long side, facing the door. Haydar took the top of the table on Uly's right. Piruz was on his left, at the low end of the table, with Ethir beyond that.

Sterling opened the door, with Nasrin and several of her Khet sailors, all armed and intimidating, entering, escorting two Ononguli males.

Seeing Nasrin put a smile on his face, so Uly gestured her to join them at the table, instead of standing back. She ended up next to Maks Sobol, on the far side from Conductor Chayka.

Maks bore a familial resemblance to Adrian Sobol. Same bones in the face. Same twist to his horns. Younger by at least a decade, assuming that Ononguli aged at the same rate as Humans.

Lukyan Chayka had referred to Maks as his Second-in-Command. Even younger than Chayka, Sobol was older than Dan, to say nothing of Uly or Nasrin.

At least he had Haydar, looking august and formal at that end of the table, however much that was really a scam. Uly knew Haydar better. He'd rather be rewriting the communications network protocols right now, so no other Ononguli ship could suddenly reach out and make them listen.

Uly focused on Lukyan Chayka.

"How old are you?" Chayka asked bluntly, eyes opening wide.

"He is young for a Human adult," Haydar replied first. "And

dangerous enough that my clan elected him to *Speak* for it, allowing me to retire from the job."

Uly pursed his lips, but didn't interrupt. Or correct. Technically all true. And Haydar would have a reason for saying it that way.

The two Ononguli turned to Haydar. Maks turned back to Nasrin a moment later. Both nodded.

"And you have, if I understand it, a crew of Humans, Mazhin, Emro, Thogin, and Ononguli?" Chayka asked.

"That is correct," Uly replied. "All of those were in the cell with me when I decided to break out of the Imperial prison barge where we were being held."

Both Ononguli blinked.

"Then I stole a shuttle and captured its crew," Uly continued in a bland voice, leaving out all the terror and risk. "From there, we had our pick of vessels in local orbit. I stole the vessel you know as *Iron Wasp*."

"And Adrian's still there?" Maks asked.

Uly shrugged.

"You probably know Imperial protocols better than I do," Uly said. "Humans are new to this part of the galaxy."

He didn't need to explain that *all* of explored space from a Human standpoint wasn't much larger than one fifth of one Imperial Sector. Compact and somewhat dense, but in the middle of nowhere.

He'd settle for exotic and alien.

"But you have some of Adrian's crew with you?" Chakya asked.

"We do," Uly nodded.

There was a pause. Pregnant. Chayka seemed to be trying to find the words. Or filing off the sharp edges before he spoke them. Something.

"Tell me about the Ononguli Sphere," Ethir suddenly asked. "All of us are from systems and sectors rimward of the Auga, so we don't know your kind all that well. Enlisted engineers didn't know much about important things, either, beyond broad strokes of culture."

Uly kept himself still and watched. He hadn't planned for the others to whipsaw the newcomers, but he could see where it would be effective. He was just sorry Dan wasn't here. Nasrin was smart and beautiful, but both paled next to Dan. Plus, Dan was his First Officer.

His right hand.

"The Sphere is really more of a flattened lump of dough," Chayka began. "If you dropped it against the countertop of Auga space. There are lines on treaties, but the Auga are forever pushing to see if they can spall off existing worlds with trade treaties or colonize empty ones. The clans of the Sphere retaliate with raids into Auga space, as well as petty piracy of the sorts that *Compass Rose* or *Iron Wasp* undertake. Or did, until Adrian apparently got himself arrested."

Uly nodded. That much had been more or less gathered from the current crew he'd inherited.

"Why was *Compass Rose required* to assist us in battle?" Uly asked, centering things into the place he wanted them.

They could get the history of the Ononguli Sphere later. Or never, depending. *Compass Rose* and Conductor Chayka had functionally changed sides in the middle of a battle, entirely on the basis that they had mistaken this Interceptor for *Iron Wasp*.

Chayka nodded.

"This is an Ononguli ship," he said, gesturing to the room around them. "That you'd taken it as a Human vessel changes some things, but at the same time you have at least a partial Ononguli crew. However mixed you are."

"And what does that mean to the Ononguli Sphere?" Uly pressed.

"It may not seem like it to outsiders, but the Sphere is well organized," Chayka replied.

Ethir's laughter probably wasn't the interruption that Chayka was expecting. Nor Haydar's.

Uly simply watched.

"We might have a reputation in many places, Conductor Fortier," Chayka finally said. "The Ononguli, that is."

"You bet," Ethir piped in. "Crazy barbarian raiders who don't wipe their boots before entering. Sure fit what *Iron Wasp* was doing, considering where they were when they got taken by the Auga."

Chayka shrugged.

"I won't suggest it is not an appropriate image, Fortier," he offered. "I will say that, in order to be allowed to command an Ononguli warship, you have to swear certain oaths and accept a variety of responsibilities. Those are unbending."

"And you think that applies to the *Corsac Fox*?" Ethir asked, turning deadly serious in the blink of an eye.

"I'm not sure," Chayka replied, seemingly honestly. "But it might."

Uly would give the Conductor credit for that much at least.

"What other requirements do you face, Conductor Chayka?" Uly asked.

"For one, I probably need to return directly to Ononguli space with the news," he said. "You, and what you did to *Lacium*, as well as Adrian Sobol and *Iron Wasp*."

"I don't think you fully understand what we've done here," Uly replied, watching both of the strangers closely. "I didn't capture *Lacium* in order to make it my base of operations as a pirate."

"No?" Maks asked, while Chayka hesitated. Like perhaps he saw something the younger pirate didn't.

"No," Uly said. "I'm working with the Trade Factors of *Z'Gosza* to clean up this region of space. That meant an attack at *Lacium*, capturing it, but then seeing if I could find locals who would run the place as a legitimate colony when I left, rather than a pirate haven. Having looked at the industry on the ground below us, as well as what's in orbit, I think that it is possible. If the right people have the right motivations."

"And what are those?" Maks Sobol asked, much like Dan would have stepped in were she here. Or how Haydar and Ethir were doing.

"I'm taking *Khile Heavy* with me," Uly said. "Then selling it on *Z'Gosza* to someone who will use it. I think that *Wereshark* might be repairable if someone cared. Or maybe someone could build something like it to defend *Lacium*. I will use this as a base from time to time, but I'm also planning to operate out of *Z'Gosza*."

"What are you planning?" Maks asked, still not seeing it.

"I'm ending piracy," Uly told him simply.

"Ending?" Maks asked, incredulous.

"That's right," Uly said. "If *Compass Rose* has decided that they need to be on my side, that means that you're also going to end piracy.

I'm not going to demand that you immediately renounce your past, though, Conductor."

"No?" Chayka asked.

"No," Uly nodded. "Haydar and Ethir have a list of all the boxes of personal effects that we inherited when we stole this vessel from the *Auga*. The crew were entirely Ononguli, as you expected. I have no use for most of it, but haven't done anything about jettisoning it to burn up on some atmosphere somewhere. Instead, I'd like to make arrangements to have you haul it, or as much of it as possible, back to the Ononguli Sphere, so that the relatives at least have it, in case the men and women incarcerated never return. Or if they do."

"How much gear are we talking?" Chayka asked sharply. "We're limited in the cargo space *Compass Rose* can haul. In the past, most of our space in the argosy was on *Legend of Ymnan*."

Uly looked at Haydar.

"Roughly the volume of the shuttle that carried you here," Haydar said. "Not the cargo capacity, but the absolute size itself."

"Then there is no way I can pack all that and travel any distance," Chayka said.

"What if I sold you a small cargo carrier cheap?" Uly asked.

"If you what?" Chayka asked.

"The ships that have surrendered here thought that they were dealing with pirates, Chayka," Uly said. "Using your notes, I have emptied a few of the vessels of crews entirely, assuming that to be the fastest way to short-circuit somebody trying to start another revolution or irritate me. I have hulls available. I plan to hire some folks to supplement my crews to help sail them as prizes to *Z'Gosza*, where a court of law will declare them to be my property for disposal as I wish. That includes *Scavenger Angel*, which is a Probe with a large cargo capacity, as well as armaments. I can sell it to you instead of the locals when we get there."

"That's going to cause problems, Fortier," Chayka replied.

"Not if I break all the pirates I can find, Chayka," Uly said. "I am given to understand that the former *Iron Wasp* was one of the most heavily armed pirate vessels most of the people I've asked have ever seen.

Since I have taken *Khile Heavy* as well, there are not that many others left that are capable of being a threat to me. And once the larger systems and governments realize what I'm up to, I expect more support from them."

"Shit, you're serious," Chayka reacted

"He's deadly serious, bucko," Ethir replied in that cruel voice. "Folks around here either shape up or start running. And it's only going to get worse."

Uly watched both Ononguli men absorb that. Chayka spoke first.

"*Scavenger Angel*?" he asked.

Uly nodded slowly.

"How cheap?" Chayka asked.

Uly considered a myriad of responses.

"Have you got the crew to sail it to *Z'Gosza* for me?" he asked.

"I do," Chayka replied. "As long as I don't have to fight or anything. Plus, we might be able to recruit some folks from around here, as long as we mix the crews up some, rather than taking any single block from one ship. I think there ought to be enough Ononguli for my needs. Don't imagine strangers would want to sail that long of a distance with me, clear over to Sector Twenty-One."

"Tell you what, Conductor Chayka," Uly offered. "I'll sell it to you for one Imperial Guilder after it's mine, plus you providing the crew to get it to *Z'Gosza*, then haul a certain cargo back to the Ononguli Sphere for me."

"All those personal effects," Chayka said.

Uly nodded.

Chayka blew out a heavy breath.

"I have a related question before I answer, Fortier," he said, pausing.

"Go on."

"In the safe in your room, was it empty when you took over?"

"It was," Uly nodded. "Cleaned and locked open, with the security combination written on a piece of tape for the next owners, once the Auga got around to selling it."

Chayka nodded.

"Okay, that explains a lot," he said, then he turned to his partner.

"Maks, I'm promoting you to provisional Conductor, in command of *Scavenger Angel* once the *Corsac Fox* turns it over to us. I'll need to make two copies of the packet in my safe, for you and the *Fox* here, so you understand what is implied when you are an Ononguli conductor."

"What if I'm not interested?" Uly asked.

Chayka and Sobol both blinked at him, flinching in surprise.

Uly watched them with a hard smile that Haydar, Ethir, Piruz, and even Nasrin matched.

"I'm not sure that you're allowed, Fortier, if I can be a little rude," Chayka said. "Ononguli crew. Ononguli vessel. More importantly, though, if you are one of us that means that the Ononguli Sphere is your ally. And you can recruit more ships and crew from over there if you wanted. It feels like you are on a mission far bigger than just one system. Maybe big enough to be a threat to the Auga themselves, which I and mine would enjoy, because they're intending to conquer or absorb the entire galaxy, one of these days."

"And does that require that I become an ally of the Ononguli Sphere, sight unseen?" Uly asked. "*Required*, like you, to answer the call of any other Ononguli ship in distress?"

Again, shock on those two faces.

Chayka finally nodded and blew out a sigh.

"That's one of those secrets that most folks don't know about," he offered. "I would appreciate it not being general news, even if we don't come to an agreement. But yes, any and all Ononguli ships are supposed to help each other, friendly or not. That's part of the reason I took *Compass Rose* this far around the curve of Imperial space. Not a lot of those folks make it out here to bother me, and I don't have to put up with some of the bozos that remained behind."

Uly nodded. Smiled even.

"You send me a packet to review, *Compass Rose*," he said. "But you haven't answered my question."

Chayka twitched a little.

"Uhm?"

"*Scavenger Angel*," Uly said. "Maks. Admiralty Court. Cargo run to the Sphere."

"Oh, that," Chayka said. "Assuming the state of the hull, that's a given."

"A given?"

"You're Ononguli at that point, *Corsac Fox*," Chayka smiled. "That's what we do."

Uly nodded.

He could work with this. He just wasn't sure how.

# KHILE HEAVY

# SIXTY-SEVEN

Dan watched the main screen on *Corsac Fox*'s bridge as the many ships of the argosy assembled at the final waypoint.

That had been Lukyan Chayka's term for the group. *Corsac Fox. Compass Rose. Scavenger Angel. Khile Heavy. Swift Passage.*

One additional captured cargo carrier a little bigger than *Corsac Fox* that had been emptied of crew. Two smaller ones. Two other big cargo vessels had still had owners or at least original crew and officers aboard from before they had been captured when taken at *Lacium*, so Uly had set them free to carry the news home.

*Lacium* itself had required a week of meetings, negotiations, and occasional heads bopped together, but they'd come around. Then two weeks of arguing before Uly imposed a Citizens Council on the civilians, with instructions to sort out their own governance.

Uly had allowed them to confiscate a few of the smaller armed vessels as the core of a local defensive fleet. Not enough to threaten anyone, but enough to keep pirates from coming back, once the colonists at *Lacium* had gotten the upper hand.

Dan didn't know how long they'd hold it, but with so many pirates in jail there, they looked to be certain to try.

The Khet conductor off *Khile Heavy*, one Elemér Petőfi, had been rounded up with about two dozen others like him, once it had become clear that they would try to overthrow the good citizens of *Lacium* after Uly left.

She had them aft in separate cells, for the folks at *Z'Gosza* to sort out. Or sell to somewhere else that wanted to request extradition.

As she and Uly had concluded, the best they'd been able to do was show everyone that there was a door none of them had ever seen before. It was up to each of them to decide to kick it in and move beyond the life they'd previously known.

And the *Corsac Fox* would remain in the area, so it wasn't like back-sliders wouldn't have other difficulties.

She caught Uly absently staring at her. Dan smiled. He returned it a moment later, then flexed his shoulders once and nodded.

Dan watched him open a comm line to the argosy.

"All vessels, this is the *Corsac Fox*," he announced.

Dan liked that. He'd given up resisting, and just embraced the fact that folks were calling him the *Corsac Fox*, instead of the ship.

They might need to find a new name for the hull. Not *Iron Wasp*, though. Or maybe so. There were going to be ongoing cases of mistaken identity, considering how famous Adrian Sobol's ship had gotten in some regions.

"*Compass Rose*, you and *Khile Heavy* remain on our flanks when we arrive at *Z'Gosza*," Uly continued. "As planned out, they might still flip out a little at this much firepower suddenly arriving on their doorstep, regardless of the fact that we sent a courier home ahead of us. We'll come out high and then drop down into closer orbit once everyone over there is happy. Any questions?"

"I'm assuming dinner is on you, *Corsac Fox*," Lukyan replied.

That one had gone all in on being an ally, as near as Dan could tell. Even more than the Khet of *Z'Gosza*, though Rabiu could probably be considered crew at this point. She turned to the Khet, caught his nod.

As a species, they tended to be broad. The troopers she'd taken with her had shown Dan how squishy and out of shape Rabiu and his bosses were, but she'd seen a change come over that fish over the last month. Eating better, but that was Vahid. Walking and climbing stairs more. Hitting the machines in the gym.

He wasn't ready to storm a station with her. However, he was looking far better than he had when she'd met him.

"Affirmative, *Compass Rose*," Uly replied. "I'll have Trade Factors to introduce you to, and I'm hoping that they'll pick up the tab."

That got a round of laughter from all the conductors. Even Drew was acting like a conductor while flying *Khile Heavy*, but he'd made it clear in no uncertain terms that he would be returning to *Corsac Fox* to fly as soon as he could.

They still needed crew. Not as badly as before, since they'd taken Chayka's apparent advice and recruited folks from various ships, putting them under Human, Mazhin, or Ononguli officers for now.

Shortly, it would all be Factor Bitrus's problem, and Dan found herself looking forward to working with Uly to see what their next adventure was. She couldn't imagine that he'd be satisfied merely sailing around and capturing small-time pirates. And other pirate dens like *Lacium* would wake up to the shitty state of their defenses and probably do something about it.

Or not. They were pirates, after all.

Dan shared a smile with Uly, then he turned to the Khet in their midst.

"Rabiu, you're on," Uly said. "Sterling, take us into warp."

# SIXTY-EIGHT

Rabiu swallowed heavily and wondered what Director Bukra or Factor Bitrus would say when he announced his resignation. Sure as shit would likely be a surprise, but he'd spent two months around the *Corsac Fox* and that Human's crew.

*Z'Gosza* paled badly by comparison.

Uly got shit done. So did Dan. So did all of them, come to think of it. Without filings in triplicate, each requiring different chops from different departments or directors in order to finalize interim details.

Point at a problem. Identify it. Assign someone to come up with solutions. Implement.

He'd been expecting the merchants of *Lacium*, all of them really just fences dealing in stolen goods, one way or another, to spend half a year sorting themselves out. Bitrus had thought that was overly ambitious, and that a year or more would be necessary, with Uly gone all that time.

There'd been a few times he'd wished that he could be a minnow, swimming quietly in the shadow of some shark, when that courier arrived to announce that the *Corsac Fox* planned to return, triumphant and commanding a small fleet of warships. In a month.

Talk about piranha in the water...

Rabiu grinned and glanced over at Shehu Okorie, noting that he'd finally convinced the camerakhet to film him from his good side.

Rabiu had lost a lot of weight over the last month. Fewer heavy meals. More exercise. WAY LESS stress.

He felt like a new fish. And had had to dig into the ship's stores for a new wardrobe. Even getting home wasn't about to help, because nothing he'd owned since university would likely fit, unless tents were in fashion.

Definitely a new fish.

Shehu nodded back and grinned. He'd been filming since they approached that last check-in point with everyone, catching the casual humor and sharp professionalism that was so unlike *Z'Gosza* society. Or business.

"All hands, stand by to emerge from warp," Sterling announced.

Rabiu finally had understood how thin Uly was for crew when they'd told him how old Sterling Huff and Solomon Wyndham were. He'd thought that Humans just had that much more variation in size, rather than some of them were still basically kids.

Sharp kids. Even Uly wasn't much older than Sterling.

Just how dangerous could Humans be, when they got out into the wider galaxy in significant numbers?

*Corsac Fox* joined up with the rest of the universe and all the stars were back.

Uly pointed a finger at him.

"*Z'Gosza* Station, this is Rabiu Khadijan, aboard *Corsac Fox*," he announced. "Please contact Factor Bitrus and let him know that we have arrived."

Three days was long enough warning, right?

Rabiu held his public face perfectly bland, but let his eyes stray to the readout of local space. All the usual stations, each of them armed enough to threaten any pirate wanting to attack. And he'd already transmitted home the stack of mistakes that *Lacium* had made.

How had they managed to stay in business as long as they had? That had been the surprise.

Anybody could have attacked, any time they wanted, and taken the place. Hell, a Striker-class warship could have crushed everything in orbit of *Lacium,* then blown the station up without getting his scales out of alignment.

Why hadn't anybody ever tried?

But Rabiu knew the answer to that.

Factor Bitrus had made an example of *Lacium* because his organization—and his allies—didn't trade with those pirates.

*Those* pirates.

Rabiu hadn't been senior enough to know which pirates Bitrus's other departments did trade with. And he was utterly certain that they did, just from the number of Khet from *Z'Gosza* that had been swept up in Uly's net. Granted, this region of space tended to be heavily Khet already, but still...

Factor Bitrus appeared on the main screen. Rabiu assumed that his former boss—*Former? Already?*—would see the bridge as it had been before, since Drew was on *Khile Heavy* and Solomon Wyndham and the two Emro women were on each of the cargo carriers with their security teams.

"Good afternoon, sir," Rabiu said cheerily. "As noted, and as assigned, we have been successful at *Lacium* and the *Corsac Fox* has returned with several vessels that need to be processed by the Admiralty Court. I hope that you have had time to review all of my various reports?"

He'd sent a couple of sets over the last month. It had been the most recent one that he'd considered a bombshell. The one where he told them that Uly was coming.

Bitrus looked old, there on the screen. Rabiu didn't have a better way to phrase it, and certainly would never say it to the Khet's face, but he'd spent a lot of time around Khet troopers who were used to excessive physical activity on a daily basis.

And even then, Dan and her folks had raised the bar on the mercenaries. In a good way.

"We have," Bitrus said in a careful voice. "How quickly were you intending to move?"

"We're still on the schedule I transmitted in my executive summary, sir," Rabiu said, smiling but unbending. "*Scavenger Angel* and the other vessels have prize crews aboard. *Compass Rose* is an ally, an Ononguli vessel that is under hire by the *Corsac Fox* at present. We'd like to place the argosy into orbit, then file our claims. *Scavenger Angel* has a new owner already lined up, and he is intending to take possession as-is, but the others will need to go through full maritime inspections before they can be properly valued subsequent for sale on the open market."

*Khile Heavy*, though Rabiu knew that Uly would be careful who he sold that one to. One Striker-sized cargo vessel excellent for delivering goods to any medium-sized world, plus a couple of tramps that could make high-speed runs to various destinations, or do deliveries to mining colonies or small places that didn't have much cash to import most goods.

Something changed in Bitrus's face. It went from contained to closed, though Rabiu guessed that nobody but a corporate Khet might have noticed.

He'd spent his entire career after university working for this Khet's organization. Working his way up. And he was about to chuck it all out the window?

Was this what a mid-life crisis tasted like?

Certainly, he felt fifty kilograms lighter today instead of the twenty he'd actually lost.

Freedom.

Running away with pirates? Who'd have ever imagined that about Rabiu Khadijan? Maybe he'd make it back to one of his reunions, one of these days, with *stories…*

Still, Bitrus nodded.

"I'm looking forward to your most up-to-date memorandum, Khadijan," the Factor said. "I will notify the local authorities to handle everything."

The line went dead, just like that.

Rabiu was sitting not far from Dan. She turned to him with one eyebrow raised.

Khet didn't have hair. It had taken him a bit to understand how Humans communicated so many things with the hair on their heads or faces.

Skeptical. He agreed.

"That was interesting," she observed neutrally.

"I might have let a few things slip accidentally," Rabiu replied. It had been accidental, right?

"Oh?"

Rabiu noted all the faces turned his way. Plus a camera, recording everything, but Shehu and the others had determined that there was so much more they needed to film about the *Corsac Fox*, if they could arrange the funding. Unless Uly was planning on hiring them directly after this?

There would be the first three-hour documentary being shopped to local video markets as soon as Uly gave them permission. He and Dan had approved the footage, laughing out loud in places when they'd watched it. Shehu had a great eye for framing images, but Sani and Bello had really turned it into entertainment.

"My vocabulary might have been a bit off, from what he was expecting," Rabiu nodded, first to Dan, then to Uly. "I spoke of filing *our* claims for the ships, rather than Uly filing *his*. I suppose that means that I would like to quit my current job and enlist with you, if I may. You obviously need a business development manager handling things around here, though I don't think I've done too bad a job at it at *Lacium*."

"You've done excellent work, Rabiu," Uly said. The others chimed in with welcoming sounds. "Would they let you quit like that?"

Rabiu nodded, understanding the gist of the concern.

"They might object, but then they'd have to kidnap me or something," Rabiu admitted. "I've had more fun over the last two months than I've had in years and years."

"Let's see how they respond when we're over there," Dan interjected. "It may be that they prefer having one of their agents aboard, as we move forward. I'd hate to have you burn your bridges before you had to."

It took him a moment to parse that out of Human. Burn bridges? Oh, cut a canal. Similar, he thought.

And he had so much to learn about his new friends.

Friends. That was it.

Rabiu Khadijan had been hard-pressed to name friends. He had business associates. Underlings. Bosses. Competitors for promotions and bonuses.

He couldn't remember sitting around and drinking tea with folks while talking about mundane things.

And he wasn't about to give that up.

Dan saw something in his face, because she turned to Uly and nodded. He smiled, and Rabiu relaxed some.

There was still this fish ladder to run, but he could see a happier future ahead of him.

# SIXTY-NINE

"*Corsac Fox*, this is *Compass Rose*," Lukyan said over the secured argosy channel that that damned Mazhin had insisted on setting up.

Lukyan supposed that it was revenge for being able to activate Ononguli command circuits that those other folks hadn't known about at the time. Haydar was still a little salty about that. Roshan had ripped whole chunks of software out so that he could understand how it was done and cut in overrides.

The clan elders might get a little pissy later, but Lukyan was pretty sure he'd be betting on Uly anyway. Especially after watching the Human work for a month.

And the team he'd assembled, which looked like it might include at least half of the Khet gunners. And a lot of Khet troopers, though *Lacium* had hired a chunk by offering land on the surface to build homesteads on. Lots of rivers and waterfront down there, which was what had attracted the Khet in the first place, over and above the great spot close to several trade routes.

How many of those trade corridors might shift over to include a place like *Lacium*, if they stayed cleaned up? Hell of a lot of money for the merchants if they did.

Uly'd slipped at one point and noted that interesting point in a meeting, surprising folks who hadn't planned far enough ahead.

Lukyan wasn't sure many people could keep up with the *Corsac Fox*.

"This is Uly," came the comm reply. "What's your status, Lukyan?"

"Since we're all friends now, I was planning to swing by *Scavenger Angel* and pick up Maks, then rendezvous with you," Lukyan replied. "Thanks for letting me borrow Michaels to get things in order. I'd personally rather be in friendly company when we meet the locals. I know you've said that they'll honor your agreements, but there might still be a few warrants out."

"Understood," Uly said with an easy laugh. "Looking forward to it. Hopefully, I can get you folks on your way in a few days."

Lukyan didn't say anything. Normally, something like that would take the merchants of a place like *Z'Gosza* months to sort out.

Just like however long those yahoos had expected Uly to be bottled up at *Lacium*.

They really had no clue, did they?

"I should be aboard in an hour," Lukyan said.

"Excellent news," Uly replied. "I'll have Vahid make us something special for dinner."

Lukyan cut the line and found his mouth watering at the thought. That Mazhin knew how to cook. And understood Ononguli cuisine.

Khet tended to like fish and sea vegetables. Humans were omnivorous.

Ononguli liked meat. And there had been enough herds of things down on *Lacium* proper to restock larders, when Lukyan hadn't had to pay for it. Or buy the bad cuts and old stuff because funds were tight.

And *Corsac Fox* had done even better in that department.

Lukyan rose and smiled at the universe. Uly hadn't even ripped his horns out when he'd read that package that Ononguli conductors had to swear to. Hadn't accepted it fully, but the Human had started behaving more like an Ononguli pirate.

Or at least one that had seen the light. Something.

There hadn't been any other Tuesdays after that. Lukyan wasn't sure if that was good or bad.

Certainly, there was a new galaxy busy being born.

"Oskar, you're in charge," he said as he started aft, "but do whatever Huff or Roscoe order."

"No worries there, boss," Oskar replied.

Dmytro was commanding the cargo beast nearby. Maks was on *Scavenger Angel*. They'd probably be able to add to the combined, permanent crew from the Ononguli he'd hired on *Lacium*, assuming he could get another handful or so from *Z'Gosza*.

Still, how many of them had *misunderstandings*, ex-wives, or blood duels waiting if they ever went home?

And yet, Lukyan was going home anyway. This was too damned big.

The shuttle wasn't full. He'd put his foot down after he'd gotten his dorks to clean it. Uly had had things brought out of storage, but *Scavenger Angel* had been stripped down at *Lacium* and prepped for a long, fast sail home. All they had to do was haul a couple of big shipping containers directly over from *Corsac Fox* and load up consumables for the run.

The trip to get Maks over didn't take long. Didn't even land. Just mated airlocks and Lukyan smiled at the kid as he came aboard.

"Being a conductor looks good on you," Lukyan told his friend, studying him closely as they backed away and got in motion.

"Feels like a twenty-kilo backpack I'm carrying around, everywhere I go," Maks replied.

"Oh, it is," Lukyan agreed. "And it never gets any lighter. But the benefits are pretty good. And you'll be able to either keep *Scavenger Angel* or trade for something better when we get home."

"You're really letting me be in charge of all that?" Maks asked.

"Maks, the various clan elders are likely to get a little ugly when all the news gets out," Lukyan said. "I might get cashiered and grounded, depending on how they feel about what I've done out here. Won't know until I see them. You were ready for your own command, we just hadn't taken anything with the right kind of crew to set you up."

"You do realize that Uly doesn't believe that a crew should all be one species, right?" Maks scowled at him.

"I do," Lukyan agreed. "However, with most pirates, that's generally been standard operating procedure for for eons. Or you get a scratch crew made up of whoever you could recruit, and those take forever to gel. All-Ononguli means that we have something extra binding us. You have the same, as soon as we offload the Khet security troopers that got you this far and lose whoever decides to quit."

"We recruiting on *Z'Gosza*?" Maks asked as the shuttle came about and started forward.

"Assuming they let us," Lukyan nodded. "And only Ononguli, because that's our next stop."

"What if others want to come see the Endless Plains?" Maks asked.

And that, right there, was the nightmare that most commonly kept Lukyan up at nights.

The Ononguli Sphere was just that. Ononguli. There were many worlds with mixed populations in there, but all bent the neck to the clan elders of the Sphere. Period. And they weren't all that common, because the Sphere had never fostered outsiders coming in to set up colonies.

But Uly would have to come at some point. Humans were too far away to come with him, beyond his current crew, but Mazhin? Emro? Thogin?

Who else would want to come to the Sphere? Maybe live there? Who else might join Uly on his grand adventure, if he did have to come talk to the old farts on Rayzian?

"Maks, that's why I put you in command of your own ship," Lukyan finally said. "Uly is a grass fire, but nobody knows how much wind, rain, or mountains will shape his impact."

"Big?"

Lukyan shrugged.

"Out of my hands," he offered. "You pay attention and learn. This is the future. When nobody was looking, it went ahead and arrived. Trying to keep it from breaking my horns off going forward."

He noted the shudder that passed through Maks's frame.

There wasn't much he could do about it.

Too much depended on Uly.

# SEVENTY

Uly had gone ahead and met Lukyan and Maks when they docked. A month had turned them from nervous strangers to folks you told dirty jokes to, once you sorted out the cultural idioms. And Uly was getting pretty good at that, as well.

Those two were also comfortable around his people. It showed in their smiles when they boarded, so different from the hard-ass pirates like Adrian Sobol or his pet killer, Ruvim Boyko.

Uly still owed that one a blood debt. Maybe he'd get a chance to collect it, one of these days, assuming the Auga didn't do it for him.

Still, friends.

"Welcome aboard," Uly said, shaking hands with both of them.

They were on his ship. They could adapt to Human customs, as opposed to the occasional Ononguli thing of throwing your head back to show that you weren't threatening someone with your horns.

Weird, but it worked.

Dan led them into a dining hall and got folks settled. Minus the various security officers currently supervising the rest of the argosy, all the key players were present. Him and Dan. Haydar, Piruz, and Nasrin. Suka Kuri. Ethir and Waltin, with the latter really being the smartest of the four, but almost as lazy as Hobse. Waltin would have had his pointed nose in a book. Rabiu, still representing the Khet of *Z'Gosza* until he quit or got fired.

Lukyan and Maks got seated in a way that the camera was generally looking at the backs of heads. Not to obscure their faces, but neither were excited to be filmed and it let Uly sit directly across from them to talk, with everyone else down both sides of the long table filling in spaces.

Vahid and folks began filling water glasses and delivering steaming, fresh bread.

Occasionally, Uly wondered what would happen when he forgot what Human food tasted like. It would probably be a slow process, until he managed to get home and nothing tasted right.

Assuming he ever got home.

The jury was still out on that, beyond the desire to let his family know he'd made it. And Dan's and the others.

"How's Emil doing?" Maks asked as they sat.

"Learning to walk again," Dan replied. "He's stable for now, but that stump needs to heal before he exercises much. Not that he'll listen to the doctors."

Khet medics, getting a crash course in Human medicine as they had to cut off Emil's leg just below the knee, once it became clear that the bones had all been too badly mangled to ever heal properly. As it was, they'd barely kept sepsis from setting in and killing the man, even as tough as Emil was.

Eventually, Uly had heard Dan explain to the medics what an osteointegrated implant was, where a big screw was driven into bone, then left to extend beyond the skin, where mechanical parts could be attached later. Like a lower leg. The problem was that they had to do a lot of work to the shin bones to get them to a point where that could happen.

Emil Beranger had never been one to lay in bed, even when it had been necessary to heal. At least the burns and the rest of the cracked or broken bones had been largely fixed.

"Normally, I'd expect a pirate injured that badly to retire," Lukyan began. "But where would he go?"

"He'll stay with us for as long as he wants," Uly said before Dan could answer. "Then, if he wants to leave, he'll tell us where we're dropping him off."

Simple as that. Emil Beranger hadn't made many demands, going all the way back to the first moment Uly had laid eyes on him, in the airlock before heading across to *King Hewitt II*. In fact, Uly was more worried about Gennady Travers, losing his best friend and sidekick.

Uly could see both of them retiring together and buying a bar somewhere, except that most species out here didn't drink alcohol. And he didn't see them happy with a tea room or coffee shop.

Still, Emil and Gennady would decide their own fate.

Dan smiled compactly at him and nodded. Those two men had earned that, at a dead minimum.

And if they could machine him the right parts for his leg, Emil might return to duty in six months, likely with an even bigger chip on his shoulder.

Food started being delivered. As usual with meetings like this, several bowls of things ranging across cuisines and spice levels, so that folks could serve themselves from a common trough and enjoy. Meat in a brownish sauce over pasta tonight. Or whatever the equivalent Ononguli foods were.

Vahid, taking extra special care of Lukyan and Maks.

*Lacium* could have gone a different way, but for *Compass Rose*. Haydar's assessment was that *Corsac Fox* would have still won the battle, but they would have had to annihilate at least three more pirate vessels and crews to make their point, plus risk excessive damage themselves.

Instead, *Compass Rose* had knocked everyone else over into surrendering.

And saving lives, which was really what Uly wanted out of all this.

Dead folks never got a chance to turn over a new leaf and make themselves something better than they'd been yesterday. Like the two pirates across the table from him right now.

Plus the Auga were coming for everyone, eventually. Pirates preying on shipping was too much like fools fighting in a burning house.

So Uly ate and watched all of his new friends enjoy themselves, asking questions, offering sarcastic replies.

Having fun.

"What about Factor Bitrus?" Lukyan asked Rabiu between courses. "Will he really follow Uly's lead and let us get away with everything we've been up to?"

"I specifically haven't asked you, Lukyan," Rabiu replied. "As a result, I have no idea if anyone from *Z'Gosza* was paying you under the table, or merely buying stolen goods cheaper than they could have bought them legitimately."

Lukyan started to reply, but Rabiu held up a hand.

"And don't tell me," he said sharply. "Ever. That was the past. Uly and Dan are the future. We'll talk about ways to get rich saving the galaxy, instead of preying on it, okay?"

Uly was impressed. Rabiu really had changed sides.

"I have a question for you, Conductor Chayka," Waltin, of all people, spoke up, yelling somewhat down the table as he had a high, reedy voice that carried well, but didn't have a lot of mass to it.

Still, folks quieted down and turned to the normally quiet Thogin. Waltin blushed furiously and grimaced, but nodded to himself.

"Call me Lukyan."

"Lukyan. I've been reading the paperwork you sent over for Uly," Waltin continued. "We all have. I appreciate that you plan to induct Uly into the Ononguli Horde at some point, but you can't, really. Not the way things are written down."

"Why not?" Lukyan asked, confused.

Uly noted that he wasn't the only one leaned in and silent, all pretense of eating gone as Waltin held their attention. But Uly had some really sharp folks on his team. Most commanders forgot to listen to their experts.

Waltin blushed some more, then nodded again. Working himself up to talking to strangers? He'd always been the quiet one.

"He's not Ononguli," Waltin finally blurted out. "All of your everything includes references back to his family, clan, and tribe, making oaths and promises based on blood ties that bind laterally and enforce behavior as part of that larger group. He doesn't have those. Not to you. Any relationship you have with him will have to be at the national level, like we're establishing with *Z'Gosza* and *Lacium*."

Uly nodded. He'd heard his experts, most of the folks at the table, point out many of those details. Then scratch their heads at how the Ononguli intended to finesse them.

"Agreed," Lukyan replied. "If I thought I could manage it, I'd ask Uly to send a diplomat of some sort home with Maks and I, but I also understand that you don't have excess people you trust like that. Not today. Maybe not for years, as you build up your crew and staff."

"Oh, but I do," Uly said, smiling as the two Ononguli's faces twisted in confusion, horns nearly tangling as they spun around. And the rest of the table.

"Who?" Maks asked, when the room fell to a silence so heavy Uly could hear the life support blowers running.

"You and Lukyan," Uly said.

"WHAT?"

Uly liked how they both managed to be in perfect harmony when they said that. He let the noise fall some before trying to talk over everyone else having opinions.

In fact, he took a sip of wine to get them to shut up. It worked.

"You, Lukyan," Uly finally continued. "And your new squadron associate, Maks Sobol. You two will go tell the Clan Elders who I am. What I'm up to. How they can come over here to talk to me and make treaties. I've asked, and none of my current Ononguli crew wish to return to the Sphere with you. In fact, a few Ononguli locals have asked if they could join my crew, but I've put them off until you got a chance to talk to them, because I can always hire Khet or Ugotha or others, as I need. *Compass Rose* and *Scavenger Angel* have all-Ononguli crews."

He paused. The way their mouths worked, open and close again, looked more like the Khet than anything.

"Me?" Lukyan finally managed.

"You will be my messenger to the Ononguli," Uly nodded serenely. "My ambassador, if you will, but at a minimum you can carry a packet home with you that will explain."

"What if they demand you come to Rayzian?" he asked.

"Let them," Uly said. "I am a Human. This is a Human ship, regardless of who built it or who I stole it from. They can ask. They cannot order. Keep that in mind."

He caught Dan's sharp nod from the corner of his eye. And he had a growing legend to keep up and build.

He was the *Corsac Fox*, regardless of it technically being the name of the ship.

Maks started to say something, but Lukyan put a hand on his friend's arm.

"No, he's right, Maks," Lukyan said. "We're a long ways from the Sphere. We chose that for our own reasons, and nothing less than the *Corsac Fox* would have convinced me to return to Rayzian anyway. You know that."

Maks subsided. The room deflated some. Lukyan turned to Uly again.

"Now what?" he asked.

"Now?" Uly asked. "We eat as friends. Tomorrow, we go talk to the Factor, then start getting these ships condemned for sale, so that you and Maks can load up cargo and start the run home in a few days."

"Just like that?" Lukyan asked, shock evident in spite of all the planning they'd done.

"Just like that," Uly nodded.

## SEVENTY-ONE

Uly looked around at his escorts as the shuttle docked.

As before, Dan had taken charge and brought Nasrin, Yanouk, Anari, and Katya. Piruz had come, but Haydar had begged off. Rabiu was present. Ethir and Waltin were back with Haydar, on the bridge.

Lukyan and Maks looked more like men walking to their own hanging, but Uly smiled as the shuttle's airlock hatch opened.

Dan rose and went first. Because Dan. Uly waited. He was in charge of the mission, but she was running the operation of getting him into a meeting with Factor Bitrus and whoever else.

Outside, they met Director Bukra, surrounded by a small staff of folks that Uly generally recognized, but could not immediately name. Not exactly flunkies, but assistants, Deputies, and other Administrators that had been brought along to handle things.

Dan was armed. Her people were armed. The bureaucrats stirred uncomfortably, but were not armed. That was good.

It wasn't that Uly didn't trust these people. After all, he had signed contracts with them, and that was the highest form of civilization possible to the Factors of *Z'Gosza*.

There were, however, any number of places where things were open to *interpretation*. That Bitrus or one of the others might end up paying significant damages for violating such agreements, like destroying *Corsac Fox* or one of the other ships, might come down to ledger entries on quarterly profit and loss statements.

So Uly wasn't taking any chances. Nor were Haydar or Sterling or the others.

Uly supposed that it would come across as arrogant, but he really didn't care at this point. He had a deal with these folks. They would execute it.

Or courts would intervene.

Dan and the Khet led him to a side room with a long table bisecting it. Uly found it informative that Factor Bitrus stood at the center of the far side. Director Bukra moved to the high end. Uly stood across from the Factor.

Rabiu stayed next to Uly. Headcrests went up when the locals processed that bit.

"Factor Bitrus," Uly said quietly. "Thank you for taking this meeting. As early investors in the project, I think you will be exceptionally well disposed to show a significant profit from the outcome, as well as greatly reduced operating expenses in certain market segments, going forward."

Ethir's words, polished by Rabiu and Haydar.

Uly wasn't entirely sure what he was saying, as it was so close to a foreign language to him. *Batyr* society didn't do profit and loss. They did a socialization that meant the greatest good for the greatest number of people, while not allowing injury to the minorities left over.

Profit and loss were numbers, not career-making outcomes.

Certainly, Bitrus hadn't been expecting it. He shook his head slightly, as though Dan had reached across the table and slapped the Khet.

Then Bitrus smiled. It almost felt genuine, but Uly had seen the change that had come over Rabiu lately to see the difference.

"Please," Bitrus declaimed. "Let us sit!"

Uly did quickly, allowing his host to go last. And most important.

At least until the Admiralty Court got involved and folks started seeing the potential returns for pirate-hunting.

Uly wondered if Factor Bitrus had started the process of extracting his fins from whatever elements of the pirate trade his organization and allies had gotten into before the *Corsac Fox* had come along.

Or had he been expecting to have a year to get his shit together?

Uly smiled.

"I have been following your reports, *Corsac Fox*," Bitrus said as everyone got settled, Uly and his on this side of the table, a school of businesskhet over there. "You expect to move quickly?"

"I believe that we can file an initial report with the Court tomorrow," Uly said simply. "As *Scavenger Angel* is being bought as-is, no formal inspections will be needed. Merely a court-ordered Adjudication of Ownership, as detailed in the original treaty. The other vessels will obviously require longer, as some of them may be technically owned by insurance brokers who previously paid out claims and wish to challenge things in local courts. However, I am given to understand that none of my current argosy were ever chartered or insured out of *Z'Gosza*."

Because Rabiu had pointed that tidbit out earlier. Ethir and Haydar had then gone over all the potential cargo carriers and pirates to specifically exclude the ones that might cause trouble here.

He'd let *Lacium* nationalize those vessels instead. Out of his hands. Poof. Go ask them and stop bothering me.

Again, the big fish over there looked like he'd run into a door accidentally. Uly's smile never wavered. Then the Factor's eyes got cagey and he turned to Maks.

"Maks Sobol, new Conductor of *Scavenger Angel* and relative of the famous Adrian Sobol?" Bitrus asked.

"That is correct, Factor Bitrus," Maks replied with a polite nod.

Uly and Lukyan had drilled him to keep things short, honest, and neutral.

"How do you feel about working with an enemy of your family?" Bitrus asked.

Uly saw Lukyan tense, but nobody else reacted. Not yet. Both sides, it seemed, had fallen into stillness.

Maks laughed.

"I'd rather be on the winning side, sir," he said with a grin. "If Adrian ever gets out of prison, I suspect he'll be the same way."

Well, that was one way to deflate a bout of pomposity. Factor Bitrus visibly shrank in reaction.

Obviously, he'd been hoping to split Uly's team up.

Dumb-ass, but Uly wasn't about to say that to him.

Uly made a note to inquire with Rabiu later. If he understood local culture well enough, Director Bukra might be Factor Bukra soon. And if Bitrus overplayed his hand right now and Uly got pissy about things, Bukra might take Bitrus's slot.

Uly rescued Bitrus instead of letting him founder.

"Just as you and your people have been on my side from the beginning, Factor," Uly reminded the Khet, gesturing to Rabiu. "Administrator Khadijan has been most helpful to date and I was hoping that you might see fit to keep him aboard my vessel as a liaison, although it might be more appropriate to classify him as an Ambassador going forward, citing sections eleven, thirteen, fourteen, and twenty-five of the original treaty."

Lots of twitches over there. Only one quiet Khet, down at the low end of the table, who nodded to himself. Probably the lawyer who had memorized the contract. Possibly almost as well as Ethir and Waltin had.

Almost.

Even Rabiu had blinked at that, but he'd been all set to quit the office in order to go be a pirate.

Might as well get paid for it. Uly didn't want to burn Factor Bitrus or up-and-coming Factor Bukra. Keeping one of their allies on his crew would help.

"Ambassador?" Bukra asked, when it became clear that Bitrus had possibly been struck mute.

"Indeed, sir," Uly smiled, turning that way. "The act of filing a claim in Admiralty Court on *Z'Gosza* functionally activates the full treaty, wherein *Z'Gosza* recognizes me as head of state of a foreign nation, just as I have done at *Lacium*. I'm not certain when I will be ready to open an embassy here, but that is no reason not to have an ambassador from *Z'Gosza* involved."

"Like you did at *Lacium*?" Bukra asked, his voice slowed and choppy as he processed the words coming out of his own mouth.

"Yes," Uly said. "After I identified the new government that would be taking power at *Lacium*, I provided them a copy of the same treaty, modifying basically only dates, names, and locations, then signing and executing it before I left *Lacium*."

"You didn't conquer *Lacium*?" Bitrus asked now, still a little off.

"Correct," Uly nodded. "I captured it, liberating that system from the pirates that had previously been holding it. As no representatives of the overthrown government could be located, I assisted the locals in establishing a new one. Their new Admiralty Court condemned a handful of the vessels I had captured when the pirates surrendered, and they are building out a small patrol force designed to keep piracy from returning."

He paused. The many Khet over there had all been stunned mute. All except that one lawyer. He spoke up now.

"Conductor, am I correct in understanding that you have fully executed a functionally identical treaty with the authorities at *Lacium*?" the Khet asked.

"You are correct," Uly said, smiling to take the sting out of the mousetrap.

*Z'Gosza* could deal with *Scavenger Angel* and the others, or Uly could immediately return to *Lacium* for them to handle it instead. And the profits. And Uly's goodwill.

Lots of potential profits, possibly accruing to merchants somewhere else.

Rabiu was a cold-hearted fish when he wanted to be. Putting him together with Haydar and Ethir was possibly a bad idea, but only for Uly's enemies. The three of them had cooked up the entire scheme while Uly was still busy sorting out the captured pirates with Dan.

*Fait accompli.* The best kind of surprise.

"Factor Bitrus, I highly recommend that we bring to bear whatever pressures we might leverage, to get *Scavenger Angel* processed as quickly as possible," the lawyer said, turning to his ultimate boss with such utter sincerity that everyone looked over.

Uly nodded. That one got it. He nodded back. The others would figure it out.

Uly wasn't going to play any games here. Bitrus and his allies could help, right now, or hinder. Attempt to hinder. They could not stop the *Corsac Fox*, short of killing him and destroying whatever goodwill they might have ever earned along the way.

Contract law was a religion on *Z'Gosza*.

Bitrus blinked and nodded. Bukra stepped in. Factor-in-Training?

"Conductor Fortier," Bukra said. "There have been a few questions about your argosy. Minor ones, obviously. Perhaps well beneath your notice, but we happen to have you handy and your staff could provide the best clarifications going forward so perhaps now would be the most excellent time to inquire?"

Uly nodded. He had a team of deadly women, most of whom were at least as smart as the men he'd left behind. And he could always get Haydar and Ethir on the comm if he needed something legally arcane looked up.

"*Scavenger Angel* has a new owner already lined up?" Bukra asked.

"Conductor Maks Sobol," Uly nodded to his new friend. "He will hold a controlling interest in the corporate entity purchasing the vessel, using sweat equity and certain other valuable considerations, while I retain a passive, minority stake."

Again, words that were like arcane totems one chanted to ward off bad luck, but they seemed to resonate with the Khet. Because they used *certain other valuable considerations* almost as religiously in negotiating their own deals.

"What of *Khile Heavy*?" Bukra asked. "That vessel is perhaps better known in the region than the former *Iron Wasp* was, if such a thing is possible."

"It is my hope that a trusted entity on *Z'Gosza* makes an offer for the vessel, once I have free and clear ownership established," Uly replied.

"What are your intentions for it?" Bukra asked, causing many of the others to gasp.

Uly supposed that such a question might normally take thirty minutes of arcane maneuvering. At least in the old days.

*Z'Gosza* was changing, just not as fast as Rabiu Khadijan had. Same direction, though.

Better.

"I would like the vessel to fulfill one of two roles," Uly said. "Perhaps both, if possible."

"Those being?"

"Anti-piracy patrols, in the manner than *Corsac Fox* has undertaken," Uly nodded. "At the same time, it is heavily armed enough to be a useful warship, if *Z'Gosza* were to start the process of building up a formal navy, rather than the assorted civilian mercenaries your various conglomerates currently employ."

"Why?" Bukra asked. "Why would we need that?"

"Because Auga is coming," Uly replied. "Not tomorrow. Not next year. But one of these days. Already, they press against the border of the Ononguli Sphere, slowly pushing the Horde back. They will not be satisfied until they have conquered the galaxy. I intend to stop them."

"You?" Bukra asked.

"Me," Uly agreed. "And my friends. I have been in an Auga holding facility. Their idea of justice is a bureaucratic thing, where I would have been thrown in prison as a pirate, for having been captured by pirates and being a prisoner on their ship. For the Auga, the letter of the law is the only thing they worship. Not right and wrong, but law and process. And they will not accept it when a society decides not to voluntarily join the empire. Your histories have shown that all will be absorbed and assimilated before the Auga, regardless. They do not believe in freedom. Nor do pirates who deal in slaves, my friends. Those will be stopped as well, and the slaves freed. Period. I will not bend on that, so perhaps others should be notified that certain things are no longer acceptable."

Uly stopped there and drew a hard, silent breath. These Khet were capitalists, but he couldn't hold that against them. They had been raised poorly, putting the benefit of the individual over that of the broader society, which history had shown caused so many civilizations to eventually collapse.

Uly couldn't save the galaxy. He wouldn't live long enough.

He could still try.

Dan glanced over and he caught her smile. Just like that, half the weight of his day vanished off his shoulders, as if dew burning off.

Around him, his other friends smiled slowly as well. Across the table, it spread, finally capturing Bukra and then Bitrus after infecting the rest one by one.

"How can we help?" Factor Bitrus asked after a stretch of intense silence.

"Spread the word," Uly replied.

# SEVENTY-TWO

Lukyan sat between Maks and Uly. He'd luckily never been in a Khet courtroom. And certainly not a Probate Court. That was normally where you went when wills and last directives needed to be assessed by a neutral party, because bad blood in the family had twisted things around. Just look at him and his oldest brother, Bohdan.

No, Criminal Court would have been where they'd have tried Lukyan around here, except that he was now a valuable and lauded ally of the *Corsac Fox*. More than one random stranger had reached out to the ship, just in the last two days, with offers of just about anything he needed, from companionship all the way up to an interior decorator offering to redo *Compass Rose* as a mobile advertising platform for his services.

*Z'Gosza* was weird, but he could honestly say that once they made up their minds to do a thing, the wheels of commerce got greased and rolling quickly.

Lukyan turned and looked over at Uly's Khet Business Manager. And Ambassador. And potential right hand, at least in this system. Rabiu Khadijan smiled back at him, then a door opened and a bailiff entered.

"All rise," the Khet said.

Lukyan rose. As did everyone else.

The judge was an older Khet. Short and almost round, even for that kind. Hallmarks of great age in the way his headcrest was graying and extra spiky.

The Khet paused, just inside the door. Mostly a stutter in his step, before turning and crossing to his bench.

"This Court is now in session," the bailiff continued. "The Honorable Justice Soun presiding."

Judge Soun gaveled once, wood on wood with a sharp crack,

"Be seated," he said in a surprisingly strong voice. "This court will come to order."

Lukyan was at the center of a small mob, but it was Uly's mob. Dan and her warrior women. A Mazhin, two giant Emro, and a female Ononguli who had no interest in men at all or in transferring to his or Maks's ship to return to the Sphere.

Nobody was armed here except for the bailiff and a pair of guards quietly watching from the front corners of the room.

Judge Soun took a moment to review a small computer tablet on his desk. The court reporter sat poised to record and correct. The civilians at the low end of the room hardly breathed, from the lack of sound.

And the place was utterly packed. Uly, Haydar, Ethir, Waltin, and Rabiu, poised for business in the same manner that Dan and her team seemed ready to storm the bench unarmed.

Maks had definitely been right. It was so much better to be on the winning side of things.

"In the matter of the *Corsac Fox* versus the unknown owners of the vessel *Scavenger Angel*," Judge Soun announced, looking up finally and zeroing in on Uly like a turret. "Are the litigants present?"

Uly rose slowly. Came to rest, feet shoulder-width apart and hands crossed behind his back.

"*Corsac Fox* is present, Your Honor," he said.

"*Scavenger Angel*?" Soun asked.

Nobody. Lukyan wasn't surprised. It had, as near as Maks had been able to tell from old log entries, never previously been within forty light-years of *Z'Gosza*. And everything around Uly happened faster than most people could process, so whoever might have a claim probably wouldn't hear the news for a year.

Too late by then.

"Are there no ownership representatives of the vessel *Scavenger Angel* present?" Soun asked again. "*Corsac Fox*, you will take your table as a litigant."

Uly moved. Rabiu went with him, along with a Khet lawyer they had dug up from somewhere. Lukyan didn't ask, because he didn't expect to spend much time around here in the future.

Hopefully, the Clan Elders wouldn't send him right back. Except that them doing so kept him away from Bohdan, as well as Nadiya and all her issues.

Okay, maybe not such a bad outcome, after all.

Lukyan watched on tenterhooks, just like everyone else in the room. He'd read the treaties that had been signed. Insane, but at the end of the day, Lukyan didn't think he'd ever seen a better way to gaff a businesskhet and drag him into helping you do something.

The judge studied Uly as the three of them got settled.

"I have a note here that you are properly addressed as Ulysses Fortier," Soun said. "Conductor of the vessel named *Corsac Fox*. However, I have also watched the same documentary that I'm certain a sizeable minority of the system population watched last night, wherein you are generally called the *Corsac Fox* as a personal moniker?"

"That is correct, Your Honor," Uly replied. "That nickname has grown far larger than it should have, to the point that it is truly a case of mistaken identity. However, it works for my purposes."

"And those are?" Soun asked. "No, hold that. Bailiff, you will swear the plaintiff in."

Lukyan had wondered if the judge would forget process. This was a new thing, and Lukyan supposed that Probate Court didn't tend to be as formal as criminal proceedings.

The bailiff Khet got Uly on a raised chair, turned sideways to the room so he could address both the court and whoever might have shown up to argue. They had some weird holy tome that Lukyan suspected was an Introduction to Business textbook. Or the equivalent.

Z'Goszans got a little weird on the topic.

"Do you swear to tell the truth, the whole truth, and nothing but the truth?" the bailiff asked.

"I do," Uly replied.

The whole courtroom sighed together, just loud enough to be audible and cause the judge to look this way sternly.

Then silence fell.

"Conductor Fortier," Judge Soun said. "*Corsac Fox*. We were discussing your purposes before this court. Could you summarize for the gallery?"

Lukyan watched a change come over Uly. He was really still a kid. Junior officer barely out of training and showing promise, but Lukyan knew that if he'd been put in the same situation as Uly, he'd probably still be in an Auga jail somewhere. Maks was the same way.

Damn it, pretty much everybody he knew would have failed at some point.

How had the kid managed?

Then the charisma turned on, and Lukyan finally understood.

Uly could make you believe. Had. Changing sides had been Lukyan's idea originally, because he'd mistaken *Corsac Fox* for *Iron Wasp*.

It was still a good idea.

"Piracy is a problem in this region," Uly stated simply, turning to talk to all the Khet hanging on his words. And any of them who would watch this on video later. "It offends me, because such a thing represents the myriad failures of the societies in question, to have allowed such a thing to happen."

Lukyan found himself leaning forward with the rest of them.

"When I broke out of an Auga prison and stole a warship from them, I had only a few options before me," Uly continued. The room gasped, in spite of watching him talk about it on the vid last night with maybe a billion of their closest neighbors. "We subsequently stole from them a laden cargo carrier, which gave us the ability to not have to immediately start attacking Khet shipping. Or Ononguli. Or Ugotha. Or anyone else. Only Auga."

Uly paused there and turned briefly back to the judge, waiting for that worthy to nod before continuing.

"In many ways, the Auga are worse than pirates, because they intend to implacably conquer the galaxy," Uly said. "Maybe the entire universe, given time. I believe that most species deserve the right to choose their own destiny, rather than having it imposed on them. I will stop the Auga, if I can. While I am doing that, I needed a base of operations. As such, I could have become another pirate, but that would have involved me continuing to tear down *Z'Goszan* society. And all your trade partners. Or I could come here and offer to hunt pirates for you. To bring a kind of order that allows free beings to live without fear."

Again, that quiet gasp, multiplied by a few hundred mouths. And Lukyan was expecting it. He could still feel Uly's magic engulfing him.

Maks's mouth had fallen entirely open. He wasn't alone there.

"Working with Factor Bitrus and his organization, I have signed such a treaty," Uly nodded, one hand up to include this room. "An Admiralty Court, whose purpose is to adjudicate that my actions are not those of a pirate but those of a mercenary Officer of the Court, stopping pirates. Taking resources away from them in the manner of ships and cargo that fund their activities. I can bring them here, take ownership in a legally recognized manner, and help bring peace and security."

"And the attack on the moorage at *Lacium*?" Judge Soun finally found his voice again.

"Pirates," Uly replied. "A whole nest of them, believing themselves to be above any law. My forces captured those pirates, liberated the merchants of *Lacium*, and hopefully have put them on the path to being trade partners to *Z'Gosza* in the future."

"Which brings us to *Scavenger Angel*," Soun stated.

"It does, Your Honor," Uly agreed.

Lukyan couldn't help but tense. This was the first. Judge Soun had been one of three randomly picked to handle it. Nobody knew how an Admiralty Court was supposed to operate, beyond the letter of the treaty agreement.

The whole audience must have leaned forward, from the way benches squeaked.

"I have read the report you filed, *Corsac Fox*," Judge Soun said. "And watched the interviews with you and Sheridan Chastain. Is she in the audience?"

As if anyone could miss a tall, dark-skinned Human woman, surrounded by outsiders in the front row of the gallery.

"She is," Uly said. "Dan?"

She was just beyond Maks. Her standing caused folks in back to whisper and mutter, a sound like a small avalanche gaining traction.

Judge Soun rapped his hammer hard on the top of his bench. Folks mostly quieted.

"Are you a threat to civilization, Commander Chastain?" Soun asked.

"Only the criminals, Your Honor," she nodded.

The audience sighed again. Uly's magic.

"Conductor Fortier," Soun continued. "*Corsac Fox*. What will you do with *Scavenger Angel*, if it comes legally into your possession?"

Lukyan knew that all of this information was contained in the filing. Judge Soun was playing to the gallery in his own way. Drawing the Khet of *Z'Gosza* along the path Uly and his legal experts had mapped.

"Immediately sell it to Maks Sobol," Uly said, pointing. "While maintaining a minority ownership. He has been hired by me to carry a specific cargo back to the Ononguli Sphere."

"And that cargo is?" Soun pressed.

Lukyan wondered if the Judge was also trying to keep a Tuesday from getting out of hand. He'd been there. It had worked out, but things had been touch and go for a bit.

"*Scavenger Angel* will transport all of the personal effects of the former crew of the vessel *Iron Wasp*," Uly said. "Such were aboard when we took the ship. I want the crew's families to get them, if nothing else, though I am given to understand that most of the crew members will eventually either be traded home for captured Imperial crew members, or serve short sentences and be released. Thus, they can get their memories back when they return home."

Whatever else Uly said was swallowed by the utter eruption of cheers and noise from the audience. Feet stomping. Hands banging on benches or clapping. It was almost painful to hear.

Judge Soun was rapping his gavel hard, but even that made no dent in the noise. Folks were on their feet now. The two guards and the bailiff seemed to be rethinking career choices, visibly worried that the mob was about to swarm forward.

Uly stopped it cold by raising a single hand. At once acknowledging the crowd and asking them to quiet down.

Magic.

Lukyan was happy to be on that winning side. Still.

Judge Soun gaveled once, but it was a formality. Uly was in charge in here.

"The gallery will remain seated and quiet, or I will order it cleared," Soun said simply.

As threats went, Lukyan was hard-pressed to remember one better delivered. Just the right hint of menace in the tones. He'd have to remember it, just in case.

"And after *Scavenger Angel*, *Corsac Fox*?" Judge Soun asked.

"I have several other vessels that were liberated from the pirates," Uly replied. "Those will also be brought before this court. Once ownership is determined, my plan is to sell them on the local starship market, at once expanding the network of cargo vessels and removing threats to it."

"Including the warship *Khile Heavy*?" Soun pressed.

"Including that one, Your Honor," Uly acknowledged. "I do not wish to keep it. To build up a personal warfleet, as many worlds might grow nervous. Instead, my hope is that the government of *Z'Gosza*, like the newly liberated government of *Lacium*, will create their own anti-piracy forces and assist me in hunting down these scourges of civilization. In making the galaxy a better place. And, eventually, being in a position to help resist the Auga, when they come for you. And they will. Maybe not until your grandchildren are dead and forgotten, but nothing so far has stayed their hand."

Judge Soun nodded once, but it had no emotional content. Merely acknowledgment of what Uly had said. The audience was restive, but holding themselves silent and poised. Lukyan could feel the mad energy, bottled up.

Soun looked out over the crowd.

"One last time, are there any ownership representatives of the vessel *Scavenger Angel* present?" he asked.

The crowd held its breath. Lukyan included.

"This Court finds for the plaintiff," Judge Soun gaveled once, a hard crack of sound. "Ownership of the vessel *Scavenger Angel* is ordered transferred to the *Corsac Fox*, with all appropriate levies being paid. This Court is adjourned."

Crack.

# SEVENTY-THREE

Uly looked up when the door chime sounded. It was late in his day and he'd been sitting in his front room, reading reports and sipping some wine.

He rose and answered, trying to judge how critical it was if nobody had called ahead or sounded an alert. Nor waited until tomorrow.

Dan.

He stepped back and gestured her in, returning to his chair and putting the reader down.

She sat and Uly took a moment to study her. Taller, which always surprised him when he stood close to her. Athletic and tough, she outmassed him entirely. But he'd been skinny his whole life.

Afro-Siberian face, with prominent, rounded cheekbones, eyes that came almost to points, and that dark, curly hair.

She smiled. He shared it.

"How are you doing?" Dan asked.

Uly started to shrug, but caught himself. Dan wouldn't be here for a mere social call.

Would she?

"I feel like we've done the impossible, yet again," he replied, feeling his face twist into something that combined a smile with a grimace.

Disbelief, maybe? Lukyan had mentioned, before he'd gone, how amazing he found Uly's luck.

Uly chalked a lot of it up to the amazing woman sitting across from him.

"At the same time, we've executed plans well," he offered. "Got to *Z'Gosza*. Took *Lacium*. Got back here. Maks and Lukyan are safely gone and on their way to the Sphere."

"That's the crew, Uly," she replied. "How are you?"

This time, he did shrug.

"I'm doing the best I can," he told her. "It would be impossible without you and the others. I'm still holding the center. It seems to be holding, but I have no idea what might knock me off-balance. Mostly, I never have time to stop and think about everything that has happened over the last year and a half. Instead, I'm trying to figure out where we need to be a year from now. And how we get there."

"Do you need some leave time?" she asked.

He considered it. Nothing he'd done on *Vanguard Lesauvage* had prepared him for this. And he'd only been on *Marshall Castillon* long enough to settle in and discover how much his peers and superior officers disliked him.

Enough to send him to his death, it seemed.

At the same time, everything had prepared him. Had gotten him here.

He was still making progress.

"I think that not rushing out immediately might be beneficial," he offered. "We've got to sell the other ships, with *Scavenger Angel* taken care of. Folks are offering us credit over and above everything we confiscated at *Lacium*. Plus things we can sell off of *Wren*. Maybe hanging out in the vicinity of *Z'Gosza* and training new crew would be good. How is that going, by the way?"

"Maks and Lukyan took most of the Ononguli that wanted to go," she nodded. "We're interviewing the remainder, but I'm not that hopeful. We'll be able to add a large contingent of Khet, but I intend to do that slowly, so we can break them in properly to how the *Corsac Fox* does things."

He couldn't help the grimace. Even Dan had taken to referring to him as the *Corsac Fox*.

On the one hand, it made a great legend, and recruiting new sailors had been much easier, with so many fired up to serve. On the other hand, he'd never set out to be a hero.

All he'd ever wanted was to serve honorably. Circumstances had conspired against him enough times to have him this many light-centuries from home, with no intention of going back.

"That scowl," Dan pointed out. "That's why I ask."

Uly nodded. Most people weren't sharp enough to read him as well as Dan could. Even Haydar and Nasrin.

"There are days I just want to be Uly," he said. "Not to be The *Corsac Fox*, and all that such a title implies. I'm not sure I'll ever be allowed. At least not until you and I steal a small Seeker and flee anonymously across the cosmos, never to be seen again."

"I'd go with you," she said.

The raw honesty on her face took his breath away. She would.

At the same time, most of this crew would probably make the same declaration. And be just as committed to it.

None of them wanted to go home any more than he did. Most of them didn't have homes. Even Lukyan Chayka had been driven here by things back on Rayzian, though he was going to go face them.

Because Uly had asked.

What would it take for Uly to go confront people like Captain Savatier? He didn't know.

"What about you?" Uly asked. "If we're hiding in my quarters and letting our hair down, what does Dan want? I try to remember to ask and not just take you for granted as Commander Chastain and my Second-in-Command. What would put a smile on your face?"

"You do when you treat me like that, Uly," she said, smiling. "None of the racism from back home. An assumption that I'm competent and can handle things without you ever asking or second-guessing me."

"I couldn't do any of this without you, Dan," he said honestly.

"I like being needed," she nodded.

"I need you," he said. "Uly does, just as much as the *Corsac Fox*."

She gasped. Studied him.

There was something in her eyes, but it vanished too quickly for him to identify it. Maybe if he had tentacles he could have tasted whatever it was, but she'd hidden it.

They stared at each other for a long moment.

Uly felt his face redden with embarrassment. Beautiful woman. Deadly woman. Amazing woman. Here in his quarters. On any other vessel—or back at University—he risked reprimand or expulsion for such a thing.

And he was in command, with her as one of his officers and crew. He didn't dare even reach out a hand right now, uncertain how she might respond.

And he needed her more as a friend and First Officer than he did any anything else.

However, he could taste that need in the air.

She could too, but it added to the reserve in her eyes.

They had something magical, and didn't dare ruin it. He couldn't do this—all of this, any of this—without her.

"Will we ever find a way to be off duty?" she asked quietly. "Just be us, short of stealing that Seeker and running away from all this?"

"I don't know," Uly offered. "Uly would like that, but I'm not sure if the rest of the galaxy will allow the *Corsac Fox* to indulge himself like that."

"You could make them," she said, rising.

For a moment, he wondered if she was about to lean over and kiss him. Uly held himself still and watched her move, but she stepped away. Towards the hatch.

As though she needed to get out of here before they did something they might regret later.

Or not regret.

Then her words registered.

"Make them?" he asked, rising in her wake, but she was at the hatch and opening it, eyes glittering with something that was highly emotional, but not tears.

Rage against fate, perhaps? Rain check for later?

He didn't know.

"Make them," she repeated, standing now just beyond the threshold of his quarters. Of his life. "You are the *Corsac Fox.*"

She stepped back with a smile and a nod, letting the hatch close.

He was alone. Disturbed at her exit as much as her presence.

She'd been right. Not tonight, and he didn't know when.

Because maybe he could make the galaxy listen.

He was the *Corsac Fox.*

# READ MORE

Be sure to read the rest of the Corsac Fox series!

https://www.knottedroadpress.com/product-category/science-fiction/
corsac-fox/

# ABOUT THE AUTHOR

Blaze Ward writes science fiction in the Alexandria Station universe (Jessica Keller, The Science Officer, The Story Road, etc.) as well as several other science fiction universes, such as Star Dragon, the Dominion, and more. He also writes odd bits of high fantasy with swords and orcs. In addition, he is the Editor and Publisher of *Boundary Shock Quarterly Magazine*. You can find out more at his website www.blazeward.com, as well as Facebook, Goodreads, and other places.

Blaze's works are available as ebooks, paper, and audio, and can be found at a variety of online vendors. His newsletter comes out regularly, and you can also follow his blog on his website. He really enjoys interacting with fans, and looks forward to any and all questions—even ones about his books!

**Never miss a release!**
If you'd like to be notified of new releases, sign up for my newsletter.

http://www.blazeward.com/newsletter/

**Buy More!**
Did you know that you can buy directly from the KRP website?

https://www.knottedroadpress.com/shop/

**Connect with Blaze!**

Web: www.blazeward.com

Boundary Shock Quarterly (BSQ):
https://www.boundaryshockquarterly.com/

# ABOUT KNOTTED ROAD PRESS

Knotted Road Press publishes dynamic fiction set in exotic locations and unique non-fiction voices in genres such as autobiography, business, cookbooks, and how-to. Our authors cover a wide range of genres including science fiction, fantasy, mystery, literary, and poetry, appealing to all readers. We offer both DRM-free ebooks and print books for a global readership.

Knotted Road Press
www.KnottedRoadPress.com
www.KnottedRoadPress.com/Shop